First to Fight

The Marines go to Sea

David C. Perry

Griz Publications

Liberty Lake, WA

ISBN-13:978-1543022858

ISBN-10: 1543022855

Praise for First to Fight

Meticulously researched, historically accurate and well written tale of the American Revolution and the operational birth of the U.S. Navy and Marine Corps team. With David Perry's *First To Fight*, the reader steps back in time to meet the powerful personalities, little known patriot volunteers and their British opponents surrounding the 1775 birth of the United States Marine Corps in a Philadelphia tavern, the Continental Navy and the conduct of the first American naval expeditionary operation "from the sea" against the British Colony of New Providence (Bahamas). An engaging and interesting read for all those interested in the history brought to life.

—Timothy Hanifen,
Major General,
US Marine Corps, Retired

First To Fight was written with stunning attention to detail in a way that only David C. Perry could bring it. He managed to capture the true essence of the Corps and put it where it deserves to be; on the title!

—L. Douglas Hogan,
US Marine Corps Veteran,
Author of Oath Takers & the Tyrant Series

First To Fight is the latest exciting historical novel by renowned author David Perry that superbly brings to life the birth of the U. S. Navy and the Marine Corps. David's thorough and detailed descriptions of the battles and people who were instrumental in the forming of the naval service are expertly brought to life. *First To Fight* is an excellent read for all history buffs, particularly those who are interested in learning more about early Revolutionary War naval battles and the legends from that crucial time in our nation's history.

—Greg Nosal,
Rear Admiral,
US Navy, Retired

A history you can breathe in. A life you feel. A legacy endured.

—A. R. Shaw,
US Air Force Reserves,
Author of Surrender the Sun and the Graham's Resolution Series

Leveraging the successes of his first two books, author Dave Perry again delivers a captivating historical fiction account of the birth of our nation's Marine Corps. Well researched, the historical backdrop and fictional depictions blend together in a fascinating interpretation of an important dimension of America's founding. Great entertainment and education for those who appreciate the daring exploits of those early patriots on whose shoulders today's defenders of freedom stand.

—Steve Eastburg,
Rear Admiral,
US Navy, Retired

Dave Perry's *First To Fight* is an excellent book for anyone seeking to contemplate the realm of the possible through the period in the American Revolution that ushered in the birth of the Navy and Marine Corps. Rich in detail, the writing style of the period, and mastery in nautical terminology, *First To Fight* draws the reader through an expression of national interest in maritime security. This paves the way for the commissioning of ships -"it is clear we must have a navy to interdict the king's shipping and supply our men in the field" and to raise "two battalions of marines." Perry's ensuing tale of battles in the fight for independence and/or a budding nation confronting a superpower transcends the ages and remains present in today's global security environment. *First To Fight* is highly recommended for readers of military history and folklore and national security professionals alike.

—Todd Coker,
Lieutenant Colonel,
US Marine Corps, Retired

For Bonnie, the love of my life. Thirty-five more years, please.

FIRST TO FIGHT

Introduction   1

DECK LOG 1768   4

DECK LOG 1773   10

DECK LOG 1775   18

DECK LOG 1776 - January   62

DECK LOG 1776 - April   135

Observations and Remarks   202

Salty Talk   204

Principal Characters   214

Naval Service Hymns   226

Final Information   229

Introduction

"First to Fight for right and freedom,
And to keep our honor clean,
We are proud to claim the title,
Of United States Marine."

I love this hymn. I am a Navy man, not a Marine, but let's face it —the Marine Corps Hymn is the best of all the service anthems. And yes, no one can deny that the Marines have the sharpest uniforms. So, I am proud to name my first historical novel that focuses on the genesis of the Marine Corps, *First to Fight*.

Several months of detailed research have been devoted to this work. This was also the case in the first two books I wrote for the series, *Not Self but Country* and *The Crucible of Tradition*. Accordingly, while a work of fiction, I have attempted to follow the timeline of events and include historical names as much as is possible. *First to Fight* now stands as the first book in the *Not Self but Country* series.

While many elements such as dialog—and indeed all thoughts —attributed to the characters are from my imagination, <u>no activity or setting was intentionally altered from a historical event</u>. In fact, during the composition of the novel, some sections had to be rewritten as I discovered historical documentation that contradicted the way the scene was initially set down.

Many sources were utilized in the research for the novel. However, *Marines in the Revolution – A History of the Continental Marines in the American Revolution 1775-1783*, served as the primary source for the chronology of events and biographical details of most of the Marine enlisted and officers. This work, written in 1975 by Charles R. Smith and published by the History and Museums Division of the USMC, is an outstanding account of American history, and I strongly recommend it to anyone with interest in the subject.

It presents the Corps history in a chronological narrative. It also reproduces many source documents such as muster lists, Congressional resolutions, and diaries. One particularly helpful section is the detailed biographical data on every marine officer that was available from diaries, wills, news articles, tax rolls, and the like.

Spelling, grammar, and punctuation were not as important in eighteenth-century America as in later centuries. Further, many of the documents prepared during the period were not intended as historical records for posterity. Accordingly, names of locations, businesses, vessels, slogans, and in many cases even people, have various spellings. Two examples are, "DONT TREAD ON ME" and "Connestogoe Waggon." In some cases, different sources even listed given names differently, forcing me to choose which I would present in the novel.

First To Fight, as with all the books in this series, was written to immerse the reader in the culture of the time. Many times the spelling or phraseology of the period was not in agreement with twenty-first century standards. Also, nautical and naval terms are used throughout. A nautical dictionary is presented near the end of this book in the chapter titled "Salty Talk." Please enjoy this as part of the reading experience.

Several devices, sections, and appendices are included to aid the reader in enjoying *First To Fight*. The first that the reader will notice is the short historical sketch at the beginning of each chapter providing some context of major events occurring that year. Next, notice that each section of a chapter begins with a flag cluing the reader in to the national perspective to be presented in the section.

The Patriot or American focused sections will begin with the coiled rattlesnake flag. This flag, called the Gadsden flag, was used by Commodore Esek Hopkins when his fleet set sail in February 1776. This was also the first flag of the United States Marines.

DONT TREAD ON ME

The Gadsden Flag

British/English perspective sections start with the Queen Anne or British Naval Ensign flag.

The Queen Anne Flag

Other helps include the Salty Talk lexicon at the end of the volume and several diagrams scattered throughout the narrative which depicts positions of various ships and other formations.

Samuel Nicholas was the first Marine officer commissioned, the first to achieve the rank of major, clearly recognized as the senior officer at the time, and a man who served his country with courage and distinction. Recognizing these historical facts, I am happy to concur with the view of all current marines, and those throughout the past 241 years, that Captain Samuel Nicholas was the first Commandant of the Marine Corps.

Please don't forget to click this link, and to write a quick review to help others discover this great story of our United States Marine Corps.

https://www.amazon.com/David-Perry/e/B00G04V4T6

DECK LOG 1768

The year in summary

*T*his year, a leap year in both the Julian and Gregorian calendars, opened with a great show as far as the Anglo world was concerned. Philip Astley debuted the first modern circus in London, complete with galloping horses and acrobats.

Two events of more significance occurred later that year which foreshadowed America's revolt against the British government. In February, Samuel Adams and James Otis Jr. wrote, and the Massachusetts House of Representatives passed, what became the "Massachusetts Circular Letter." In response to Crown import duties on glass, paint, paper, lead, and tea, Adams and Otis wrote that the new taxes violated the British Constitution because colonial residents were not represented in Parliament. The letter circulated to the other American colonies and was favorably received in Virginia, New Jersey, and Connecticut. It prompted the home government to establish a new cabinet position of Secretary of State for the Colonies to deal specifically with the American Colonies.

Elsewhere, Russia began a long war with Turkey, and several small kingdoms in Asia united to form the modern country of Nepal. In August, Captain James Cook set sail from Plymouth on his first voyage of exploration and discovery. An early signal of the demise of the golden age of imperialism was that the 162-year reign of the Dutch East India Company came to a close in Indonesia.

The flames of revolution blazed higher as the year in North America began to wane. The new British Secretary for the Colonies ordered regular army troops and navy warships to Boston in the autumn. By year's end, Boston saw their Assembly dissolved, violent protests and assaults on Crown customs officials, and two thousand British troops living among the populace.

February 11, 1768
Near Philadelphia, Pennsylvania

With the lonely chime of the midnight stroke barely a distant memory, the darkness enfolded them in its cloaking embrace. Spun wool abounded, encasing the men from toe to ear—woolen stockings and drawers next to skin, silken riding breaches covered by knee-high black leather boots.

Above the waist were linen shirts and silk cravats snug beneath the wool vests and jackets. Over it all were the heavy topcoats with collars turned up and split tails brushing the tops of the boots. Fur gloves, scarves wound about the ears and throat, and tricorne hats atop, completed the uniforms. But the men still felt it was the darkness that cloaked them.

It was not that the darkness was impenetrable, far from it. A large lantern followed the troop, and another was suspended before it, illuminating the small flakes of snow that seemed to materialize from black nothingness above their heads. Samuel Nicholas raised a gloved hand and used the leather on the back of it to wipe a drop of moisture from the tip of his cold nose. His other hand loosely gripped the reins of a tall chestnut hunter he chose specifically for this morning's affair.

Although relaxed, he was far from tired. Samuel could not have avoided the day's event, however. He was instrumental in forming this troop, and he had no intention of allowing them out on the day's adventure without him. At any rate, he enjoyed these forays, regardless of the snow, darkness, and early hour.

The pursuit would be arduous, but this was not the first time Samuel's company had made such a foray. The foe was crafty and knew the ground better than the mounted company from Philadelphia. Samuel's riders always outnumbered their opponents, and thus far, they always prevailed in the field.

None of the men in the troop spoke, and the only sounds were the sluice of water, flapping of sails, and the occasional thump of ice bouncing off the wooden sides of the ferry. This group, making its way across the Delaware on the Gloucester Ferry, was only one contingent of a larger group that would soon assemble in New Jersey.

Similar groups of mounted gentlemen rose before dawn in various homes of Philadelphia and New Jersey, pulling themselves from the warmth of plush beds, and were now making their ways to the rendezvous. They did it before, and they would do it again. It was not as if there were any shortage of targets to pursue.

Robert Morris was barely conscious of the coordinated internal flexing of different muscles and slight shifting of weight as his body automatically adjusted to the slight slowing of the ferry's progress. They were nearly across the river, and the bow of the ferry would soon bump to a stop as it collided smoothly with the wharf on the New Jersey shore of the Delaware River.

Thump—hands reached out from the darkness and made the ferry fast to the dock with deft round turns, and as quickly ran the broad, sturdy gangway aboard. Robert glanced left and right, making eye contact in the darkness first with Samuel then with his long-time friend Charles Willing. Both deferred to Morris, inclined their heads slightly toward the shore, indicating that he should debark first.

As one of, if not the wealthiest man in North America, Robert was well used to deference and privilege. Without pause he stepped forward, leading Brutus. Robert's groom selected the strong sure-footed horse this morning with confidence that he would carry his master safely across the hard turf, dotted unpredictably with treacherous patches of thick and slippery ice.

Others followed, leading their mounts until the ferry was empty and the group was formed on the frozen road. Smiles and nods—then they mounted and trotted off down the road toward the assembly.

Two hours later, Betty Hugg, daughter of the establishment's owner, poured more steaming tea into the men's mugs from a heavy pitcher. Morris, Nicholas, John Cawalader, John Dunlap, Willing, Jonathan Potts and others were seated in chairs and benches around this table. Other groups crowded around the other tables. Perhaps forty men or more, all told, were gathered in the taproom.

Pewter and crockery plates and platters covered the tables laden with ham, pork chops, various fowl, and toasted soft tack. Tubs of butter found spots here and there. The men gulped the hot tea, some of it fortified with rum or whiskey, most plain or simply flavored with sugar and fresh milk.

Eventually, the men satisfied their appetites, and the loud hubbub of conversation settled to more muted notes. The exterior door opened quickly, admitting a smattering of snowflakes and a confident but demure black man. Old Natty, as everyone knew him, was a slave of Samuel Morris. He got up much earlier than all the other men to make sure everything was ready for the morning's proceedings. Moments later, Samuel Morris, the president of the group, rose and addressed the men.

"My friends," Samuel began, "Ol' Natty has just informed me that the pack is ready. It is time to say farewell to our warm breakfast and mount our steeds. The trumpet will sound in five minutes' time."

Chairs scraped, boots scuffed and clomped. Scarves, coats, and headgear were once again donned. Several men gathered around chamber pots in the corners, others went outside and concluded their business in the snow and frozen mud.

In five minutes, the group was mounted and assembled with Robert and Samuel Morris and Samuel Nicholas riding at its head. Clouds of frosty fog hung about the men's heads as their breath immediately condensed with each exhalation. The sky overhead transitioned from the nebulous black nothingness to pale gray; and still, the small snowflakes materialized from somewhere above them, though they were more difficult to see against the gray sky than when they contrasted with the black night.

Mingo, Piper, Sweetlys, Sugnell, Davy, and a dozen other select foxhounds bayed, circled, and sniffed, waiting to be released.

The trumpet bellowed and President Morris gave the word, waving a gloved hand in the air, "Follow me, gentlemen. Tally hoe!"

With that order, the hounds and the troop of assembled Philadelphia gentlemen bounded off into the Gloucester, New Jersey countryside in pursuit of their weekly fox hunt. In this gentlemanly pastime, without conscious consideration, they honed the skills of discipline, communication, riding, and regimentation that would serve their futures in a much more serious endeavor.

Samuel Nicholas swung easily in his saddle as he rode next to Robert Morris. These fox hunting forays cemented the bond between the up-and-coming young gentleman and the successful, well-connected Robert Morris. Both were charter members of the club, but Samuel was the spark that ignited it. He was happy to admit to himself that his idea and diligence paid off in three ways. The events were great fun, they were certainly of benefit to his health and constitution, and friendships he made were a bounty for his reputation and future.

April 19, 1768
Alexandria, Virginia

Mid-April in the Colony of Virginia was still mild. The sun was kind this day as it shone from directly overhead on the young gentleman. At barely twenty-two years old, three years older than the town in which he now stood, Matthew Parke shifted his weight from foot to foot on the flat cobbles of Duke Street. This broad thoroughfare that extended from the bluff down to the wharves and dockage on the waterfront was the primary commercial street in the growing city. He stood just out of the scant shade cast by the imposing warehouse on the north side of the broad street—John Carlisle's warehouse.

On the western bank of the Potomac River, Alexandria was burgeoning, and her leading citizen, John Carlisle was profiting enormously from the event. Born in Scotland and now settled in the colony, Carlisle had married well, to Sarah Fairfax, the fair daughter of one of the most influential men in Virginia.

John's connections, as well as his mercantile ventures during the late war with France, and trading relationship with the king combined to leave him a very wealthy man indeed. The large warehouse was only a tiny fraction of his property and wealth, even though it held a daunting array of commodities bound for England and, finished wares recently arrived from Europe and the Caribbean.

Although not related, Matthew's grandfather and John Carlisle had been cordial acquaintances since youth. "Friends" would have implied more than the substance of the association truly represented. It was to this relationship that Matthew owed his current circumstance.

Matthew shaded his eyes and watched as the ship-rigged trading vessel sheeted home her main and fore courses to let the faint whispers of an offshore breeze carry her from the wharf out into the Potomac's current. His grandfather's visage was becoming blurred, but there was no mistaking the bright scarlet of his British Army uniform as he stood on the quarterdeck with his hands resting on the cap of the starboard bulwark.

Matthew genuinely treasured his past few years with his grandfather—The Colonel—as everyone in the family called him. Matthew was extremely proud of his heritage. The Colonel served with distinction as an aide to the third Duke of Marlborough in France during the Seven Years War. In recognition, no doubt, of his noble service, the Colonel was appointed Governor of the Windward Islands and took his grandson with him on that assignment.

As an older teenaged gentleman, Matthew was enthralled with everything about the Caribbean. He spent time rubbing shoulders with the Army officers, occasionally drilled with the militia, and went to sea with several friends he made among Royal Navy officers.

Grandfather taught him duty, courage, honor, sword drill, and noblesse oblige. His martial friends educated him practically in marksmanship, leadership, and tactical combat; and his comrades in the Navy exposed him to ship handling and the sheer delight of being at sea.

He thrilled to the ship's motion when the deck came to life beneath his feet. The thick air, heavily laden with moisture and salt, served as a tonic flowing over his skin and through his hair. The sun was always more intense at sea. It baked his pale English skin to a tanned glow.

This life was great preparation and exposure to a world of excitement and opportunity, but for reasons he could not articulate, Matthew subtly avoided a commission in the Army, and he was too old to enter the Navy.

Now he was here—the new world. Grandfather's friend made him a clerk to the steward of his warehouse. "Pay attention, boy. Mind your business. Work hard. Don't shirk, and you have a great future in America," Carlisle told him when Matthew and The Colonel dined with him and Mrs. Carlisle in the great mansion on the bluff. In a weak moment of generosity and benevolence, Carlisle even offered to allow Matthew to bed in a vacant room of the warehouse until he got his feet under him.

"Have you finished paying respects to your grandfather, young man?" the firm voice came down to the street from an open window on the second floor of the warehouse.

"I have, sir," Matthew replied, looking up.

"In that case, come up to the office. We've ledgers and bills of lading to reconcile before we are finished this day."

Matthew turned and pushed the door inward, determined to make a good start of his new future.

DECK LOG 1773

The year in summary

*I*n the year *1773*, many significant and diverse events occured throughout the world. In a monumental effort to preserve and document its history, China began compiling the Siku Quanshu, the largest compilation of literature in their history, while in Turkey, Sultan Mustafa III formed the Istanbul Institute of Technology, which was destined to become one of the three greatest engineering universities in the world. And in Guatemala, an estimated 7.5 magnitude earthquake destroyed the city of Antigua. Aftershocks continued from July through December, rocking the entire country.

Closer to home, political unrest continued to boil in the North American Colonies. In the fall, the satirical essay entitled "Rules By Which A Great Empire May Be Reduced To A Small One,' was published by Pennsylvania dissident, Benjamin Franklin. Elsewhere, Daniel Boone attempted to establish a British settlement in Kentucky. His efforts were repulsed by the indigenous residents with a longstanding claim to the area.

The big event, as far as Americans are concerned, was the night that became known as The Boston Tea Party. The British East India Company was suffering great financial hardship, and to save the company, Parliament lowered taxes on the tea. This allowed the Company to undercut even the smugglers in North America.

Patriot groups in Charleston, New York, and Philadelphia forced local consignees to refuse the tea shipments. But in Boston, the consignees were sons of the Royal Governor. So, the local Sons of Liberty took a different course. In December, they dressed as Mohawks and dumped about 45 tons of tea in Boston Harbor. The estimated value of the tea in 2016 currency was approximately one million U.S. dollars.

February 9, 1773
Alexandria, Virginia

Mary Hawkins' public-house was not an elaborate affair, nor had she named it yet. Built from rough sawn lumber and scraps scavenged from other building projects around the thriving port of Alexandria, the seamen's tavern didn't even boast a plank floor. Pounded clay and sand would serve for the time. The only stones or bricks in the edifice formed the large fireplace, and it was blazing cheerily on this cold February night.

Mary saved every penny and half penny she could since she was a barefoot girl wringing and hanging laundry for her aunt. She watched as Alexandria grew from a dusty road and an anchorage pool to an important world gateway. She was determined to link her future fortune to the growth of the new city.

Mary's place was close to the waterfront at the southwest corner of Royal and Cameron Streets, and the seamen knew she was honest, and her prices were fair. The choices at Mary's were few and simple. She served local ale, rum from the Caribbean, bread that she baked herself every morning, and whatever she could find each day to put together some type of soup or porridge.

Mary stood behind the rough planks of the bar pouring drinks and dishing food. She had a girl to serve the customers and a boy to do the heavy lifting, cleaning, and fetching. She was happy but not content. She slept in the lean-to that also served as pantry and storeroom, still saving every farthing she earned to continue building and improving her establishment. She was going to be someone in Virginia.

Mary allowed herself one indulgence. A stray mongrel dog called this location his home before construction had begun on the tavern. Mary began giving him bits from her meals while she was supervising and helping the builders, and the beast decided to lay claim to her as well as the location.

Now he rarely left her side. She began calling him Lord Dunmore after John Murray, the recently installed governor of Virginia who was also the 4th Earl of Dunmore. The animal (the dog, not the governor) was currently lying across the opening at the end of the bar, effectively blocking the path of any customer who might want to wander behind the bar where Mary was working.

As there were a number of ships at anchor and moored to the wharf, Mary's place was crowded and loud on this night. Most of the rough men were drinking, a few were eating, and all were animatedly doing their best to spin yarns that would outdo those of their friends and shipmates.

Hands and arms were gesticulating to explain the direction of the wind and the set of the sails. Crusts of bread, dishes, and spoons slid across the tables illustrating reefs, shoals, and the movements of the vessels involved in the tales. Mary's serving girl weaved in and out among the tables, dodging the windmilling arms, gathering empty bowls, and refilling glasses and tankards as voices roared and laughed.

The door burst open, admitting the harsh cold blackness of the night along with three men. The leading man was well dressed—his cocked hat sat athwart his head, and his clothes gave the impression of a naval officer, though not perfectly. The other two wore the scarlet of the British Army.

The room grew quiet as the intruding party scanned the interior faces. The fire crackled, and the wind carried a few stray flakes of snow around the red shoulders of the soldiers, only to have them melt in the air before landing on the packed earth floor. Mary's beast gave the impression of great effort and bother as he used his forelegs to raise himself to a sitting position, his haunches leaning against her ankles and his face toward the door.

"Bring your lobsters in or out, then Gov'nor, and close the door," Mary addressed the leader of the trio. "'Tis a cold night, and don't I pay one shilling tuppence to the rick for this here firewood—split and delivered."

The man scowled for a moment, then complied, taking a step farther into the room to make space for the soldiers.

Over his shoulder he said, "Close the door, Private."

The last soldier into the tavern complied with the order.

A man at a table near the bar looked at the trio then jerked his thumb in their direction. He leaned his head toward the center of his table and said something to his companions in a low voice. The men burst into laughter at the private joke.

Gradually the conversations began again, but quieter, less volume and not as raucous. The trio did not sit down. Rather their leader studied the room, looking closely at the men's garb and faces, listening to their quiet dialects and accents. All spoke English. American might be a more apt description since their homeports ranged from Massachusetts to Georgia.

He reached into his breast pocket and withdrew a paper containing a list of names and descriptions, which he perused for a few moments. Ultimately, he made up his mind and spoke.

"You there," the leader of the trio said loudly, addressing men at a table in the far corner, near the fire. The conversations died again. "You men are on the Yankee sloop at the wharf." It sounded like an accusation.

Abraham Whipple had his back to the corner and eyed the speaker coldly. He began to rise but was suppressed by a firm hand on the shoulder, pressing him back onto his seat. It belonged to John Trevett, who stood as he held his captain in his chair.

"And just who might be doing the asking?" Trevett said to the speaker.

"I am asking the questions, here," the man answered. "But it will do no harm for you to know that I am Captain Lawson Bellows of the Virginia Navy, and I carry the commission of Lord Dunmore himself."

At the mention of the governor's name, Mary's dog cocked his head, and his ears rose and pointed slightly. Mary reached down, scratching the top of his head, and whispering for him to stay. Mary's serving girl glanced over at the dog and grinned.

"Well don't that just make you somethin' the cat dragged up out o' the bilges last night?" Trevett replied. A few men chuckled, and Bellows stiffened but refused to take the bait.

"I have here a list of the piratical felons suspected of attacking and burning His Majesty's tender, *Gaspee*, and some of you easily satisfy the descriptions. Lord Dunmore orders me to bring you to him to answer charges."

"That tells me two things about your Lord Dunmore," responded Trevett. "First off, he's mighty late to the game. That's all news from nearly a year ago." He paused. "And secondly, he's poking his Virginia nose into Rhode Island's business."

There were snorts and chuckles around the room. A couple of men laughed out loud. Trevett looked down at his captain—Whipple—who glanced up at him for a moment. Silent understanding passed between them. Both remembered the night in June the previous year when several dozen Rhode Islanders burned the British Navy tender to the waterline after it ran aground in Narragansett Bay.

To date, none of the men had ever been convicted or even captured. Abraham Whipple was reputed to have been in charge of the expedition.

"Lord Dunmore represents the king. Bringing the king's enemies to justice is the business of any of the king's governors," Bellows explained in a didactic tone. "Now then, none of you have answered my question."

"You've got me dead to rights, Captain. My name is Trevett. John Trevett. I am the mate on the *Katy*," Trevett admitted. "Just what is the penalty for being a merchant mate in Virginia?"

More chuckles.

"Impertinence of young fools will be dealt with as required."

Mary spoke up. "Gentlemen, please. Can't this wait until tomorrow, in a location that does not involve pestering my patrons?"

Bellows turned his head and glared at her. "You keep a still tongue in your head, wench; else I will close this place down for harboring pirates!"

Matthew Parke was seated at a table against the front wall near the door. This placed him roughly between Bellows and Mary.

Matthew could see the disdain in the captain's eyes, and spittle sprayed from his lips with the invective he sprayed at the proprietress. Mary's jaw clenched, stifling any further remark. The fur along Lord Dunmore's neck and spine was standing up as he eyed the captain and the two soldiers.

"And you had better keep control of that cur."

"Oh Captain . . . Captain Bellows? Over here. Did you forget about me?" Trevett mocked to divert Bellows' attention from Mary. "I am not sure the lady's dog is the only cur in here tonight."

Again—chuckles from the patrons.

Bellows looked back at Trevett, then returned his eyes to the document in his hand. A moment later he said, "I am not interested in you, Trevett. What about that fellow seated next to you?" He looked into the older man's face. "You match the description of Abraham Whipple. I think Governor Murray— Lord Dunmore—would be very interested in talking to you."

Parke continued to watch the drama with close attention and a mixture of emotions. His grandfather had been a royal governor on the Windward Islands, and Matthew did not like seeing the royal authority disdained. At the same time, he knew there were legitimate grievances against the heavy hand of authority in the colonies.

These men did not seem traitors or pirates. Matthew recently began frequenting this establishment in the evenings. His office duties were growing dull, and a strong yearning for adventure and significance was growing in him. He liked the type of men who crewed the trading ships and enjoyed mixing with them in Mary's tavern.

Whipple gave a stern look at Trevett to still him and finally spoke to Bellows on his own behalf. "His lordship is just going to have to queue up and wait his turn. The Right Honorable

Governor Wanton of Rhode Island has already papered half of New England with his broadsides offering one hundred pounds for any scoundrel willing to betray his neighbor regarding this *Gaspee* business. Been near on six months now, and he has yet to entice one man with his Judas' reward. That said, this here o humble ship captain is not likely to sail away with the likes of you to visit bloody Lord Dunmore and likely be treated to some English Justice."

The dog stood when he heard his name again, and Mary restrained him by holding the scruff of his neck.

Crimson rose in Captain Bellows, beginning low on his throat and rising until his ears glowed red. "I have authority to compel you to accompany me, sir."

"You would be well advised, Captain," Whipple responded levelly, "to forget you have that authority and scurry off to the safety of your ship. Authority and means are not the same things."

"By Heaven, sir, you will not threaten me! I represent the governor and the king." He turned his face over his shoulder and continued, "Soldiers, present!"

Until now, the two soldiers were quietly standing behind Captain Bellows with their Brown Bess muskets across their bodies. At this order, they both swung the butt plates up to their shoulders and pointed the muzzles toward Trevett and Whipple.

"Think very carefully about what you are doing, Captain Bellows," John Trevett said.

"Make ready," Bellows ordered.

The soldiers cocked their flintlocks and sighted along the barrels toward the two Yankee seamen.

"This is your last warning," Bellows threatened.

Several men around the tavern stood. Matthew Parke could not believe what he was seeing. Lord Dunmore's menacing growl grew louder.

Mary screamed at the captain and the soldiers. "Stop it! There is no need for this."

Her shrill cry startled one of the soldiers who turned his muzzle toward her. Parke sprang to his feet in an instant and dove toward the soldier. Catching him in the side of his ribs, he drove him into his companion.

The first soldier's musket discharged, sending the .75 caliber lead ball plowing up splinters across the planks of the bar, plucking Mary's sleeve before lodging in a support post of the exterior wall.

Losing his balance, the soldier crashed into his companion, who also pulled his trigger while still aiming the muzzle at Whipple. His ball flew towards the Yankee captain's face, whipping past

Whipple's left ear and blasting through the thin wall sheathing and spending its remaining energy in the dark, snowy night. Matthew landed atop the pile of soldiers.

Captain Bellows barely managed to keep his footing, if not his dignity, as the three men scuffled and tumbled behind him, kicking, and bumping his heels and calves several times. By the time the two soldiers regained their feet, most of the men in the room were standing and beginning to press in on them. Their backs were to the door.

Addressing Matthew Parke, Captain Bellows demanded, "You there, young man, what's your name?"

Before Matthew could answer, a deep voice from the crowd interjected, "You're through asking questions here, Bellows. This here committee just took a vote and decided this is your last chance to back out of here under command of your own helm—and lay a course for deeper water."

Several murmurs of agreement rumbled through the crowd.

"You've not heard the last of this," he said to the room in general, "not by a long splice."

That said, he spun on his heel, shoved his way between the two red-coated soldiers, and pulled the door open. Seconds later, the three men were dim shadows disappearing into the snowy darkness, not even bothering to pull the door closed behind them.

Matthew swung the crude door closed as Mary set aside her characteristic parsimony just long enough to shout, "One round for the house."

The men roared, Lord Dunmore barked, and John Trevett walked over to shake Parke's hand and invite him to join the Yankee's for a drink. Matthew introduced himself and sat down with Trevett and Whipple as the girl came and refilled their drinks.

"I believe you may have saved my life, young man," Whipple stated. "That fool of Murray's was determined if not much else."

"It was just a reaction, sir," Matthew replied. "Truly I didn't weigh the right or the wrong of it. My insides just told me this was not an issue a man should die for this night. If I may be so bold, Captain Whipple, you Americans are certainly not shy of rejecting the king's authority."

"Tis not always the king himself we mind so much, sir," Trevett replied. "Rather it is the imbeciles his ministers select to represent him in his colonies. But if I may ask, without being rude, Mr. Parke, why do you say, 'you Americans.'"

"I am not offended, Mr. Trevett. I was born in England, near Ipswich. My grandfather was governor of the Windward Islands and took me to the posting with him. He brought me here, not many years past—with recommendations—to make my way in the world. I am very grateful to him for it."

Matthew sipped his refreshed drink and continued. "There are many more opportunities for a man like me on this vast continent than in the mother country. My family in England was not poor, but the fortune does diminish as each generation divides it amongst the heirs. Any rate, I am not the type to just hang about the estate shooting partridges and riding to the hounds."

"Well spoken, son," Whipple said affectionately. "Are you a seafaring man, then?"

"Hardly, that, Captain. I am a clerk—recently raised to agent—for Mr. Carlisle. He has sent me on a handful of voyages to the Caribbean so that he could profit from my acquaintances there for business dealings. But my capacity at sea was that of passenger."

"You are definitely a man of quick action, sir. Mr. Brown—John Brown—of Rhode Island is my employer. He owns the *Katy*, the sloop I command. I am confident I could offer you a berth aboard. I have no doubt you would soon be a mate on one of his vessels. But I tell you this, my boy. I think your future lies in Philadelphia. I think you could set up as an agent there. If Mr. Brown won't back your venture, I will back you myself."

"You are too kind, sir. We've only just met."

"Nonsense, Mr. Parke. I am a sea captain. My life and the survival of my crew and cargo depend on my ability to make swift and accurate decisions. There is a quality of character and determination about you that I like."

"If I may contribute," Trevett interjected, "There are men in Philadelphia whom I believe you would enjoy meeting, Mr. Parke. They are men of substance and vision; and, more to the point, men who hunt the fox regularly. I am sure you would be a welcome and valuable addition to their company."

"You have both given me much to ruminate on."

"You think hard on it, Mr. Parke. We sail in a few hours but, with the Blessing, will be back here in a month's time. That should allow you the time you need to consider your options and close your accounts with Mr. Carlisle honorably—if that is your decision."

Matthew stood, and the other two followed, shaking hands all around.

"Good night, sirs, he said. I will find you and inform you of my answer when the *Katy* is back in Alexandria."

That said, he took his leave and returned to his rooms to consider his future in this new and growing world.

DECK LOG 1775

The year in summary

*T*he year *1775* was the genesis of the United States of America. Great things were happening in the world, but from the Anglo-American perspective, they were eclipsed by rebellion. British troops occupied Boston, and Parliament declared the entire colony of Massachusetts Bay to be in rebellion. Patrick Henry delivered his famous "Give me liberty or give me death" speech when the Virginia House of Burgesses was disbanded by the Royal Governor.

While still striving for a peaceful solution to their grievances, the Second Continental Congress began to build and organize a government for the fragile alliance of colonies. But in April, Paul Revere and William Dawes made their ride into immortality warning the Massachusetts countryside of the coming British soldiers. This culminated in the first battle of the American Revolution—The shot heard 'round the world at Lexington.

More battles followed; Ethan Allen and his Green Mountain Boys captured Fort Ticonderoga. Americans lost the Battle of Bunker Hill while inflicting devastating casualties on British Army officers, and Benedict Arnold built a fleet on Lake Champlain, lost the naval battle with the British fleet, but forestalled an invasion of New York that would have crippled the Revolution.

Later in the year, Congress appointed General George Washington, a Virginia planter, as Commander in Chief of the Continental Army. He arrived in New England to discover that his army's supply of powder afforded less than a dozen shots per man, yet they held the British Army under siege in Boston.

As the year wound down, the Continental Navy and Marines were born, and men recruited to fill the ranks. John Barry, one of *the infant Navy's first captains, was the first to capture a British warship on the high seas. The year closed with the British forces in Quebec repulsing an invasion led by Continental generals Richard Montgomery and Benedict Arnold.*

June 15, 1775
Providence, Rhode Island

Twelfth of June, The Year of Our Lord One Thousand Seven Hundred Seventy and Five, By the General Assembly of the Crown Colony of Rhode Island and Providence Plantations, etcetera,

It is voted and resolved, that the committee of safety be, and they are hereby directed to, charter two suitable vessels for the use of the colony and fit out the same in the best manner, to protect the trade of this colony.

That the said vessels be at the risk of the colony, and be appraised, before they are chartered, by Messrs. Joseph Anthony, Rufus Hopkins, and Cromwell Child or any two of them; who are also to agree for the hire of the said vessels.

That the largest of the said vessels be manned with eighty men, exclusive of officers; and be equipped with ten guns, four-pounders; fourteen swivel guns, a sufficient number of small arms, and all necessary warlike stores.

That the small vessel be manned in a number not exceeding thirty men.

That the whole be included in the number of fifteen hundred men, ordered to be raised in this colony, and be kept in pay until the 1st day of December next, unless discharged before, by order of the General Assembly.

That they receive the same bounty and pay as the land forces, excepting that the first and second lieutenants and master receive the same pay as the first lieutenant of the land forces; and petty officers the same as sergeants of the army.

And that the lieutenant general, brigadier general, and committee of safety, or the major part of them, have the power of directing and ordering said vessels; and in case it shall appear to them that the officers and men of said vessels can be more serviceable on shore, than at sea, to order them on shore, to defend the seaports in this colony.

And it is further voted and resolved that the following officers be, and are hereby appointed to command the said vessels, to wit:

—Of the largest vessel: Abraham Whipple, commander with the rank and power of commodore of both vessels.

John Grimes, first lieutenant.

Benjamin Seabury, second lieutenant.

William Bradford of Providence, master.

Ebenezer Flagg, quartermaster, at the wages of four pounds, lawful money, per month.

—Of the smallest vessel: Christopher Whipple, commander.

William Rhodes, lieutenant.

John Trevett finished reading the carefully trimmed parchment with perfectly executed copperplate flowing across its broad flat face. He handed the sheet back to Captain Whipple who folded it and slid it neatly back into his breast pocket. Whipple wore a smile of satisfaction and benevolence.

"So, you see, my boy," Whipple said, "It is quite out of my hands. The General Assembly have been quite specific in their proclamation. Grimes is to be premier, and Seabury and Bradford complete the commissioned officers. There will be more ships. This war is not over, not by a long chalk. Heavens, son, it is barely begun. You mark my words."

"But Captain, I've sailed many years with you. Now we have the chance to strike back at these scoundrels, and I'm to be left out. It is not right, I say!"

"Listen to me, John, your time will come. By thunder, son, there are privateer companies forming now. Letters of Marque and

Reprisal will be written before you know it."

The pair sat at a small square table outside the new Sabin Tavern. The current location of the establishment removed any trace of sentiment Abraham Whipple might have felt for the tavern.

The old Sabin, in its former location—now that is a different story altogether. Abe spent many a leisurely hour there. But the most memorable was the night of the *Gaspee* Raid. He, with John Brown and the other local captains, had planned *Gaspee's* demise sitting around the long table at the tavern's former location.

Sabin sold the old property and opened this new, larger concern on Market Square. It was definitely a smart move for the proprietor, as Market Square was the new center of activity in Providence. And it didn't hurt his business or his reputation that the local Sons of Liberty adopted the gathering place as their Providence meeting location.

Even now, with the sun approaching the zenith, and people, horses, and carts entering and crisscrossing the cobbles, Abe could feel the familiar sense of exhilaration infusing his being. He was savoring his last cup of chocolate before joining his command, and Trevett nearly drained the hot pot of coffee as he downed mug after mug of the invigorating beverage.

"You will be working for the Assembly now, Captain. There will be more paperwork than Mr. Brown ever imagined when you worked for him. Someone will need to keep a log of the progress of the battle—and copy all the reports fair. The Assembly didn't think of that when pickin' your crew for you—now did they, sir? Make me your clerk, Captain."

Abraham Whipple looked out at the square, watching the shadows recede as the sun climbed its predictable arc. Absentmindedly, he laid his hand on his breast and felt the crackling of the parchment in the pocket. He was fond of Trevett. He knew the young man would find a way to get into the struggle.

"Okay, John. You're my clerk. But you will have to be mustered as supernumerary. Victuals and prize money only—as an able seaman."

"Thank you, Captain. Thank you."

"Well, get your dunnage then. I don't want to be waiting for you when we cast off our moorings."

John inclined his head, indicating a small chest that sat against the Sabin's front wall. Whipple grinned. So, the young rascal knew all along.

"Right, then. Let's be about it."

Whipple stood and downed the remainder of his cocoa in one swallow. Trevett emptied his coffee mug as well and hefted his sea chest onto his right shoulder. The two men set off toward the dockside with the morning's sun warming their shoulders and backs.

"Mornin' Cap'n," Ebenezer Flagg greeted evenly as Whipple and Trevett approached *Katy's* gangway. He was on the wharf, busy overhauling the mooring lines to ensure they were ready to be pulled quickly onto the sloop when she unmoored and headed down the river.

Although from New Hampshire, Flagg sailed many years with Whipple and John Brown—in fact, many of his shipmates were on *Katy*—and he was proud to sail now in the fledgling Rhode Island Navy.

As the sloop's quartermaster, he was the bridge between the hands and the officers. This morning he was ensuring all the preparations to get underway were made properly. There was no way he would allow this sloop of the new navy to be embarrassed on their first official action.

"Good morning, Eb," Whipple replied as he stepped onto the gangplank.

Trevett nodded to the quartermaster and followed his captain onboard. Once aboard, the pair stopped amidships. With his hands on his hips, Whipple swiveled his head, eyes flicking up and down from deck to main truck, taking in everything.

When he was satisfied with the sloop's readiness, he called to his new first lieutenant. "Mr. Grimes."

John Grimes straightened up from some task he was supervising on the fo'c'sle and strode quickly back to his captain. "Morning, Captain," he said, touching his forehead. "What is it you want, sir?"

"I'll see you and the second lieutenant—and the master too, I suppose—in the cabin in a quarter of an hour." He pulled his watch from his waistcoat and peered at it. "I think you know my clerk," he grinned. Trevett and Grimes smiled and nodded at each other. "He will bring Captain Whipple—the younger—from *Washington* to the meeting as well. Pray, receive him with naval honors."

Grimes looked confused at Whipple and scratched the back of his head.

"Make a path at the gangway lined with sideboys and ring the bell a couple of times when he comes aboard. For heaven's sake, John. Have you no imagination or sense of decorum?" He smiled again.

"Yessir; I mean no, sir; I mean aye, aye, Commodore," Lieutenant Grimes replied.

Whipple continued grinning and shook his head. Trevett raised his hat to Captain Whipple and turned to go to *Washington* and deliver his message to Captain Whipple—the younger. Abraham went below to his tiny cabin.

Trevett stood in *Katy's* tiny cabin facing the commodore. His hat was held in his hands before him, and his head was bowed under the low overhead beams.

"He was not aboard, Commodore. And William—Lieutenant Rhodes—stated that a messenger told him that Mr. Whipple would not be accepting the commission."

Abraham Whipple was dumbfounded. How could any kin of his pass on an opportunity to strike a blow at the tyrant? Well, so be it. This was no time to muck around with indecision.

"Very well—thank you, John. Lieutenant Grimes, you will repair onboard *Washington* and take command of the sloop. Mr. Trevett, would you please prepare written orders to that effect?"

"Aye, Aye, Commodore."

"Very well. Let us proceed with our meeting."

Whipple sat on the locker under the small window that spanned the large glass windowpanes of the sloop's stern. Trevett, Master Bradford, *Captain* Grimes and Lieutenant Seabury sat on chairs, two of which they brought from their own small hutch-like cabins. With the small table in the center of the space, there was no room for anyone—or anything else.

The lieutenants, the clerk, and master each paired off and were looking at three copies of a thin, leather-bound volume. Each pair leafed through their book, reading the notations, scanning the sketches, and imagining what they would look like in reality when employed on their sloops.

"These are all copies I made about a week ago when I learned a navy was to be formed for the colony. I took the original off *Gaspee* . . . er . . . someone took it off *Gaspee*, so I was led to believe, at any rate," the newly minted commodore informed the officers of his pocket-sized fleet. "Tis the British signal book. Not the entire book, but those I thought would be useful to us."

The others continued to flick pages back and forward.

"John," Whipple looked at Trevett who immediately looked up from the book, "you will handle the signaling on *Katy*."

"Aye, Commodore," Trevett nodded.

"Right. Now then, suppose I sketch out the way things stand. My orders require me to rid the bay of Wallace's tenders. It is no secret to you that he sits comfortably in his great cabin on *Rose*, plowing a furrow to and fro in the Sound, just off Newport, while his tenders ply Narragansett Bay plundering our innocent shipping and strangling our livelihoods."

"Commodore Whipple," the newly appointed Captain interrupted, "suppose we put a stop to Wallace and his imperial piracy once and for all. We know where the frigate haunts, and we can be there afore the sun sets. He won't a be expectin' two sloops to attack 'im. T'gether we mounts near as much iron as he, and we can come at 'em from different directions, like."

"I appreciate your zeal, Captain," the Commodore continued. But I must consider—not only counts of guns—but weights and measures—as well as my orders. And, not to be too pedantic, the Admiralty rates *Rose* a post ship, her being eight carriage guns light of a true frigate."

"My Heavens, son," Bradford broke in, chiding Grimes and interrupting the commodore's lecture while contradicting him simultaneously. "*Rose's* broadside alone weighs near four times that o' our'n, with over twice'd the compliment. They'd plum swamp us with seamen if ever they got alongside!" Then, to Whipple, "As a practical matter, Abe, all the rascals commanding post ships on foreign stations calls 'em frigates."

The commodore leveled his eyes on Bradford and silenced him with a cold stare. "Thank you, Master, but I do not require your assistance at present to explain the case to Captain Grimes. Nor to lecture me on the British Navy."

Apparently, Gentlemen," Whipple continued, broadening his remarks to all the officers, "I neglected to properly explain the venue at the outset of our gathering. This is neither a committee meeting nor a council of war. We are assembled here for me to issue my orders and explain my intentions, and for you to indicate your understanding thereof. Are there any questions as to my point?"

No one spoke.

"Excellent. To continue, then, *Rose's* tender, *Diana*, is known to be sweeping the bay—has been since Wallace armed and crewed her after stealing her from Mr. Lindsey. She was seen to anchor near Newport at twilight last evening. That is the latest intelligence I possess. Do any of you have any other information on her whereabouts?"

"Only that she is known to cruise the middle bay, sir," Seabury offered.

"Thank you, Lieutenant. I concur. It is likely, that is where we will find her."

"Is *Washington* ready to sail, Captain?" Whipple asked Grimes.

"If she is not, she soon will be Commodore," Christopher confirmed.

"Right," Whipple continued. "Mr. Seabury, you are now *Katy's* first lieutenant. As soon as Captain Grimes departs—with honors —you may unmoor and proceed to sea."

The first lieutenant nodded.

"Captain, *Washington* will follow *Katy* down the channel at a reasonable interval. After we clear the river's mouth, we will sweep to the south'ard, and *Washington* to the east five cables."

John Grimes nodded his understanding to the commodore.

"You will continue south, sweeping east about Prudence Island. If you encounter *Diana*, drive her south or take her. I would prefer not to sink her if that is possible. We shall rendezvous in the channel betwixt Prudence and Conanicut. Any questions?" His eyes explored the room, resting on each face in turn. No one spoke; a couple shook their heads.

"Very well. Captain Grimes, you may rejoin your command. Lieutenant Seabury, please get the sloop underway as soon as you are ready."

Chairs scraped. Men stood, bent deeply at the shoulder to avoid the overhead. One at a time, they scooted around the table and slipped through the narrow door.

Abraham Whipple was left alone with his thoughts. To him, Providence had given the lot of commanding the first government-sanctioned navy of the loosely confederated colonies. The moment was not lost on him.

Abraham was a man of imagination as well as discipline. He was no stranger to armed resistance, and he knew that the colonies' grievances were not to be settled without force of arms.

But he scorned the pot-house fools and dandies who swore that a few weeks of rattling swords in scabbards would bring Parliament to her senses and set the world right again. He knew this struggle would consume a year or more of his life.

Perhaps it would extinguish his life. Abraham Whipple went to sea during the French and Indian war. He knew that one stray musket ball could immediately and finally snuff his life like the flame of a cheap tallow candle.

The sounds of a ship readying herself to sail echoed throughout his miniature world, as did the thumping of footsteps, heavy coils of rope dropping on the decks, the flat tone of the bells as Grimes stepped onto the wharf, and the scraping sound of the gangplank as it was shoved ashore.

Men chanted rhythmically while they cheerfully heaved on the halyards that brought the heavy mainsail skyward and two-blocked its peak at the main truck. These were sounds of comfort that were familiar to Whipple since he had forsaken his father's farming life and gone to sea decades before. *Will this be the last day I hear these sounds?*

It was not like Abraham to be nostalgic . . . nor morbid. But he was not being morbid; he was merely reflecting on the gravity and the moment. He knew his family was well provided for. They could certainly retire to his father's farm if they wanted to . . . if the worst happened to him.

But there was no need for that. His success as captain of *Game Cock* during the late war was renown and had earned him enough prize money to set up his family for generations. No, Sarah would miss him, but she would want for no material thing. She could afford to live anywhere she liked.

He thought of his children. Catherine would always be special to him . . . Katy. It was an act of true friendship that prompted John Brown to name *Katy* after Abraham's dear daughter. He dwelt on his children and the future that he and thousands of men like him were building for them on this wild yet promising continent.

John Trevett stood at *Katy's* binnacle, scratching notes of times and activities that occurred around him onto scraps of paper that would serve as the sloop's rough deck log. He would copy them fair into the formal document at the day's end. Assuming he was able at the day's end. Assuming his limbs were intact, and he could still draw breath at day's end. He rapped lightly on the wooden binnacle box with his knuckles . . . and breathed a silent prayer for good measure.

Trevett considered his lot. Glad to be aboard for this adventure, he was still convinced his destiny did not lie in being a scribe, documenting the prolonged war that was recently birthed in America. Recording times and wind directions for bureaucrats to bundle up with long strands of red tape and file away in dark drawers.

John's legacy would be that of a substantial cobble in the foundation that was now building for a new nation. Yes—he knew there would be no reconciliation with the empire. Ministers, Lords, and Members of Parliament were not the type of men to succumb to reason and compromise.

Americans, as many were calling his fellow patriots, would emerge from this war as slaves or as citizens of new and free states. And John was bound that it would be the latter.

The sun shining in John's eyes brought him back to the moment. The breeze from the east carried the boom and mainsail over his head away to leeward as it climbed the mast. With the sheet still slacked, it blew out over the starboard bulwark.

"Take in the bow line," Lieutenant Grimes shouted forward. He was standing amidships, just behind Trevett.

John noted the time and wrote, *Wind light from ENE; tide in flood.*

Grimes watched patiently as *Katy's* bow drifted to starboard, the gap widening between it and the wharf. One line still extended from the larboard quarter to the wharf, acting as a hinge. Men took the forward mooring line below to stow it out of the way.

"Mr. Trevett, take in the main sheet two fathoms." The sheet became taught, and the breeze flattened the wrinkles in the trapezoidal sail. Trevett was happy to assume the role, even temporarily, of an officer in the sloop's company. "Take in the stern line," Seabury ordered.

The crew handling the ship's end of the line surged it, and men on the wharf slipped its eye from the bollard, dropping it into the brackish water while *Katy's* crew deftly pulled it in and carried it down the after companion for storage.

John watched and his mind registered a handful of men around the deck who apparently had no ship-handling duties. He knew several of them and made a mental note of their names. Clerk Trevett again noted the time in the rough log and wrote *Underway.*

The slight breeze was just sufficient to drive *Katy* downstream, stemming the flow of the flooding tide as it streamed up the Narragansett River. The rudder bit in the water as the men at the helm deftly steered their sloop toward the center of the channel.

Katy was drawing abreast *Washington* as Commodore Whipple's shoulders emerged from the companionway. A low murmur from the east quickly grew to a roar. John noticed now, for the first time, that Providence's citizenry lined the long wharf —not only the town's people ashore, but Captain Grimes had his crew filling the rigging and lining *Washington's* starboard bulwark.

Hats and arms were waving; "Huzzah for Commodore Whipple" could be heard in the general din. Abraham smiled and stepped over to the larboard quarter. Still smiling, Whipple doffed his hat and bowed to the cheering crowds.

At first, stunned into silence, *Katy's* crew quickly picked up the cheering themselves. Commodore Whipple turned forward and bowed to them as well.

As *Katy* drew ahead of *Washington*, the smaller sloop's bow could be seen falling off the pier as well. Moments later, she was riding in the wake of her larger consort. America's first navy—that of Rhode Island Colony—had sortied. Two small sloops with less than six score men between them were standing out to challenge the largest naval power the world had yet known.

William Jones sat behind the table, his back to the corner farthest from the door, the cold hearth of the vacant fireplace a couple feet from his left shoulder. Two dogs, one small, the other large, lay on the hearth. The large one was clearly asleep on his side with his inert head flat against the flagstones. The other relaxed with his chin resting on the ribs of his companion. His eyes swiveled around the Newport taproom, and his head rose and sunk as the larger dog inhaled and exhaled.

Any casual observer would note that William Jones was likely at the end of his teens, or just into the third decade of his life. His friends and acquaintances knew him to be keen of mind, industrious, a superb marksman who rarely returned from the hunt without a stag, and well respected in the community.

Having been sired and reared in Newport, he drifted in and out of the local chapter of the Rhode Island Militia, often elected sergeant or lieutenant during the half-decade or so of his affiliation. The men who were gathered around the table with William this morning, drinking coffee at this early hour, also knew him to be a firm patriot, scornful of the local loyalists. Some of the small group belonged to the Sons of Liberty.

They all spoke in quiet tones. Though this particular tavern was reputedly a patriot establishment, Captain Wallace was believed to have loyalist spies in Newport, some of which were low enough to accept payment for informing on their neighbors.

The man with his back to the door, marked as a seafaring man by the gold hoop earring and tattoos on the back of both his hands, spoke in a hushed tone as he looked left to the patrons at other tables.

"I been down the harbor meself at first light, Will. Five of them ships Wallace has stoled are still in the harbor. Three of 'em dockside have *Rose's* marines guardin' the gangways. T' others is swingin' t' their hooks in harbor . . . mos'ly w' a mixed lot o' Tories and Tars at anchor watch. 'Spec' the other two's out makin' mischief."

"Good report, Mate," Jones praised his colleague, "but it makes no matter so long as *Rose* is hanging about at short stay just in the roads."

"She can't stay there forever, Will," another man at the table whispered, swallowing a gulp of his now lukewarm coffee. "She's got to go on patrol at some point. Wallace is too greedy to satisfy himself with six small prizes."

"Like as not she'll send them off to Boston to the Admiral, and they will be out of our reach," Jones lamented, almost too loud for the comfort of his friends. "But we need to be ready anyway—at a moment's notice. Providence smiles on those who are prepared."

"The Sons are ready Will. You give the word, and I can have two dozen armed men on the dock in quarter of an hour's time."

Will smiled at the fourth man, sitting with his back to the cold fireplace.

Savage Gardner curled the gnarled fingers of his left hand around the forward shroud in the larboard chains. *Diana* skipped along, barely rolling in the slight waves that the north wind was just beginning to kick up. The breeze was capricious most of the day, backing and veering from east, through north to west, and back again.

For the last glass, it remained relatively steady from the north. As far as the British Navy Board was concerned, Gardner was the master on *Rose*. But today he was acting captain of *HMS Diana*, sloop tender to *Rose*. Captain Wallace appointed him as such.

With his crew of eleven, Gardner occupied this day in and around Hope, Patience, Hog, and Connanicut Islands searching for smugglers. But his main mission was to locate any small vessels being fitted out as warships. Captain Wallace had intelligence that the colony was authorizing a navy. A navy of pirates was what Captain Wallace called them—pirates and traitors.

The day was drawing toward evening, but Gardner wasn't yet ready to return to *Rose* and relinquish the freedom of his command. His arm flexed, and the shroud bowed slightly as *Diana* rolled to starboard and his weight shifted. A gunner and loader stood near each of his four swivel guns, but they had not fired them all day. He was now cruising in the waters between Patience and Connanicut Island.

"Sail ho," came the lookout's cry. He was one of only three men not in a gun crew. "Sail to the north."

Gardner squinted and shaded his eyes. Sure enough, there was a sloop to the north heading to intercept his course.

"'Nother one about a mile or two farther north, sir."

Perhaps Acting Captain Gardner will not return empty-handed, he thought.

DONT TREAD ON ME

Abraham Whipple, leaning his right hip against the starboard rail, glanced over the side. The cloudy brown water was drifting away astern, giving way to the clear blue of Narragansett Bay. He saw the charred remnants poking above the lapping wavelets and remembered the night, just a few years ago, when he watched the flames engulfing *Gaspee*.

He was not sorry for his part, would never be sorry, but there was always a touch of lament at the loss of a ship. They were gorgeous creatures in his mind—always were and always would be.

"Commodore," Trevett wanted his attention. "*Washington* is signaling, sir, 'Enemy in sight'."

"Very well, Mr. Trevett. Acknowledge and reply, 'engage enemy'." Then Whipple continued, "Tell her to take the western pass."

"Aye, aye, sir." Trevett flipped some pages in his book and began sorting out a bundle of colored bunting.

"Mr. Seabury," Whipple said, "You may send the men to their guns. They are to cast them loose and load them. The rest should go to the stations we discussed." Helmsman, steer for the eastern passage about Hope Island. We shall ensure she doesn't slip past."

"Aye, sir."

Trevett was practically hopping up and down with pent-up excitement and concern that he would be left to only take notes of the battle. His flags were streaming out to the wind, and his notes were caught up. Looking around the deck, he saw that the initial pandemonium was settling into purposeful actions. He approached Whipple.

"Captain, Commodore, Sir," he began.

Whipple lowered his glass and turned his head slightly to look Trevett in the eye.

"Sir, I can't just take notes about the fight. I have watched the crew, Captain. I know four men who are not on a gun crew and who are crack marksmen. Let me take them into the top, sir, and mark down the enemy with muskets."

"You have your assigned duties, Mr. Trevett. We need signals, and the Assembly will need their record."

"But sir . . ."

"Enough, John!"

Trevett held his tongue, but the expression on his face did his pleading for him. Ultimately, Whipple relented—partially.

"Very well, John. You may load your pistols and direct the fire of your sharpshooters from the quarterdeck. But you will stay by me and perform your other duties, as well."

"Aye, sir. Thank you, Captain!"

Trevett quickly gathered the four men, all friends of his, and gave them their orders. One he sent below to locate his chest, load his brace of pistols, and bring them to him.

Grimes stood between the helm and starboard bulwark. His feet were spread, and his knees, hips, and shoulders flexed and rotated unconsciously as *Washington* drove through the gentle swell of the bay. He glanced at his sails, then at those of *Diana*, then took in the enemy. She disappeared behind Hope Island.

The two sloops ran easily before the gentle winds, both pitching slightly in the feeble waves. Just under a cable of Narragansett Bay separated them.

"Heave to," came the order across the water from Gardner.

"That will be the day if I yield to that insolent puppy," Whipple said to the quarterdeck at large and put the speaking trumpet to his lips. "You will heave to, sir, or I shall sink you directly," he shouted back at the tender. Both sloops sailed on to the south. *Washington* was seen in the west on a converging course. No one hove to.

Trevett glance aloft at his marksmen in the top. He knew that at a range of a cable there was virtually no chance of the marksmen hitting their target. Some would even fire rifles, but the distance and the relative motion of *Diana* and *Katy* would render any hit as mere happenstance. Nevertheless, it made him and the shooters feel like just a little more than mere passengers.

"Mr. Seabury, a shot across the scoundrel's bow should give him to know that I mean business."

Seabury grabbed the linstock from the captain on number five four-pounder and crouched beside the cascabel to line up the shot. When he was satisfied the shot would not strike *Diana* but still get their attention, he lowered the slow match to the priming. The charge exploded, driving the iron ball toward the target, and recoiling the gun to the end of its breeching.

The ball skipped across the waves just forward of *Diana's* bow. That was enough for Savage Gardner. He would not allow such an insult to the Crown to go unanswered. *Diana* had four swivels, but only three mountings on the larboard bulwark.

John Trevett watched as three puffs of smoke spurted from the tender's side and quickly disbursed in the following wind. There was no indication where the shot fell. This was a historic battle—the first between any Colonial government vessel and a King's warship—and he was determined to be more than a clerk during the action. He shouted encouragement to the marksmen, which was the limit of his involvement

John saw more puffs of smoke cough out from the larboard sides of *Diana*. The wind tore the sound away with the smoke so that he heard nothing. Just over two seconds later he flinched as a goose egg sized cannonball glanced off the mast, and a small splinter nicked his left ear. He clapped his hand to the side of his face instinctively, and when he examined it, saw a slight smudge of blood on his palm.

Katy's starboard broadside was now fully engaged, and both ships sailed along to the south, popping their guns at each other. *Katy* used her four-pounders and small arms while *Diana* employed one-pound swivels and muskets.

Commodore Whipple held the glass to his right eye, not bothering even to lean against the bulwark. His veteran sea legs kept the bulk of his frame steady against the deck's rolling, heaving, and pitching. He watched the young officer on the chase direct his crew.

A second later a ball splashed five yards wide of *Katy's* larboard quarter. Then Whipple blinked involuntarily. A bright flash on *Diana* startled his eye through the glass. When he opened it, he could see smoke on the sloop's deck and several men rushing about.

On *Washington*, Captain Grimes observed the motion of the other vessels. If he were to have a role in this battle, it would have to start now. The distance between *Washington* and *Diana* was a little far for untrained gun crews, but what else but untrained crews were available to a navy only a few hours old.

Look at that, would you, Grimes thought—or did he say it aloud? He was not sure which. An explosion on *Diana*?

"Helmsman," Grimes abruptly broke the silence, "Alter course. Close with the enemy." *Washington's* head slewed toward the east, and the distance between her and *Diana* diminished. "Hold her thus."

"Aye, sir. Steady on south southeast a half east."

"Larboard battery," Grimes shouted the preparatory command. "As your guns bear—fire!"

A ragged broadside barked out from the sloop's larboard guns. The forward fired first followed shortly thereafter by the after carriage guns when the crews made final adjustments to their aim. Using only his bare eyes now, Grimes saw several splashes, but no visible damage caused by his guns.

The petty officer blinked his eyes then squeezed them tight. The pain was sharp. A high-pitched incessant tone in his brain blocked out all other sounds. He blinked again. Again. Each flutter of his lids found the light more bearable. Even more relief was felt when he sensed a shadow over his face. Focus! He willed his eyes to ignore the remaining pain and desire to sleep.

Savage. It is the captain, Savage Gardner. Gardner's mouth was working, and the petty officer could feel the damp breath, but nothing was audible.

He shouted at his captain. "I can't hear you." Even his own voice did not penetrate the screeching in his ears. He shook his head from side to side.

Abruptly he noticed the pain. Intense and sharp on his face and neck. Dull and pulsating in his thigh and hip. His memory could account for none of it

Gardner held the petty officer's lapels in both fists and shook the man as he shouted into his face. "Wake up—wake up. You'll be fine, just a little singed and knocked about is all."

The man's face and neck were scorched, and hair was burned from the front half of his scalp. His pigtail was still intact. He had been manning the farthest aft swivel on the larboard side. He was beginning to take aim at *Katy* when one of her small cannon shot had crashed into the bulwark just below his swivel.

Most of the ball's impact was absorbed by the bulwark, but enough was left to leave a deep bruise on his thigh and shove him back. Losing his balance and spinning, he'd fallen face-first into the chest containing the swivel charges.

The serious event had been dropping his linstock into the charges. The slow match quickly burned through one of the linen bags and ignited the powder in a charge. This caused the entire chest to explode and blasted him and another man onto their backs with severe burns.

"Get them some water," Gardner ordered as he stood over the petty officer and another wounded man.

He looked around. Other than the powder his musket men had in their powder horns he was now out of ammunition. Yankee sloops were closing in on each beam, pinching him tighter and tighter. He estimated he was outnumbered by at least five to one. It was getting dark, and the wind was dropping—no chance of reaching the safety of *Rose* before the enemy was alongside. *Captain Wallace will not be pleased.*

DONT TREAD ON ME

The tiny platform that comprised *Katy's* top was crowded with four marksmen. By mutual consent, they settled into a rotation of firing by turns, creating an almost continual harassment on the enemy.

Looking up, Trevett was thankful to be aligned with such resourceful and skilled men. He decided that when things settled down, he would suggest to the commodore the idea of building a marine detachment for Rhode Island's navy around these men.

At their current relative angles, most of *Katy's* starboard battery would bear on *Diana*. Trevett watched another broadside boil the water around the enemy sloop. Except for the occasional pop of a musket, their fire ceased after the explosion.

John glanced to the east and noted that the sun was hanging only a couple of diameters above the horizon. Then he saw *Diana* alter course. Her boom swung out over the larboard rail, and her bowsprit rounded to the starboard. She was headed directly west toward the northern end of Conanicut Island.

There was no hesitation in Whipple's voice. "Follow her, helmsman. Mr. Seabury, standby to heave to."

Trevett saw the men from *Diana* slipping over the sloop's side as she slid up on the shoals of Conanicut's northeast shore. They were abandoning her and escaping into the forest. Whipple looked over the side. Decades of experience told him he was close enough to the shoal water.

James Wallace, Captain, His Majesty's Navy, sat in *Rose's* great cabin. Although he was born in England, he was considered an American loyalist due to his plantation and American wife in Georgia. His eyes were slightly glazed as he reviewed sheet after sheet of administrative drivel that his clerk placed on the desk in front of him.

The Admiralty and Navy Board must have their reports and accounts, regardless of duties or circumstances. Heaven forbid that the clerks and bureaucrats in London should be deprived of papers to review, criticize, and file.

Wallace had commanded the frigate for over three years and been on the American station over six months. He was confident his presence was felt during that time. Smuggling operations in Narragansett Bay would be shut down altogether if he had anything to say about it. He already had over half a dozen small prizes to his credit, several crewed with his own officers and leading loyalist sailors.

They made excellent tenders to *Rose* and could follow the rogues into the myriad creeks and small inlets where his frigate would ground in the mud. The sooner he ended this rebellion, the better the world would be in his mind. There were hints from the admiral that better things were in store.

He withdrew the quill from his ink bottle. It was poised in the air allowing a drop to drip back into the bottle before signing another ledger. It never made it to the signature place. A distant rumble registered on Wallace's ear. He and his clerk cocked their ears to the north simultaneously.

Wallace dropped the quill on his desk and threw on his blue uniform coat with its heavy gold epaulets. His clerk collected the documents and wiped away the drop of ink that the quill left on his master's desk. Both men rushed up on deck and listened to the report of the watch officer.

"Gunfire to the north, Captain. I have sent a midshipman to the masthead with a glass and am just getting ready to call away the detail to up anchor."

"Very well. Carry on," Wallace replied. "Fire a gun and signal the recall of all boats in the harbor as well."

Captain Wallace focused his glass and was scanning to the north when he heard the midshipman hail the deck.

"Deck there! Three small vessels to the north, between Prudence and Conanicut, exchanging gunfire. Can't see any colors but one is *Diana*.

"You may slip the cable," Wallace ordered the watch officer. "Call all hands for getting underway."

"Aye, sir," the watch officer replied. He nodded at the petty officer that was already heading to the hatches to call the crew.

"*Diana's* let go 'er sheets," the midshipman continued his narrative from the masthead. "Looks like she's run up on the shoals of Conanicut."

DONT TREAD ON ME

The tavern's door burst open, and a man stood holding the latch, pausing to catch his breath. He allowed himself three deep breaths that were sufficient not only to restore his wind but also to compose his mind. He walked over and addressed William Jones who was still sitting at his regular corner table.

Both dogs were awake now, the smaller one still on the hearth. By now he had acquired an ox bone and was gnawing and licking at it. The larger ambled over to claim the floor next to William's chair, leaning against the legs. William's hand rested on its head. The man's eyes flick down to the dog and then leveled on William's.

"Now's our chance, Will," he began. "Some flap goin' on up the Bay. Wallace recalled his boats and *Rose* is slippin' 'er anchor cable."

"And the prize crews?" William asked.

"Down to skeletons. Most of the boats carried several hands back to *Rose*."

"William Jones closed his eyes and considered. He was not overly cautious, but neither was he reckless. There may still be bloodshed, but he had to admit his compatriot was right. There was not likely to be a better time to take back the small vessels captured by Wallace.

"All right," he said. "Call your men."

"Already on their way to the dock, Will," he grinned.

"Put down your helm," Commodore Whipple ordered.

Katy's rudder forced her stern to swing around to the south and her cutwater and jib boom to arc to starboard. She heeled steeply to larboard as the wind caught her beam but continued turning until facing directly into the wind.

"Meet her, Helmsman—Lieutenant Seabury, back the jib."

The crew tailed onto the jib sheet and pulled the triangular sail through the forestay, forcing it onto the starboard side. The sloop hung in the water, slightly off the wind, which balance the pressure on the opposing main and jib sails. *Katy* was hove to, remaining almost motionless, but drifting very slowly towards *Diana*.

"Mr. Bradford," Whipple addressed *Katy's* master. "Take five men and a tow line to the prize."

He referred to *Diana*, whose small crew ran her into the mud and splashed ashore on Conanicut Island to escape capture. Once his master transferred to the prize and made the tow line fast, he would pull her off the shoal and return to Providence.

"Abe, Sir, Commodore—Captain . . ."

Whipple looked up to the main top to see the marksmen gesturing frantically to the south and trying to get his attention.

"What is it, blast you?" He shouted!

"*Rose* is coming up hand over fist," one of them finally reported, pointing to the south.

Whipple swiveled his gaze from *Diana* to the south, toward Newport. Sure enough—Gould Island shoreline still occluded his view of her hull from the deck, but he knew the men in the top could see her well. He brought his glass to his eye and watched as she slid across the confined circle of the lens from left to right. She was going to come up the channel on the west side of Gould.

And there she was. What magnificence. Rose Island and Brenton's point overlapped in the background, appearing as one headland to provide the backdrop. She blended partly with the land and trees behind her, but there was no mistaking the towering pyramid of white canvas. The full-bellied rectangles of sail piled one atop the other, reaching for the deep azure of the sky's dome.

By Heaven, a ship under sail is a beautiful thing, Whipple thought, *cracking on like her tail's afire—and what a bone in her teeth*. Her cutwater raised a frothing white wave that swept away on either bow and down her sides as *Rose* crashed through each gentle swell. Her yards were braced up sharp to take every advantage of the easterly wind. *That Wallace is a determined man —a man possessed,* mused Whipple.

Commodore Whipple lowered his glass and looked back to Diana. He saw *Katy's* boat secured alongside and his men working on lashings for the tow. *Washington* was standing off and on close to the beach, and her boat was already run up onto the shore. Several of the sloop's men were standing and firing muskets toward the fleeing British tars.

Grimes will attend to them, Whipple reasoned and turned his attention back to *Diana.*

"Mr. Bradford, the tow?" Whipple shouted across the water.

Bradford looked back toward his commodore. "One minute, sir. You may take a strain."

"Lieutenant Seabury," Whipple addressed his first lieutenant, "Shift the headsails if you please."

"Heads'l sheets," Seabury shouted to the hands forward, "Let go and haul."

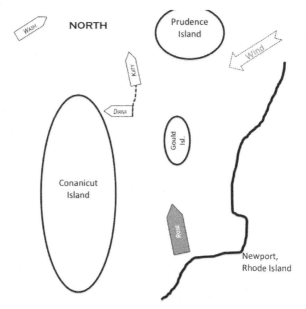

The seamen on the starboard side eased their sheets, and the pressure of the wind on the triangular foresail blew it through the forestays. The men on the larboard side took a strain and heaved around, pulling on the clew and stretching the canvas foot taught from where it was made fast by the tack.

Katy was no longer hove to. Her stem began to push the bay to either side as she began her forward motion.

"Meet her," Whipple ordered the helmsman. "Thus." He looked at the compass. "Steady on east by northeast."

"East by northeast, she is, Cap'n."

Looking around quickly, Whipple saw *Rose* still over three miles to the south and *Diana* was beginning to slide aft as the towing hawser tightened. The strain was not even sufficient to raise the line completely out of the water. He saw Trevett standing near, still making notes on the day's events.

"Signal *Washington*, John. 'Return to Providence.'"

"Aye, sir."

"I'll have a leadsman in either chain," Wallace ordered *Rose's* first lieutenant.

"Already ordered, sir," the stout lieutenant responded.

"Then make sure they know what they are about," Wallace growled. "And tend to those sails while you are about it."

Captain Sir James Wallace was not happy, and he took out his frustration on his second in command. The man touched his hat to Sir James and scurried forward to supervise the leadsmen and sail trimmers.

Captain Wallace could see the luffs of the lower square sails begin to flutter. These windward leeches provided the indication that *Rose* was getting too close to the wind. It would help some when the braces pulled the yards forward on the windward side, bracing them up sharp. But would they be able to hold their course to the north?

With their fore and aft rigs, the sloops and schooners were much more maneuverable in the confined waters of Narragansett Bay. That was, after all, why he used them to patrol for rebel smugglers.

DONT TREAD ON ME

Trevett stood at the taffrail. *Washington* acknowledged his signal flags and was reluctantly sailing north, beating into the wind as it slowly died. Looking at *Diana*, he could see the master cutting the lashing that bound the towline to her stern.

Bradford clearly knew what he was about. Having first run the hawser through the anchoring hawse hole on the bow, he then ran it outboard down the starboard side, like a spring, finally securing it to—something, Trevett could not make out what—at the sloop's stern.

This arrangement caused the grounded vessel to be towed stern-first until she was clear of the shoal and rocks. Now they cut the heavy line free of the stern, and the bow began to slew northwards and followed in *Katy's* wake as the pair sailed back to Providence.

William Jones flinched involuntarily, wincing as a couple of small splinters pricked his face. One stuck in his right eyebrow and the other in the apple of his cheek. They stung and allowed a trickle of blood, but he was thankful that both missed his right eye. He brushed them with the palm of his right hand as his left continued to hold the tiller.

The splinter in his brow became dislodged, but that in his cheek stung as his actions merely drove it deeper into his flesh. They were caused by a musket ball smashing into the boat's gunnel as it approached the sloop at anchor in Newport Harbor—one of Wallace's prizes.

Jones was surprised at the number of Sons of Liberty that he found waiting on the wharf when he arrived. Not just waiting, but seemingly awaiting his orders. Over two score of them were milling about, armed with cutlasses, pistols, pikes, a few muskets, even a cudgel or two.

Getting over his initial surprise, he concluded they would not act until they heard his plan. He efficiently formed them into several groups and sent them off to liberate Wallace's captured vessels—about half in boats toward the ones at anchor, the rest toward those moored to the piers.

The sun was high overhead. William looked at the sloop anchored northeast of Brenton point. He chose the vessel farthest from the wharf. Now his longboat was fairly skimming across the harbor. Propelled by eight oarsmen, several other patriots were crowded into the bow, waiting to storm onto the sloop.

He didn't see any red uniforms among the men on his target. Apparently, Wallace had recalled his regular crew, including the Marines. This was not necessarily a good sign. Animosity between loyalists and patriots often involved more vitriol than between the patriots and the British regulars.

Looking over his shoulder, William saw some of the other vessels had already been liberated and were making their way north between Goat Island and Long Wharf. Having ordered them to head north toward Providence or smaller ports where *Rose* could not pursue, he knew they would soon be racing through Coaster's Harbour and slipping around Coddington's Point.

William turned his attention back to the sloop he assigned to himself. About half the men on board were strung along the starboard bulwark firing muskets toward his boat. The rest were on the anchor engaged in weighing. *You would be slipping your cable if you knew what we had in store*, he thought.

Half a cable now. He pushed the tiller over so the boat would curve north. The boat would now slide into the sloop broadside— starboard gunnel to starboard gunnel—allowing all the men to climb aboard at once. Thirty yards. A metallic clang and one of the men yelped as a musket ball glance off his cutlass and wrenched it from his fist.

"Boat oars!"

The men pulled the oars in, and they clattered noisily as they were dropped along the centerline of the boat. There was no bowhook. Instead, his men grabbed any handhold they could find to arrest the forward motion as his boat ground alongside the sloop.

Musket muzzles and pike heads were jabbing down into the boat. William recognized a couple of the defenders as he drew his cutlass and searched with his free hand for a purchase that would allow him to swing up and over the sloop's bulwark.

Then they were over the rail and on the deck. The dull thud of wood slamming against wood or smashing into flesh and bone. The clash of metal striking metal. Sporadic burst of pistol discharge. William registered the recognition of his neighbor's face as it disappeared over the larboard bulwark, one of his patriots shoving the man into the harbor.

He sensed rather than saw the butt of a musket swinging toward him and instinctively parried with his cutlass. His blade stuck in the wood of the stock, and both men tugged to wrench their weapons free. He felt his cutlass come loose and smashed the guard into his assailant's face as he readied to swing the weapon again. The man staggered backward, blood flowing from a broken nose, and before he could recover his balance and composure, angry hands toppled him backward into the harbor as well.

Then quiet. William heard only heavy breathing and the occasional slap of the halyards against the mast. Men were floating in the water. Some face up, some face down, a few clinging to the boat that drifted downwind. Two lay motionless on the sloop's deck. One was a patriot and one a loyalist. After his men caught their breath, two of them grabbed an inert loyalist by the boots and began to drag him to the starboard side.

"No," William commanded sharply. "Enough. We will tend his wounds with our own."

He pointed to a group of his men with his cutlass then waived it carelessly toward the mast and the windlass.

"Get underway. I'll take the helm."

They dropped the man's feet with a clunk to the deck. The victorious patriots ambled toward halyards and anchor windlass to complete the task of getting underway that was begun by the loyalist anchor watch less than half a glass earlier.

Rose was close-hauled on the starboard tack. The rising northeast wind blew fresh over the bow as her sheets and braces were hauled as tight as the crew could pull, even with bosun's mates' rattans cracking across their bare shoulders.

Little good it is doing, Captain Wallace whined to himself and cursed silently as he watched *Diana* and *Katy* slowly widening the gap to the north. Even made up in a tow he could not overtake the pair. Now, as he watched, he saw that the tow was cast loose so the two could both make better speed to the north.

"On deck," the lookout shouted. "Several small sail to the south and east."

All the officers on the quarterdeck swung aft and aimed their glasses, sweeping an arc from east to south.

"It's the prizes, I'll wager," remarked the first lieutenant.

"I right well know it's the prizes, Lieutenant," Wallace spat back. He swore aloud. Then he strongly rebuked himself for giving audible vent to his vile frustration. He knew Whipple was behind this and vowed that he would have his revenge.

"Take the ship back to Newport," he shot the words at the first lieutenant. Then he tucked his glass under his arm and stormed below to sulk in his cabin.

Whipple, along with Grimes, Bradford, and Trevett sat at the commodore's usual table in the Sabin enjoying their victory dinner. The affair took more than twice the normal time to complete, as a fairly continuous stream of well-wishers flowed through the tavern to buy drinks, slap backs, and deliver verbose congratulatory toasts.

By act of a colonial legislature, America had created a navy. That navy sallied forth, met the greatest navy in the world, and returned robed in the laurels of victory. Certainly, Rhode Island would bring the interloping tyrant to his knees.

Triumph could only be a matter of hours away. At any rate, if one were to listen to the populace of Providence flowing through the Sabin this evening, that was the favorite scenario.

The seamen who pulled off this feat—by the grace of God, they were quick to interject—were sober-minded enough to know that all they accomplished was to liberate some shipping and arouse the considerable ire of an already irritated King's officer.

The tables were all occupied, but finally the officers had theirs to themselves. Whipple leaned back in his chair and rubbed his belly, undoing another button of his waistcoat. He took his clay pipe and a crock of tobacco from the wall shelf behind him and filled the pipe.

John Trevett sat nearest the hearth, while the commodore was behind the table. John stood and took a spill from the pile on the mantle. As it was June there was no flame in the fireplace, so John lit the spill in a smoking lamp and passed it to his friend.

Commodore Whipple sucked in, drawing the flame through the tobacco until it ignited. He then shook the spill to extinguish it and laid it on the table. None of the group spoke for a time, allowing their fibers to relax while reflecting on the day's events, and being thankful they lived through it.

John saw a man come through the doorway opening onto the square. He didn't recognize the fellow. He was dirty, and his clothing appeared ragged, none of which was out of place in a waterfront tavern, but it did arouse a few glances in the Sabin, which had become a more upscale establishment.

"I am looking for Captain Whipple," the new arrival declared to the room.

The room became quiet. John Trevett stood.

"Over here my friend," Trevett replied, beckoning the man to join them.

He walked over and then shook hands. "You appear gallied, my dear sir. Pray be seated," John invited, sliding an empty chair up to their table.

"I thank you, sir," the newcomer said, dropping into the seat. "My name is William Jones," he introduced himself, "of Newport."

"I am Abraham Whipple, lately made commodore of the colony's navy." Whipple stuck out his hand and shook that of William. "Are you in bad bread, young sir?"

"I am not, Commodore. In point of fact, finding you allows me to successfully conclude a profitable venture."

"Pray enlighten me then, my new friend. How may I be of service?"

"I have come, Commodore Whipple, to report the liberation of six of the colony's trading vessels and turn over custody of a sloop to you, sir."

Whipple was struck dumb and sat silent. He pressed his lips closed when he realized his mouth was hanging open.

"You understand, sir, the Sons in Newport have been scheming to make mischief for Wallace since he began sending his booty into Newport. The network of patriots is extensive. Well sir, this morning a watcher saw *Rose* slip her cable and set sail to the north. Must have been chasing you fellows, Commodore."

"Go on young man," Whipple ordered having regained his composure. He decided to let the tale unfold in the manner prescribed by its teller.

Jones related the day's events, as he knew them, from the beginning of the day in Newport. He told Commodore Whipple of the patriots' exploits in Newport, and how they liberated Captain Wallace's prizes.

"Am I given to understand that you commanded this enterprise?" Whipple asked when Jones fell silent, gulping an ale that was set in front of him.

Jones was silent during which time he considered the question. Finally, he answered, "I suppose, sir, that after a fashion, you could say so. I confess I have no detailed knowledge of the Son's network, but upon reflection, I realize that the plan did not go into execution until given the order. It appears that the patriots understood implicitly that I would assume authority, even though no discourse passed to that end."

"By Jove, boy, that is a story. You shall lodge at my home this night. Sarah will want to make your acquaintance." He held up his hand to forestall objection. "I dare say, the news you brought will surely serve to enhance the satisfaction of the governor and the assembly."

Jones looked at his mug and smiled sheepishly.

"It occurs to me that I have been rude as I was preoccupied by your report. Please allow me to introduce my colleagues." Whipple introduced his officers.

"It is an honor to meet all of you. I believe I met you briefly in Newport, sir, some years ago," he said when introduced to John Grimes.

A plate was brought, and Jones attacked it ravenously. The men went over the day's events again and again. Secondary topics discussed—future plans, tactical considerations, the disposition of the Tory and British prisoners. At last, after most other patrons deserted the room, the group rose. Whipple settled the account, and each made his way home for a well-deserved respite.

September 5, 1775
Philadelphia, Pennsylvania

The red brick structure, built in the Georgian style, was nearly twenty-five years old. The clock itself, housed in the central steeple, had been displaying the time for the city's residents since Thomas Stretch built and installed it in 1752. Although not truly deemed unsafe or uninhabitable, serious signs of failure had become evident in the steeple, and local builders were beginning to make overtures about its replacement.

Cracks and settlement, however, were not on the minds of the men gathered in the main assembly room of the building. In fact, even the continuation of the clammy, oppressive heat that plagued Philadelphia throughout the summer scarcely elicited a comment on this afternoon. The minds of these men were occupied with the more important business of restoring the rights and prosperity of their several colonies—their country as many of them considered it.

These were the men of the Second Continental Congress, delegated by their respective colonies to accomplish what was proving to be an increasingly complex mission. The colonies represented by these gentlemen were in various stages of enmity with their mother country—England. A number of them were in open rebellion, while others ranged from attempted reconciliation to open support of the grievances of the others.

They struggled to find common ground, agreement, and solution while maintaining a resolve to demonstrate a united confederation to the corrupt ministries and parliament that governed them so poorly from across thousands of miles of sea.

Now, according to some, they had the rashness of their Boston cousins to thank that they were becoming embroiled with their king in a shooting war. Already the Congress had dispatched a commander-in-chief from Virginia to organize and take command of the army that was largely composed of New Englanders. To some of the delegates, this was seen as an imperative need to maintain cohesion of the colonies. To others, it was a dangerous provocation that only served to move them further from the reconciliation that had to be achieved.

This morning's debate had begun rationally enough, at least in the estimation of some. The British army forced the Massachusetts militia to take up arms in defense of their families and property—their rights as free citizens. General Washington had been sent to turn the militia into an army.

As maritime colonies or a maritime country, it logically follows that a navy is required as well as an army. Already Washington's army was suffocating from lack of supply while the British had unfettered access to seemingly inexhaustible resources from the world.

"Mr. John Rutledge, the delegate from South Carolina is recognized," John Hancock announced from his chair on the dais.

"Thank you, Mr. President," John Rutledge replied, managing to hold a semblance of politeness in his voice. "The delegations from our northern brethren have incrementally drawn us from an honorable, prosperous settlement with the king toward irreconcilable rebellion. We concede that relations in the early part of the decade grew intolerable, but the solution lay in the way of negotiation and compromise—even peaceful disobedience, yet instead, we have been led down a path of bloodshed and treason. The line must be drawn."

Thomas Cushing couldn't wait to be recognized. He rose to his feet as he slapped his palm on his table. A delegate from Boston and long-time friend of Hancock, he shot him a quick glance before responding to Rutledge.

"Mr. Rutledge," Cushing launched into his statement, "I have firmly and consistently asserted my stalwart opposition to independence from England, but it must be clearly understood that we in Boston—New England—are not following some carefully orchestrated plot to slowly drag our neighbors down a path from which there is no other escape."

Well, perhaps not all of us are, Hancock thought as he glanced at the table occupied by John and Sam Adams.

"But sir," Cushing continued, "Surely you must grant that events, to date, have been forced upon us, and we have responded with the only course left open to us. Further, now that we have an army, they merit our support. We cannot simply leave them in the field to starve or be overrun for lack of powder and shot."

Edward Rutledge rose and waited with his hands at his sides to be recognized by Hancock. When he received that recognition he began, "Gentlemen, perhaps my elder brother's zealousness led him to choose the unfortunate term, 'treason.' I will definitively stipulate to the fact that Parliament and the king's ministers have stupidly and, no doubt, unwittingly maneuvered the American colonies into a course of action leaving us no choice but to defend our lives and property with force of arms."

He paused for the subtle drama then continued, "But it is to that course of action that I now register my vehement disagreement with the current proposal. We have an army in the field—an army comprised largely of our esteemed compatriots from the north, and it is most competently commanded by a gentleman of substance from Virginia. Of that, there can be no dispute."

Delegate Rutledge paused for a breath and to reassess the current state of his listeners, then continued. "It is, therefore, essential that this body focus its attention and energies on providing materiel and sustenance for that gallant army. I am in possession of correspondence that would shock the populace if they knew the direness of its content."

Rutledge waved the letter for effect, "Mr. President, if the Congress continues to divide time and resources on every Johnny-come-lately idea that scampers though its mind, our army will not be defeated, it will simply melt away and cease to exist. We must not divert our nearly non-existent resources into the establishment of a navy when we are scarcely able to field an army." He sat.

The room was quiet for scarcely a moment before Mr. Archibald Bulloch, delegate of Georgia rose and was recognized by Hancock.

"Mr. President," he began, "it is with great reluctance that I find myself in a position to humbly contradict my neighbor and friend, Mr. Rutledge. I should couch the disagreement first with support, however. Support for his well-stated sentiment that this body, yea, this country, owes to our gallant General Washington and his brave troops all the materiel and sustenance we can sacrificially provide. And I pray that our Holy Father will bless those meager supplies with the multiplication of His Divine Providence."

Bulloch paused for what he believed to be the appropriate length of silence after invoking the support of God. Then he went on.

"But gentlemen, it is precisely in support of our brave soldiers that we must have a navy. Floating just off the coastlines of our colonies are the undefended ships that daily supply our enemy. Even a small, lightly armed navy will wreak havoc on his supply, and, more to the point, redirect that supply into the bosom of our army. Further, my friends, England plunders our shipping with impunity, starving our families and the treasury of our legislatures."

Both Rutledges rose to their feet together. John yielded to his brother, Edward, and sat.

Edward replied directly to Bulloch. "My neighbor from Georgia, you have apparently spent too much time in the taverns drinking at the tap of our Yankee colleagues." He looked at the delegate from Georgia and could see that the insult had registered. "Do they just snap their fingers for you to come running and say 'Yes, Master?' Is it not enough that our southern neighbors have acquiesced to allowing Negroes into the Army? Now we will allow them to bankrupt our treasuries order protect their trading fortunes! No—no, sir. I will not support this measure." After slowly glaring around the room with a scowl, he sat.

Thomas Lynch sat at the table next to the Rutledges. He was looking at his hands folded atop the table. He focused on the ink staining his fingertips, a reminder of the letters he had written the prior evening. He was still amused that he was selected to accompany the same delegation that included the Rutledge brothers.

Lynch's mind swerved momentarily to his plantation in Berkley County. *Why do things have to change so? Our life was good—so good on the estate. I suppose I must continue to nudge Progress in the right direction.* He stood and waited for Hancock to recognize him.

"The Chair recognizes yet another delegate from South Carolina," Hancock stated, the hint of a wry smile escaped his lips as he closed his mouth.

"Thank you, Mr. President," Lynch replied. "It has been a pleasure to serve South Carolinians with my two friends and colleagues—the Rutledge brothers. Their consistent support of our culture and interests is renown and appreciated by our friends and neighbors."

Both brothers stared down at their tabletop, shuffling papers, and making their hands busy.

"I find it necessary, therefore, to continue this discourse on behalf of the friends who have sent us all to represent them. I concede the veracity of that which Edward has stated. I am afraid, though, that many in the colony are not of the same opinion. I offer Captain Alexander Gillon as a first-rate example. Even at this very moment, he serves a committee of local mariners and visionaries who have progressed a good distance along the path of instituting South Carolina's own navy. While it is true, therefore, that a Continental Navy may require funding from the various colonies, it is equally true that the need for maritime protection and projection is universally recognized."

"Further," he continued, "I am sure my neighbor did not intend to imply that our Yankee brothers are asking us to bear the entire burden of their defense. Why, Rhode Island has already had its own navy for months. I for one applaud their zeal and foresight. I find that the rational logic of the issue compels me to support the institution of a Continental Navy." Thomas glanced sidelong at the Rutledges and he resumed his seat.

A breeze drifted in through the open windows, stirring the heavy draperies and prompting a few to glance out the window. Had it not carried more of the steamy air, it may have been a welcomed respite.

Long shadows registered somewhere in the corners of their minds as they crawled across lawns and streets. The day was moving inexorably toward its conclusion. How much longer would this debate continue? Odors of dinner would soon be borne on the same breeze, making the continued discussion seem even more interminable.

It was the turn for John Houstoun from Georgia to deliver his address. "Gentlemen," he began, "I am sincerely concerned that this topic is even debated. It is clear that a war is upon us. It is clear that there will be no diplomatic end to the war without General Washington forces General Gage to sue for peace. It is clear that no maritime nation, as ours is, has ever survived or flourished throughout history without a strong navy to project its power."

Houstoun drew a breath. "We have already pledged to place our militia forces under General Washington's central command. If we don't mean for him and our army to starve and die in the field, then it is clear we must have a navy to interdict the king's shipping and supply our men in the field. The logic is inescapable. This body, by asserting its collective will, cannot thwart the immutable laws of Nature that have been set on their courses by our Creator." Having delivered that which he believed irrefutable logic he resumed his seat.

John Penn from North Carolina pounded his table and said, "Hear him, hear him!"

"Gentlemen," Hancock began firmly, bringing the room back to order, "I believe we have spent enough of our time—and wind—debating an issue that, as of yet, does not even have the benefit of a formal resolution to lay before us." He glanced at Sam Ward and Stephen Hopkins, the delegates from Rhode Island who began the argument. Both shook their heads. They had not yet received the final wording from their legislature to introduce a resolution.

"That being the case, we will recess for the evening, to reconvene at ten in the forenoon on the morrow." Hancock banged his gavel once; the volume quickly rose in the assembly hall as the debate continued in smaller groups, then evolved into invitations to, and plans for, the evening's dinners.

November 10, 1775
Philadelphia, Pennsylvania

Friday afternoon—five men stood in the corner of the hall just to the side of the main entry. They spoke quietly in their private circle—not in whispers, but not loud enough that their voices echoed through the hall. The great bronze bell in the tower above their heads gonged twice and brought their discussion to a halt. Silas Deane, a member of Congress from Connecticut, held a rolled document in his right hand.

Deane used it like a riding crop, whipping his thigh to emphasize his points. John Adams from Massachusetts and Stephen Hopkins of Rhode Island faced him across the small circle. The member from New Hampshire, John Langdon, and New York's John Jay—the only committee member not from New England—flanked Deane on his right and left hands.

Born a scant eight days earlier, the ad hoc committee considered the letter from the Committee of Safety in Passamaquoddy, Nova Scotia. The small maritime community in Nova Scotia petitioned Congress to allow them to join the association of North Americans in order that they may "preserve *their* rights and liberties." As politicians are wont to do, Congress formed a committee to take up the matter.

The five men in the circle had done just that, and they presented their response to the letter in the form of a resolution on November 9th. There was not much debate. Near supper time, the light fled the large windows, and the politicians tabled the resolution. That was Thursday. Today is Friday.

Adams rubbed his hands vigorously. A man of assiduous decorum, he eschewed his pockets, but his hands were cold, and his fingers numb from the walk back. It was November in

Philadelphia, and there was no stove in the entry hall of the statehouse.

"Your neighbor will gavel us in at any moment, Mr. Adams. Lord love the man, but Mr. Hancock dearly esteems that gavel of his," Deane stated with a faint smile at the corners of his mouth. "We are next on the agenda."

"I do not foretell any significant debate," Langdon predicted.

"You mean to say," John Jay corrected, "any *more* significant debate."

The men nodded and murmured. There was much unofficial debate concerning their proposal over dinner and into last night. Their plans and resolutions, conceived and honed over the past several days, were ready now—detailed tactics to despoil the enemy of his supplies and gain new allies for the Cause. Sure, the force would make a show—look into Passamaquoddy and reconnoiter the situation. But the main thrust was to capture and plunder Halifax.

His Excellency, General Washington, would be charged to raise marines and sailors, predominately from the inadequate ranks of his army. Like most men of a political mind, those of this committee could not resist detail. The vision of their resolution pierced the future and the fog of war.

Their plan included the minutia of the expedition down to the thirty-two rounds of ammunition per man that would be issued. General Washington, no doubt, would wonder why Congress needed him or his officers, given the omniscient foreordination of the politicians.

"There it is," Adams said and inclined his bewigged head toward the sound of the gavel. He stood aside and allowed Deane to precede his committee into the main meeting.

The five men took their seats, and immediately John Hancock asked, "Mr. Deane, I believe that by this time debate is exhausted. If you will read your resolution once more to refresh the minds of the members, I will entertain a vote."

Silas Deane glanced at his table mate, the only other delegate from Connecticut. His colleague smiled and nodded encouragingly. Deane unrolled the document and cleared his throat quietly.

"Thank you, Mr. President," he began. Deane started off in a strong, level voice. He read the mundane, even tedious, sections and used skillful inflection when required. The conclusion of the resolution read:

"That two battalions of Marines be raised consisting of one Colonel, two lieutenant-Colonels, two majors and other officers, as

usual in other regiments; that they consist of an equal number of privates as with other battalions, that particular care be taken that no persons be appointed to offices, or enlisted into said battalions but such as are good seamen, or so acquainted with maritime affairs as to be able to serve for and during the present war with Great Britain and the Colonies unless dismissed by Congress; that they be distinguished by the names of the First and Second Battalions of Marines."

Absentmindedly, Deane rolled the document back on itself and laid it face down on his table. Coattails swept aside, he resumed his chair, scooted the document forward, and leaned his elbows on the table. In the quiet moment that followed, Deane noticed a few snowflakes swirling in the breeze outside the glass panes. Hancock looked quickly around the room and then stood.

"I believe we will just take a voice vote if there are no objections." Again, his eyes scanned the room. There was no indication of objection. "Very well, then—all those in favor of the committee's resolution please signify your support by saying, 'Aye.'

Lamps, fueled with very expensive oil of spermaceti, burned on both of the elegant tables in the front sitting room. Imported from New England, the oil was one of the most expensive products of the sperm whale and highly valued for its excellent lighting properties. Wax candles of the same derivation burned in the central chandelier and the sconces that lined the stylishly papered walls of the small room. A handful of influential men sat in the room and sipped brandy, Madera, and rum.

Darkness arrived hours earlier and brought increased wind and heavier snow with it. Heavy flakes assaulted the windows and sounded light thumps. The warm fire blazed in its appointed place, and the bright lights contrasted with the dark, snowy night. The assembled men shared a sense of cozy satisfaction and congeniality.

When the front door opened and closed, the cold night spilled in and ran along the floor of the entry hall. It touched the men's feet and reinforced their appreciation of the warm fire. Boots stamped then trod along the entry hall toward the doorway that regulated admittance to the drawing room.

The conversation died, and the men looked up at the imposing figure in the doorway. A servant accepted his hat and winter cloak then shook the snow off both. He then folded the cloak over his arm and retreated to hang it near the fire in the kitchen.

The master of the house sprang to his feet and hurried over to shake the newcomer's hand. Samuel Nicholas was very satisfied with himself for having assembled such a group of notable Americans for this dinner party. He was especially happy to have the renowned captain, John Barry, under his roof.

"Captain Barry," Nicholas gushed with honest pleasure in his face, "You do indeed honor this home with your presence. Thank you so much for coming, sir!"

Barry accepted Nicholas's hand and reciprocated the firm grasp. Both men were about thirty years old, sturdy, and confident, but Barry enjoyed several more inches in height. In fact, even though unnecessary ashore, he bent his head as he walked through the doorway into the glowing room. The habit was born out of the defensive practice of ducking his head as he passed under the overhead beams of ships.

Most of Barry's life was spent afloat. When very young he worked in his Irish uncle's fishing boat. He grew up, moved to Philadelphia, and presently commanded merchant ships for Robert Morris. Morris, the great man himself, smiled from his chair near the fire and nodded to his friend when he came into the room.

"Good evening, sir," Barry said to Morris after releasing Nicholas's hand. "It's a gale we'll have before morning I'm thinking. Wind has backed three points since the light has gone."

"I'll not dispute your judgment on the weather, John," Morris smiled.

Barry swept the room with his disarming smile, locked his eyes on Nicholas, and replied to his kind welcome. "It is me whom *you* honor, sir, by your invitation. Thank you very much for including me in your gathering."

"May I offer something to warm you, Captain?"

"Some coffee with a generous portion of rum or Irish whiskey would serve admirably, sir."

Nicholas prepared the drink himself from vessels on the sideboard and handed it to his guest.

"Pray be seated, Captain Barry," he gestured to a vacant cushion on the settee beside John Adams. "We were just discussing the day's proceedings at Congress while waiting for our supper."

"I thank you, Mr. Nicholas—and please, sir, call me John. If I may delay for a moment, I would relish the opportunity to thaw the old bones. Me joints don't recover from the cold as quickly as they used to." His frame occluded the fire as he stood on the hearth rubbing his hams with his free hand.

Morris smiled at his friend and responded, "You are a young man, yet, John. Don't affect the afflictions of age so soon."

When his guests were all seated, Samuel Nicholas resumed his seat and put his mug on a small, lacquered table. Morris was satisfied with the group. He considered these men not only some of his best friends but also kindred political allies. His eyes and lips bore the expression of subtle contentment.

The united colonies now had an army, a navy, and a corps of marines—at least in principle. The men and equipment of the latter two had yet to be funded and supplied. Morris would see to the funding; the recruiting would be left to the men like Barry.

John Adams' cousin, Sam, drained his mug, smacked his lips, and looked at his host wryly. His unspoken request was clear.

"May I offer you more refreshment, Mr. Adams?" Nicholas asked and rose to his feet.

"Don't mind if I do, young man. And don't bother to put any coffee into this one." He handed his mug to Nicholas.

"You and Mr. Jay did good work this week, Cousin," Sam congratulated and took the mug full of rum from Nicholas.

"I definitely second those sentiments, Sam," Robert raised his drink in salute and held it in the air until the others copied him.

"To the Continental Marine Corps," Nicholas made the toast, and everyone repeated the words and drank.

Matthew Parke was a little awed to be in such company. He had become closely acquainted with Nicholas since moving to Philadelphia. They rode to the hounds until the war started. Since then, they followed the events together. Not as well connected as Samuel, he was glad to be included in the gathering but a little behind in the news.

"I no doubt risk the display of my ignorance, Mr. Adams, but would you be so good as to relate the moment's events for me?"

"With relish, my boy . . . with relish. Why, these fine gentlemen with their speeches, and gavels, and how-do-you-do's, only spent about a month to accomplish what it took New Englanders a few hours to do. You recall, when the redcoats marched on Concord, an army fairly materialized from the morning mist. A real army, mind you, son, with bodies and bullets and muskets." He paused to drink.

"Now we got a congress we are doing things proper, with motions and votes. Last month we created a navy. This month we created a marine corps. No bodies, or bullets, or muskets mind you, but real, honest to goodness ink on parchment." He grinned around the room.

Morris chided, "I believe, in your own inimitable fashion, you are having sport with your colleagues, Sam."

"As I am, Robert," he agreed. "To be sincere, I am as pleased as the rest of you. If we are going to be independent, we must have an organized government with ministries and departments."

"And funding."

"And funding."

Sam Adams came down from his platform to fill in the recent details for Parke, who listened with close attention. He and Nicholas had already spoken several times about the roles they wanted in the current struggle.

The dining room was warmed by the lights, the fire, and the camaraderie. Wax ran down the base of the candle stands spilling onto the rich table in a few places. Brandy, walnuts, and dried apples crowned the meal and added to the shared pleasure of the company. Parke stifled a belch, rubbed his eyes, and took several deep breaths. He was not used to such rich food and so much spirits and wine.

John Adams cracked a walnut and spoke. "You are correct, Robert, when you say we need to buy ships and man them. The officers, of course, will raise their crews so, we must select the best men."

"The best men," Robert Morris replied with a twinkle, "no doubt come from New England."

John Adams opened his mouth to protest, but Morris stopped him by raising his hand, palm out.

"It is okay, John," Morris continued. "There is no denying that New England breeds men born to the sea. It will fall to the whole Congress, though; to be sure it is merit and not patronage that commissions our officers. A southern gentleman of ability is commanding our army. I am sure there is a man of equal ability to command the fleet. I am also sure that you won't neglect to consider Captain Barry when deliberating your list of naval officers."

"It would be foolish of me to neglect such a mariner, sir," Adams replied.

"I'll warrant that it is not by coincidence that we are in the company of our highly esteemed host and his young friend, Mr. Parke," Sam Adams interjected.

Both men studied the grain in the table and fingered nutshells.

"You are very observant, Sam," Morris answered him. "Each will make a fine marine officer. In fact, I have no doubt that Samuel could field a troop of experienced riders from his fox hunting company in twenty-four hours."

"Indeed, I could, sir."

"Your . . . er . . . confidence is noted, Robert," John Adams said, "as is your interest. In point of fact, all three names are already on a list I have been preparing for the committee's consideration.

December 2, 1775
Philadelphia, Pennsylvania

Saturdays were busy at Peggy Mullan's Red Hot Beef Steak Club, but on this particular Saturday, the eating-house fairly roared with activity, and rough men spilled out onto the covered front porch. There were no tables outside, but men sat on the planks and leaned back against the railing fronting Water Street. Some sat on the steps, and a few milled about Tun alley at the bottom of the steps.

"Peggy's" and "Tun Tavern" were, in essence, the same establishment. Robert Mullan managed both on behalf of the Mullan family. The tavern and the eatery were standing room only today. Robert even coaxed some of the neighborhood girls who didn't normally work there to serve the patrons. New England's accent and swagger were prominently on display in the crowd.

John Trevett and Matthew Parke managed to squeeze into the only empty table in the Tun. Over two hours since lunch and still they talked, catching up on each other's lives since their last meeting. Matthew had taken John's advice and relocated from Alexandria to Philadelphia. He never regretted his decision. It was a good move financially, but what was more important, it put him at the seat of the new government.

It was not that there was a shortage of revolutionary fervor in Virginia—far from it. But Philadelphia was where the Congress sat and having one's face regularly before the decision-makers proved to be the boon he desired. John gave Matthew a blow-by-blow account of the Rhode Island Navy's activities, including the first battle.

"I'll tell you this much, Matthew, 'tis fortunate for me that my family was nearby. When the old man—Commodore Whipple—decided it was time to weigh, by thunder it was time to weigh. I had barely time to stow my chest below, and Katy was filling her topsail with her bow pointed down the stream."

Matthew listened intently to the account, asking questions for clarification. He was glad to see his friend again. "I knew I would be seeing you soon enough when Congress passed the resolutions for the Navy and the Marine Corps."

"It's right you were, Matthew. We would have been here sooner had we not played cat and mouse with his Bloody Majesty's Navy in the Sound. The commodore shipped Captain Saltonstall and every other son of liberty and freedom he could jam aboard that little packet."

"Several other small ships and packet boats have made Philadelphia this week, as well. I have noticed a few men from Maryland and Virginia, too. It is well. The United Colonies can use every mother's son these days."

"Sir—the gentleman at the window table sent for you."

"Thank you, miss," John said to the harried serving girl and looked across the crowded room to see Commodore Whipple's smiling face.

John and Matthew grabbed their tankards and weaved their way between tables and servers to the larger table. Whipple told two men to vacate their seats.

They slid into the two vacant places in time to hear Whipple address Robert Mullan. "It 'pears you are doing a brisk trade today, Robert—thanks to the men I brought down from Rhode Island."

"And I do thank you very kindly for that, Commodore. Free trade is the hallmark of a healthy nation. But I thank you more so for bringing men who are willing to fight for our freedom."

"I thank you doubly, Commodore," Samuel Nicholas interjected. "The trade down to the Connestogoe Waggon is just as lively as the Tun."

A girl came around with a stoneware pitcher and splashed more ale in all the tankards. She smiled and blushed when she poured Matthew's, and he met her glance with a steady stare.

Samuel continued, "But it's not the trade that gives me the most joy, sir; 'tis the men—men by the score."

Trevett shot him a quizzical glance. "How's that, sir?"

"I was waiting to tell you, John," Parke answered his friend. "But I can't hold it any longer; Samuel is the first marine. Congress made him Captain, dated from last week. And I am to be his first lieutenant of marines on Alfred!"

"Alfred?"

"She was Morris and Willing's Black Prince," Dudley Saltonstall answered Trevett's single word question. "Barry's had her since she came off the stocks. He's supervising the refit now at Humphry's. My wife's brother, Silas Deane, made sure she was one of the first ships Congress bought. She'll be rated a frigate, mounting thirty guns—nine pounders, six pounders—whatever they can lay their hands on."

"Sounds like she'd make a great flagship, Commodore," Trevett replied.

Icy silence covered the table, and a squall shadowed Whipple's face briefly. His monotone reply did little to thaw the mood. "Hopkins is to have the fleet."

"What? That's ridiculous, Commodore!" Trevett replied. "Foolishness—when you had Gamecock in the late war, you brought in near three dozen prizes. You recently fought—and won, mind you—the first naval battle of this war!

"It's true, Abe," Saltonstall weighed in. "Esek has nowhere near your experience at sea—nearly ruined the Brown brothers' slave trade and killed nigh every slave aboard that slaver when he had her. Why, if his brother weren't governor of Rhode Island and delegate to Congress . . . "

Robert Mullan stuck his oar in. "My man behind the bar is first cousin to the chambermaid at Mr. Adams' lodgings. He tells me that Hopkins' brother, Stephen, is pushing the Naval Committee to make Esek commodore, but there's been no vote yet."

"It will be, gentlemen; it will be," Whipple said. "I do thank you for . . . "

"But Commodore, you have to fight this," Trevett burst in again.

"That's enough, Mr. Trevett," Whipple cut off the diatribe. "I'm being given Columbus—twenty-eight guns, another Willing and Morris ship, formerly Sally. Congress had a choice to make, and they made it. We have plenty to do with the work we have been allotted. Now there's an end to it."

No one at the table spoke. Most looked into their ale. Matthew Parke took a swallow of his and wiped his upper lip with the back of his wrist. The room around them continued to buzz with braggadocio and excited conversations.

Dudley Saltonstall brought the pause to a close. "You were telling us about the Marines, Captain Nicholas."

"Yes, sir, Captain. Congress is appointing lieutenants and captains, and the officers will raise their own companies. I plan to establish a recruiting station at the Waggon. Perhaps I can impose upon Robert to let me enlist some men right here at the Tun, also. The men you brought from Rhode Island will be most welcome, Commodore."

"Do you have the list of postings, sir?" Trevett did not even attempt to contain his excitement. Whipple and Saltonstall glanced briefly at one another, their lips pressing in tight lines.

"I do, John." Nicholas began to recite from memory. "As Matthew stated earlier, he and I will serve Alfred under Captain Saltonstall. A local young man by the name of Fitzpatrick will be second lieutenant. Robert Cummings, James Dickenson, and Joe Shoemaker will be with Captain Whipple—on Columbus. Joe will be senior, and James will be first." He paused and nodded toward Whipple.

Nicholas drew a deep breath and continued. "The commodore's son, John, is to have the six-pounder brig, Cabot. A countryman of Captain Barry—John Welsh—will be her captain of Marines with James Wilson for a lieutenant. There is another brig, Andrew Doria; and you all are probably aware that Commodore Whipple's sloop Katy has been purchased by Congress and rechristened Providence."

A sharp yelp screeched out from a dog lying on the warm hearth when a man stepped on his tail. Another sailor he was scuffling with shoved the man, and he lost his balance.

The dog scampered across the room and sat next to Mullan, leaning against his hip. Mullan rose to his feet and shouted, "Here now, you two scrubs, take that outside!"

They ignored him. One man pulled a knife from its sheath behind his back and grinned at his opponent. Nicholas swallowed the remainder of his ale and stood. In a flash he drew his arm back and whipped it forward, sending his heavy pewter mug toward the man with the knife. A loud thump sounded as the mug struck him behind the ear and he dropped like a sack of grain onto the floor.

Robert Mullan looked at a couple of men seated near the bar and nodded toward the hearth. They got up and encouraged the conscious sailor to leave then picked up his companion and tossed him onto the cobbled street. Conversations in the taproom quickly resumed.

"Pray continue, Samuel," Saltonstall requested.

"Well, sir, I believe I have named the five ships comprising the Continental Navy—Alfred, Columbus, Andrew Doria, Providence . . . oh yes, Cabot. Very well, then, Isaac Craig, another Irishman, will have the marines on Andrew Doria and Henry Dayton those on Providence."

John Trevett grew more concerned as Nicholas continued to recite the list. When the list was finished, he was downright distraught.

"What? That's it?" Trevett said. "Surely there will be more."

"There are no more ships, John," Nicholas replied.

"But . . . Commodore . . . You know I came to be a marine. This is not right!"

"Compose yourself, John," Whipple countered.

The others studied the grain in the table or sipped their drinks.

"Be patient. I'm sure we can find you a berth as a midshipman while we work something out. Have faith, my boy."

Trevett was not happy, but he was mollified for the time being. He was still lost in his own thoughts when a rough looking group of men approached the table. The four of them stood in a row holding worn hats in front of them. They did not look like seamen but were clearly men used to working for their keep.

Nicholas thought he recognized at least two of them from the taproom at the Connestogoe Waggon. "Is there something we can do for you men?" Nicholas asked.

"You's Mr. Nicholas—Captain Nicholas—ain't that right, sir?"

"I am indeed."

"Well, sir. I'm Alex—Alexander Neilson. This here with me is Thomas Owens, John Dougherty, and Israel Vanluden."

"I am pleased to make your acquaintance, Mr. Neilson. How may I be of service to you?"

"Well, you see, Captain—it's like this, sir. Me and Tom, we've done some work with Fitz—John Fitzpatrick—from time to time. Fitz—Mr. Fitzpatrick—told us he is goin' to be an officer of marines in the new fleet Congress is puttin' together. It's like this, Mr. Nicholas, we want to sign on . . . to be marines, sir."

"I see. In that case, I can accommodate you gentlemen. This man here is First Lieutenant Matthew Parke." Parke nodded to the men who all returned the gesture. "If you men will present yourselves here at eight o'clock in the forenoon tomorrow, Lieutenant Parke will be happy to enlist you in his company and provide you with the particulars of your duties."

All four men smiled and bobbed their heads. "Eight o'clock tomorrow it is, sir. Thankee, sir."

DECK LOG 1776

- January

The year in summary

*T*his was a pivotal and turbulent year in Western history. In July, British Captain James Cook began his third and final voyage to the Pacific on "Resolution." A week earlier, a new journey began—that of the newborn United States of America. The former colonies declared independence from Cook's Great Britain. But first, the year would open with the mother country, Great Britain, putting the torch to a great city of her first North American colony, Norfolk, Virginia. This while General George Washington was mired in a stalemate with the British Army around Boston.

In March of the year, the American's first blue water Navy and Marine Corps team would successfully achieve their first amphibious assault in Nassau, The Bahamas, capturing valuable supplies for the Revolution. General Washington finally forced the British to abandon Boston and enter a seesaw battle in and around New York.

January 1, 1776
Philadelphia, Pennsylvania

Two young men walked along the cobbled street. The walk of one was more of a shuffle as he caught himself from time to time by grabbing his companion's shoulder or sleeve a moment before falling on a patch of ice.

Patrick Kaine and George Kennedy were friends. It was an unlikely acquaintance; nevertheless, it survived over a decade of very different tastes and activities.

Today was Monday morning. Patrick was fresh-faced and optimistic, having spent the day prior attending his usual Sunday worship service and enjoying the remainder of the day with his family in a home that was physically and emotionally warm.

It could not be said that George spent the entire weekend in drink and debauchery. But there is no question that by late Sunday night he was clearly four sheets to the wind.

It took Patrick considerably more powers of persuasion than he knew he possessed to wrestle his friend from his bed this morning. But this was the day they were to sign up for the Continental Marines, and Patrick was determined—apparently determined enough for them both.

Patrick stopped and faced the façade of the Connestogoe Waggon. George stumbled to a halt beside him. Even though the black night had barely graduated to a dull gray, he shielded his eyes when he saw the light inside pass through the glass-paned windows.

"This be it, Brother," Patrick said. George mumbled a reply, but Patrick gave it no heed. He mounted the steps and closed the door behind him when both were through.

Leading George to an empty table—there were many at the early hour—Patrick and his friend sat, and he ordered strong, black coffee for them. Tea was not politically popular, considering the tax, and Patrick found that coffee made his mind start better in the morning. After Patrick coaxed a few cups into his friend, he saw who he was looking for.

"There's Mr. Wilson, George," Patrick said with a jerk of his head toward a table near the fire. "Let's go get this done."

A flag hung on the wall above the man's head. Its charge was a coiled rattlesnake sewn in the center of the yellow field. The letters "DONT TREAD ON ME" were stitched across the length at the bottom.

James Hood Wilson sat below the banner making notes on papers. He wore no uniform, but he was the lieutenant of Marines on the Continental Brig, *Cabot*. He was recruiting, and his company was almost complete.

Kennedy and Kaine stood before Lieutenant Wilson. Kennedy still swayed slightly. "Good morning, sir," they said in unison.

"Good morning, men," Wilson answered. "How may I help you?"

"We're here to join up with the Irish Company, sir."

"The Irish Company?"

"Yes, sir. We been told that an officer name o' Welsh come all the way from the Old Country to fight the English. We heard you was signing up Marines t' fight fer 'im".

"Well, men, your information, so far as it goes, is accurate. Albeit this is the first I have heard it called the Irish Company. I am sure Captain Welsh will be pleased with the moniker, however."

"Well. How about it, Lieutenant? Where do we sign?"

"Can you men truly sign your names?"

"Both men displayed their offended faces. "Course we can sign our names. Didn't our mothers teach us ciphers and letters when we were little ones?"

"Then sign next to those Xs, men. And just in time it is, too. The last of *Cabot's* berths will be filled today, and we will be weighing very soon."

First Kennedy, then Kaine dipped the quill and carefully printed their names on the muster sheet. Their faces were still beaming after Lieutenant Wilson sent them home to say good-by to their families with strict orders to report aboard *Cabot* before nightfall.

January 4, 1776
Philadelphia, Pennsylvania

Captain Nicholas Biddle stood with his hands thrust into his greatcoat. Gold epaulets of his design adorned its shoulders. When he was appointed one of the new nation's first five Navy captains, he set to work immediately having a uniform tailored to his personal specifications. The navy of the united colonies had yet to prescribe a uniform for its officers, and Nicholas was impressed with the simple formality and strength of the British naval uniform.

Now he was here, standing on the quarterdeck of his own brig, the Continental Navy Brig *Andrew Doria*. Under his feet, the quarterdeck served as the overhead for the great cabin—his very own cabin. It stretched twenty-three feet from beam to beam at the widest extent and sixteen feet from the sparkling stern windows to the door that gave him coveted privacy from the ship's company.

Going to sea as a cabin boy when he was fourteen, Nicholas quickly converted his aptitude into maritime skill and knowledge. After six years of plying the trade between his native Philadelphia and the Caribbean, he secured a berth as a midshipman in the Royal Navy. To gratify his hunger for adventure and knowledge, he left his position and signed aboard HMS *Racehorse* under Captain Lord John Phipps.

In 1773, Phipps led an expedition comprised of *Racehorse* and *Carcass*, to northern Canada. This expedition included an unsuccessful attempt to find a northwest passage from the Atlantic Ocean to the Pacific Ocean. There was much ship visiting between *Racehorse* and *Carcass* during the four-month summer voyage of almost continual daylight.

It was at that time Nicholas became acquainted with a young Midshipman named Horatio Nelson. *That young man will leave a mark on the Royal Navy, so long as he can channel his enthusiasm*, Nicholas thought as he slowly paced his quarterdeck. Returning his mind to Captain Lord Phipps, Nicholas imagined facing him now—broadside to broadside—matching their courage and skill in a duel of frigates.

Right, you've not done poorly for yourself, Mr. Midshipman Biddle, Nicholas thought as a scowling sky of black clouds dusted him with tiny white snowflakes. The lacy white flecks were no longer settling directly on the ship's surfaces. Instead, the gentle but rising breeze caused them to skip along and pirouette in groups until tiny heaps built up in sheltered corners.

Captain Biddle looked along Front Street toward Wharton and Humphrey's, where the refit had taken place. His brig, having been warped along the waterfront, was now along the main city dock. His eyes found few pedestrians challenging the weather. Those that did were scurrying along purposefully to accomplish their business.

A shadow crossed Biddle's mind. No—it crossed his vision. He halted his aimless pacing and let his eyes climb from the black boots blocking his path to the impassive face of his midshipman. John Trevett served as midshipman and Captain Biddle's clerk. Trevett was touching a corner of his hat in salute. Marine Lieutenant Isaac Craig stood a few feet away.

Biddle touched his forehead and said, "Yes, Mr. Trevett. What is it?"

"All the Marines have reported aboard, sir, and are stowing their dunnage and settling below."

"Very well. Anything else," Biddle asked and glanced toward Craig.

"Yes, sir, Captain." John gestured toward Craig with his right arm and continued, "May I present First Lieutenant Isaac Craig of the Continental Marines?"

Biddle shook hands with the Marine officer and said, "Nicholas Biddle. Very happy to have you aboard Mr. Craig."

"Thank you, Captain. I am very honored to be aboard."

The three men stood in silence a moment—motionless—as the snow assaulted their eyelashes and prompted involuntary blinks. Neither pleasantries nor official comments came to mind.

After the pause, Biddle said, "You may carry on, Lieutenant Craig."

"Aye, Captain," he said; then touched his hat and disappeared below while the swirling snow thickened around his descending form.

Trevett stood still. "Is there something else Mr. Trevett?"

"You know I should have that posting, Captain,"

"I have had this discussion many times, John, with you and with Abe. I have spoken with Mr. Morris and Mr. Adams as well. I swear John, you are worse than the Scotsman. You and John Paul Jones have missed your callings as town crier. There are politics at play here, man."

"But Captain, I've been to sea since I was aged sixteen years. I was bred to the water, sailing on the Narragansett with cousins since I was breeched. I signed on as cabin boy on the Boston Packet and earned a mate's berth on coastwise traders. New England born and bred."

"And there be the trouble, John. Congress wants able men with salt water in their veins, sure; but they also must keep this group of stubborn colonies together in a confederation. Why is it, do you think, that there is a gentleman farmer from Virginia commanding the army of New England militia? No, John. There are just not enough ships and Marines at this point. Congress had to draw a line on New England commissions and extend some to the middle Atlantic and southern colonies."

"I served Commodore Whipple in the Rhode Island Navy. We were fighting the British before Congress even thought of a navy."

"Perhaps, Mr. Trevett, you should have stayed in the Rhode Island Navy. But no, your position has not worsened for your move. Whipple told me you were his clerk—and a supernumerary at that when you began. Now at least you're a midshipman with steady wages. You must be patient, John. It's a new bureaucracy. Give it time to settle into its course. I've no doubt there will be plenty of time for promotion before this war has progressed too far. In the meantime, do your duty well."

Trevett saluted and turned to walk away when Captain Biddle recalled him. "It would gratify me if you and Lieutenant Craig would join me for dinner in the cabin, John."

"Thank you, sir. I would be honored. Shall I carry your invitation to Mr. Craig?"

"If you would be so good, I would appreciate it."

"Aye, Captain." This time Trevett was not restrained when he left.

It was ironic that the group of men was meeting at the *London* Coffee House. From their second story window, they could see gray silhouettes of every sort of sailing rig through the swirling snow. Seven men sat around the solid table. Paper, ink, quills, tankards, and plates bearing scraps of food littered the table.

Four of the men remained from the ad hoc committee that created the Marine Corps—Adams, Langdon, Hopkins, and Deane. This New England majority, now balanced with Virginian Richard Henry Lee, North Carolina's Joseph Hewes, and South Carolina's Christopher Gadsden, comprised the Naval Committee. Gadsden served with Deane and Langdon on the three-man committee that created the cost estimates for the Navy and Marine Corps.

Hopkins was the chairman. It made perfect sense. He was a man of great maritime experience from a region that owed its fortunes, and largely its existence, to maritime trade. In Stephen's mind, it was not favoritism, it was just perfect sense that his brother, Ezek, should command the young nation's navy. Apparently, the majority of the committee agreed because that is the way it was.

Many hours, much lamp oil, and countless candles and ink were expended in creating the naval service. Ships were procured, refitted, and provisioned—at least on paper. Naval and Marine officers were commissioned; seamen and private Marines were recruited and armed—at least on paper. Naval regulations, rules of prize, and rates of pay were committed to piles of paper and ink. The Navy and Marine Corps were ready to sail—at least on paper. The only detail lacking, at least on paper, was a mission.

John Adams was unusually quiet during the meeting—at least for him. Franklin was teaching him a useful form of politics. Franklin called it "listening." It was not easy for Adams. Clients often don't believe their attorney is truly representing them if he spends more time listening than talking.

But Adams was learning that if the discussion was already moving in your favor, there was no need to add to the clatter. Further, with all his other duties and responsibilities, he missed several meetings of the Naval Committee, and his stalwart sense of decorum led him to feel less entitled to vigorous debate. He drank coffee and listened.

"Gentlemen—General Washington and the New England Minuteman have sent General Gage back to England. No doubt, we will never see him again. But General Howe is a wily leader. As long as he is strong and well supplied in Boston, His Excellency must maintain his siege. Our navy must interdict General Howe's supply from the sea."

Stephen Hopkins paused to sip from his tankard filled with rum and laced with a dash of coffee.

Joseph Hewes, of South Carolina, was the secretary of the committee and worked tirelessly to create and organize the navy. "Stephen, we have co-labored these many weeks to make it to this point. The navy is ready to sail, and we must move before the river ice binds them to the Philadelphia wharf. I honestly don't know why you people choose to live in this climate."

Hewes shivered and rubbed his hands. Several of the men smiled politely.

Richard Henry Lee was one of the most prominent planters in Virginia. A friend of Washington and Patrick Henry, his family was at the pinnacle of the ruling class of the colony for generations. "Gentlemen," he said, "the situation in Tidewater grows more dire by the day. Dunmore must be stopped . . . or at least contained."

Adams reached the point where his skill of listening quietly was exhausted. "General Washington must have our support! If he can contain Howe in New England, then we can end this war in months. He needs warm clothes, ammunition, and arms. He needs powder. This navy can supply that from the very ships that bring the same to the enemy daily."

"Mr. Adams, when is it time for the delegates from New England to admit that the war is not contained?"

"Here, here," Hewes supported Lee. "The southern colonies have supplied their treasure and their militias to aid our northern brethren. Mr. Lee's Virginia has given her most able military leader. There would not be a Colonial Navy without my support and that of other southern gentlemen."

"Not to mention that this navy is commanded by New England officers, the senior of which is your brother, Mr. Chairman."

Hopkins looked at his plate and held his tongue.

"Whether you choose to admit it or not, Mr. Adams," Lee took up the argument, "The war is in Virginia. You have seen the report that arrived just this week. Lord Dunmore burned Norfolk to the ground on New Year's Day. General Howe of Mr. Hewes' noble colony led a brilliant defense from Dunmore's Tory rogues. When they saw there was no other way to dislodge the patriots, they torched our beautiful city. Now Dunmore has his own private navy to terrorize and plunder Tidewater with impunity. Virginia, Delaware, Maryland—no one is safe, and no one is there to stop him. It would not surprise me to see him sailing up to the docks of Philadelphia at the head of his armada!"

"Mr. Lee," John Langdon joined the debate, "Sir—I grieve—we all grieve the senseless and brutal destruction of Virginia's jewel. It was a magnificent city that I entered on one or the other of my ships many times since I took up the trade. It is a loss not only to Virginia but to our united cause. I must urge, however, that we all pause and consider the larger strategy."

"Just what do you consider the larger strategy, Mr. Langdon?" Deane asked.

"Our navy is small, gentlemen. It will grow and no doubt be augmented with countless letters of marque, but it will never challenge the British Navy with a line of battle. We must use our ships wisely where they have advantage."

"Our fleet can deny supply to the enemy. It can supply our army, and it can harass the enemy's ships at sea," Adams stated flatly. "We must confine our activities to those arenas."

It was quiet for a moment. A servant entered, poked the embers in the fire, and added another log. The wood smoked and smoldered while he scooped up the empty plates and refilled drinks. As he turned to leave, the fresh wood flamed to life. The wind picked up, and snowflakes became larger, quietly falling against the glass panes of the windows.

"Gentlemen," Lee was almost whispering to emphasize his words. "Congress' resolution gave us our strategy—the protection and defense of the United Colonies."

"That resolution did not countermand the original resolution to 'intercept enemy shipping!'" Adams was on his feet and slapped his palm on the table.

Hopkins could see they were getting nowhere. Lee and Gadsden crafted the current draft of the fleet's orders, but several of the northern members balked when they presented it over breakfast. The sun was now well over the yardarm and hiding behind thickening clouds and falling snow. He sensed an impasse.

"My fellow patriots," Hopkins interjected. "We will take a recess to refresh and compose ourselves. I, for one, need to pump my bilges." There was a smattering of subdued chuckles and grudging grins. "We will reconvene in a quarter of an hour."

Langdon, Deane, and Hopkins circled the porcelain chamber pot in the far corner and relieved themselves. Adams took his coffee, stood on the hearth, and stared into the renewed fire that blazed invitingly. The southerners gathered around the window and gazed at the thickening snow.

Few people were venturing into the street now. On the ships and docks, the only activity they could see was the sentries and the watches on decks of the nearest ships.

Hewes spoke quietly and continued to stare through the glass, as did Lee and Gadsden. "We have inertia with us Richard, and I framed the discussion with the first draft of the orders—sending the fleet into the Chesapeake to challenge Dunmore. We are all agreed on the text as it stands, no?"

"Yes."

"Yes."

"Good. We need one more vote. We might swing Deane; he is a consummate politician. Or we might yet sway Adams to see the right of it."

"I am not so confident Joseph," Gadsden countered. "I shared a bottle with Stephen last evening. He is very sensible of the fact that northern colonies have consumed the majority of the officer commissions. More important, yet less debated, has been the fact that Pennsylvania and New England have profited by selling or leasing Congress all of the bottoms for the fleet."

"Two are coming from Baltimore," Lee objected.

"Yes," Gadsden agreed nominally, "*Wasp* and *Hornet*. Their sting amounts to fifty-six pounds of iron between them—a small sloop and a schooner."

Some muffled chuckling from the trio near the chamber heralded the breakup of the group. The continued dull thumping of snowflakes against the glass panes contrasted with the sharp crackle of the warm fire.

Gadsden walked toward a vacant corner of the room and called out, "Stephen, a word with you please?"

Deane joined Adams by the fire. The crackling covered their quiet words as they discussed the question at hand and considered how it might fit into the larger issues in Congress as well as the war and the people of the colonies.

Less than two minutes later, Hopkins called the group back to their places around the table.

When they were seated Hopkins asked, "Would you be so kind as to read the orders one more time for us, Mr. Secretary?"

"Certainly Mr. Chairman."

Hewes flattened the paper as he cleared his throat.

Commodore Ezek Hopkins, Commander in Chief. You are instructed with the utmost diligence to proceed with the said fleet to sea, and if the winds and weather will possibly admit of it, to proceed directly to Chesapeake Bay in Virginia, and when nearly arrived there, you will send forward a small, swift sailing vessel to gain intelligence. If you find that they are not greatly superior to your own, you are immediately to enter the said bay, search out and attack, and take or destroy all the naval force of our enemies that you may find there. If you should be so fortunate as to execute this business successfully in Virginia, you are then to proceed immediately to the southward and make yourself master of such forces as the enemy may have both in North and South Carolina . . . Notwithstanding these particular orders, which it is hoped you will be able to execute, if bad winds or stormy weather or any other unforeseen accident or disaster disenable you so to do, you are then to follow such courses as your best judgment shall suggest to you as most useful to the American cause and to distress the enemy by all means in your power.

"Thank you, Joseph," Hopkins said. "Does anyone have any arguments to present that we have not heard already?"

The men glance at one another, but with the question framed as it was, no one replied.

"Very well then, by a show of hands please indicate support for the motion."

Hewes, Lee, and Gadsden raised their hands and held them aloft. The others hesitated, and Hopkins hoped that, as chairman, he would not have to vote. The seconds that ticked by seemed like minutes. Deane slowly raised his hand, followed shortly by Adams. Ultimately Langdon followed suit. Hopkins did not vote. Thankfully he declared the motion passed and the meeting adjourned.

Lieutenant Craig drained the remainder of his rum and set his tumbler on the small table in *Andrew Doria's* cabin.

"I thank you very much, Captain—a fine meal and a genial welcome. I do look forward to serving you, sir."

"Quite welcome, Isaac." Captain Biddle replied. "It is a joy to get better acquainted with you. I do apologize that the dessert was somewhat lacking, but with the winter and the war, sugar and sweetmeats are somewhat hard to come by."

"There is no call for apology, sir; I can assure you."

Biddle let a moment of silence settle in the cabin while he took a pull on his pipe and stared at a knot in the beam overhead. Then he spoke. "Would you gentlemen indulge me in a moment of ship's business?"

Trevett and Craig nodded.

"Your men will no doubt have discovered through means of scuttlebutt by now. It is a standing order that all men on the brig be inoculated against the smallpox. It is a practice I came to admire when I served the King in his navy."

Captain Nicholas forewarned Lieutenant Craig of this, so his answer was prepared. "As you wish, Captain. If I may, however, what of the wellbeing of the patient?"

"I can assure you, Isaac, it is nothing short of miraculous. Far better than nine in ten men survive the procedure. A true case of smallpox after recovery from a very mild initial illness is almost impossible to find."

"When will we undergo the procedure, sir?"

"The surgeon has it laid on for tomorrow in the forenoon watch. It is quite simple. The skin of the hand is nicked and a small amount of the puss of a corpse lately succumbed to the disease is administered."

"We will be ready, Captain. There is no time like the present to begin."

"I appreciate your enthusiasm, Lieutenant. I want to be sure that all is accomplished while we are in Philadelphia with a ready supply of physicians and corpses. There is no telling when the commodore will decide to weigh."

January 20, 1776
Reedy Island Delaware River
Downstream from Philadelphia

The warm weather was no longer even a memory. For about three days early in the month, a warm front wandered through eastern Pennsylvania and New Jersey. The commodore, Ezek Hopkins, was a decisive man. He took advantage of the temporary breakup of river ice to take his fleet a few more miles toward their objective.

First, the four ships moved a few cables from the wharves of Philadelphia to Liberty Island. It was there that Commodore Hopkins received his official orders. His brother delivered them himself, along with the naval regulations Congress approved.

Supplies trickled in at Liberty—some uniforms, a few stands of arms for the Marines, powder, and victuals. It was not nearly enough to take the fleet to sea and sail in harm's way. The commodore knew it. The officers knew it. The men who would have to fight and work the ships knew it.

Slightly less than a fortnight later, the ice broke up. That was when they crept through the floating ice to Reedy Island. All four ships plus *Providence* and *Fly* picked their way downstream at bare steerageway, casting lead lines and fending off ice. The crews were exhausted when they finally moored at the island.

Now they were again iced in. Emotions were raw and conflicted. There was frustration that they could not get to sea and come to grips with the enemy. There was frustration that they were underequipped to challenge the enemy at sea.

Like the icy wind, the reality of naval life slapped the common sailors and Marines in the face. This was not adventure, nor was it action, glory, or prizes. This was backbreaking work, dysentery, frostbite, and mind-destroying routine.

Lieutenant Jones did not turn his face when the wind assaulted his bare skin with snow crystals lifted from the frozen river. He was either too tired to care or thankful that the brutal elements made it easier to stay awake. John Paul Jones grew up on the sea—lived virtually his entire adult life on ships in nearly every climate. But this was different.

These decks were not alive. They did not heave and roll and pitch in time with the ocean's tempo. This was more like indenture to a frozen workhouse. But it was his duty—not yet his destiny—but his duty. He should be *Alfred's* captain rather than her first lieutenant, but he would be the best lieutenant in the Navy until Mr. Morris or one of his other friends could bring Congress to its senses.

Jones stood his quarterdeck watch. It was humiliating for the first lieutenant of a Navy ship to be standing watch on the quarterdeck in port. He had to admit, though, that it was necessary. All the fleet's lieutenants rotated through the watches; their primary purpose was to curtail the desertion.

The Marine lieutenants led around-the-clock patrols along the Pennsylvania shore as far as Delaware, rounding up and returning what deserters they caught. Militias in New Jersey performed the same service for the fleet. However, there was no punishment to speak of when the men were returned. *What punishment could be worse than merely returning them to this frozen hell?* These were Jones's thoughts as he watched the working party in *Alfred's* waist.

"Keep a sharp lookout, Jones," Captain Dudley Saltonstall ordered as he walked past Jones.

"Aye, aye, Captain," Jones responded mechanically as he touched his stiff fingers to his hat. *That is all I have been doing for a bloody sennight*, Jones thought. *This man is a master of superfluous orders.*

"I shall be at the wharf collecting the commodore's brother and will return within the hour. I expect the ship will be admirably turned out to receive a member of Congress."

"Yes, sir. Of course."

Saltonstall descended the slippery gangplank with the sure footing of a man bred to the sea. Jones watched him grow smaller as he walked off to provide a formal welcome for Stephen Hopkins. *We all have our roles to play, however menial and tedious*, the lieutenant thought as he turned his attention back to the working party.

The largest cabin on *Alfred*, the commodore's accommodation, was spacious. The ship was new and very modern—for a merchantman. The frigate began her life as Willing and Morris's *Black Prince* only a few years prior. She was a magnificent choice to serve as the flagship of the young nation's fleet.

Ezek Hopkins' cabin spanned the stern of the ship, just under the quarterdeck. This allowed him the light from the large glass panes above the transom, but these admitted the cold nearly as well as they did the subdued winter light.

Two partitioned spaces just forward served as Commodore Hopkins' dining room and sleeping quarters—as well as housing a nine-pounder gun in each. These were the aftermost of a fifteen-gun broadside on either beam. A hanging stove in the space kept it warm enough that the two brothers could not see their breath when they exhaled.

"Keep your voice down, Stephen. It is difficult enough to keep secrets on a ship."

Stephen frowned but did not respond to his brother's chiding. Instead, he removed a document from his pocket, unfolded it, and slid it across the desk.

"Read this, Ezek."

Commodore Hopkins squinted and held it to use the feeble light to its best advantage. It was a resolution from the Secret Committee of Congress dated from November 1775.

Ordered—the naval committee secure and bring away said powder and have it brought to the port of Philadelphia or as near Philadelphia as can be accomplished with safety.

"Why isn't this in *my* orders, Stephen?"

"It is, Ezek. You must look closely and assume the proper interpretation."

Ezek laid the paper on the table and placed his hands on either side, palms down. He fixed his elder brother with a determined gaze. "Why is it not *explicit* in my orders, Brother?"

"I needed the southern vote to finalize any orders at all. They needed to tell their constituency that the Navy would free them from the tightening noose of the British Navy."

"So now I sit frozen in the ice with a fleet that could provide His Excellency with the powder and guns he needs. Yet, when Providence finally decides to free us, I must instead sail to Virginia and do the work their navy won't—while in the meantime, their general must battle the British Army with sticks and clods of frozen earth. Is that the strategy your politicians have devised, Stephen?"

"Now I must ask you to keep your voice down, Little Brother. Show me your orders."

Ezek removed the document from his desk drawer and slid it to his brother.

Stephen leaned on the desk with a palm holding either side of the orders flat against the wooden surface. He then stabbed it with his index finger.

"There, Ezek.

'Notwithstanding these particular orders, which it is hoped you will be able to execute, if bad winds or stormy weather, or any other unforeseen accident or disaster disenable you so to do, you are then to follow such courses as your best Judgment shall suggest to you as most useful to the American cause and to distress the Enemy by all means in your power.

"I am confident that at some point between now and the day you take this fleet through the Capes, you will find some *unforeseen accident or disaster* to *disenable* you sufficiently to allow you to exercise your best Judgment."

The cabin became still—but not silent. The muffled thumping and scraping sounds of a working ship provided a background of ambient noise. Ezek read the section for himself. His eyes swiveled up from the document and stared into those of his elder brother, seeking to probe his thoughts. When he broke his stare, they gazed through the great stern window into the cold winter sunlight.

Marine First Lieutenant Matthew Parke stood at the bottom of the gangplank and mentally counted off his Marines as they preceded him up and through the gangway. *All accounted for—and no prisoners, this time,* he told himself before trudging carefully up the slippery accommodation to join his men.

The men waited in a rough line with the corporal standing in front of them. They managed to make the British dragoon uniforms they wore look slovenly. No doubt, they represented the spoils of some Yankee privateer's profitable cruise in northern waters. The officer of the mounted troops for whom they were intended would not be proud of the manner in which they were currently displayed.

Lieutenant Parke put more effort into looking dashing in the green uniform he wore. Captain Nicholas designed the officers' uniform. It was green and resembled the clothing worn by the captain's fox hunting club before the war. Congress had not yet prescribed any uniform, but Matthew was grateful and proud to serve on the same ship as Nicholas and adopted his uniform as a way to solidify his identity with him.

Parke stopped in front of Corporal Marshall and said, "Be sure the muskets are not loaded this time before dismissing the squad below."

James Marshall, the corporal of the patrol, grimaced at the memory that comment conjured.

"Then see that they are carefully oiled and wrapped before ensuring that the men get some hot coffee and victuals."

"Aye, aye, sir."

Parke looked past the heads of his men toward Captain Nicholas standing in *Alfred's* waist at the opposite bulwark. He was staring across the frozen river at New Jersey.

"Fall out the men, Corporal."

The corporal touched his hat. Parke did likewise and then walked the frosty deck to report to his captain.

"First Lieutenant Parke reporting, sir," Matthew said to Nicholas's back.

There was no immediate response. Finally, "Yes, Matthew?"

"All men accounted for, sir. No incidents. No prisoners." After another moment of silence, he continued. "I would much rather be searching for British soldiers than our own deserters, Captain. This is not what was in my mind when I entered the service, sir."

When Nicholas again held his peace, Matthew looked around the deck. Men were still working at various duties. They were wrapped as warmly as possible in whatever scraps of fabric they could procure. He knew the sick berth was crowded with frostbite amputations and various other maladies. Few were malingering. There was no need to imagine an illness with the myriad of actual infirmities from which to choose.

"That is New Jersey, Matthew. We used to ride to the hound on that shore. I would relish a day like today. Winter's bite on my face and the steam from the horse's nostrils were exhilarating. Now this . . . this idleness. Can it be even the same world?"

Matthew knew the officers were affected as well as the men. There was even one of the Marine lieutenants from the fleet who disappeared with his bounty and recruiting advance payment.

Matthew thought back to his younger days in the Caribbean. He imagined the balmy tropical breeze lapping at his skin while the frothy breakers crashed onto the coral cliffs. In his mind, Matthew's bones began to thaw, and he could feel blood start to circulate in his fingers again.

"By yer leave, sirs!" A brawny petty officer bawled at the two Marine officers as he led a party of men carrying equipage forward along the larboard side. The rude interruption plunged Matthew back into his frozen world.

After the men moved away with their burden, Captain Nicholas said, "Go below, Matthew. Have some hot coffee and rum. I will join you directly the sergeant sets out with his patrol."

"Aye, sir. Thank you, sir." Lieutenant Parke touched his hat again to his captain's back and shuffled off toward the relative warmth of the wardroom.

Below decks where it was comparatively warm, the Marine patrol gathered in their berthing area. It was actually their berthing, messing, working, and skylarking area. They slowly peeled off their frozen scarves and outer coats.

"Right, then," Corporal Marshall said. "You men heard the lieutenant. Owens, I want you to personally inspect Dougherty's musket *before* he cleans and stows it. There will not be a repeat of the prior episode."

All the men in the squad looked at the beam overhead and saw the splintery hole that still contained Dougherty's musket ball that he accidentally discharged after his last patrol. All the men—that is — except Dougherty, who looked at his feet.

"Will do, Corporal," Owens replied. "Let me see that thing, John, t' be certain you've drawn the ball."

Benjamin Dunn, *Andrew Doria's* master, and Isaac Craig sat at the small wardroom table near the hanging stove. Both men had their overcoats on and were hunched over the table with gloved hands cupped around mugs filled with coffee—steaming hot when it was poured but now only tepid.

Thomas Vernon Turner, Sergeant of Marines, knocked once on the wooden frame of the thin canvas door and stepped into the cramped space. He stamped his feet, rubbed his gloved hands, and extended them to the warmth of the stove.

"Young Mr. Bevan said you wanted to see me immediately I came aboard, Lieutenant."

"Indeed, I did, Sergeant. The surgeon informs me that you are the only man on Captain Biddle's brig who has not yet been inoculated."

"Couldn't be helped, sir." Thomas glance at the lieutenant then faced the warm stove. "Sergeant's meeting on the flag most o' the day yesterday. Doctor was gone off'n the ship when I got back."

"Sergeant Turner, that is the second time you were unavailable when ordered to attend. You know that I am the only Marine officer in this company, and you are the only sergeant. You *will* be available at the very next opportunity. Is that clear, Sergeant?"

"It is, Lieutenant. . . . Will that be *all*, sir?"

February 13, 1776
Delaware Capes

Captain Whipple sat erect in the sternsheets of his gig. Though his men rowed dry, and he wore his thick woolen sea coat, the damp, icy wind cut through the fabric and assaulted every inch of exposed skin. But he would not allow himself to slump and shrug deeper into the thick cocoon of his winter garb.

The entire fleet was watching him as he was rowed from *Columbus* to *Andrew Doria.* In addition to those two ships, *Providence, Fly, Alfred,* and *Cabot* were anchored in a rough line along the Cape Henlopen beach at the mouth of Delaware Bay.

Captain Whipple's eyes were still sharp—he spotted *Hornet* weathering the cape with her sails sheeted in hard as she raced to reach her anchorage before the sun set. Her consort, *Wasp,* also from Baltimore, came in half a glass before her and was just now backing her topsail over the anchorage.

Whipple watched her. The topsail was blown back against the mast, and she began to move astern. A seaman on the fo'c'sle swung his mallet against the stopper, and the heavy bow anchor splashed into the bay arresting *Wasp's* sternway.

Whipple swiveled his head and brought his eyes dead ahead as the cox'n began his approach to *Andrew Doria's* starboard entry port. *Eight ships. That would be an acceptable navy if we weren't charged with battling the largest navy the world has ever seen,* he thought. *So much to do. Why am I investing an hour of my time in this errand when a midshipman could execute it just as well? It is for the young man. I owe him this much for his loyalty.*

Then he was there. The bowhook grabbed onto the chains, and Whipple was grabbing the manropes and skipping up the batons to *Andrew Doria's* main deck. Bells ringing, Marines at attention, sideboys saluting, bosun blowing his silver call. And there was Biddle, saluting and then extending his right hand.

"Welcome aboard Captain." They shook hands. "May I present my officers?" They walked down the line, and Captain Whipple shook hands with each as they were introduced in descending order of seniority.

"Very credible turnout, Captain," Whipple told Biddle. "Would you be so kind as to ask Lieutenant Craig and Midshipman Trevett to join us in your cabin in five minutes' time?" Without awaiting an answer, he turned and walked aft toward the stern cabin.

After the captains disappeared from the weather deck, First Lieutenant Craig turned to face his sergeant.

"Dismiss the honor guard, Sergeant Turner. And be so kind as to find Midshipman Trevett and ask him to join me in four minutes at the door to the great cabin."

"Aye, aye, 'tenant."

Andrew Doria's great cabin offered about half the space to that of *Columbus*. Captain Biddle poured two generous tumblers of rum and handed one to his guest.

"Death to the British, Abe."

"Death to the British, Captain," Whipple echoed his host, and both men downed their drinks in one swallow.

Biddle refilled their glasses, and both men took seats. Neither spoke for a moment as they sipped their rum. The twenty-five-year-old captain waited patiently for his guest to open the conversation.

Delaware sand dunes on Cape Henlopen were visible through the salt-crusted stern window but were rapidly fading in the evening twilight. A few lights in the village of Lewes were winking into life.

"The commodore has authorized me to take your midshipman from you, Nicholas."

"Yes, I suspected as much, Abe, when you asked to see him."

"I've no one to send to replace him."

"We'll manage, sir. Perhaps I can discover a clerk in Lewes. The man is a good seaman, but his heart is to be a Marine."

There was a knock at the door. Biddle invited the two men to enter.

Craig and Trevett crowded into the small space and stood roughly at attention—their heads were bent under the overhead beams. They wore their best suits of clothes and held hats under their arms.

"First Lieutenant Craig and Midshipman Trevett reporting as ordered, sir," Craig said.

"Take seats, gentlemen," Whipple directed.

Each man slid into the closest seat and laid his hat on the small dining table that also served as Captain Biddle's desk.

"I'll get right to the point." Whipple drew a document from the breast pocket of his coat and slid it across the table to Trevett. "This is your commission, John. I advised patience, and here it is, rewarded by Commodore Hopkins himself. If you accept this, you are a lieutenant in the Marine Corps of the United Colonies."

Trevett cracked the seal, unfolded the document, and held it close to scan the lines of copperplate in the fading light. Finally, his face split into a broad grin as he rose to his feet and thanked Whipple vociferously. Craig also stood and pumped Trevett's hand in congratulations, welcoming him to *Andrew Doria's* officer's mess.

"That is premature, Lieutenant. Shoemaker is shorthanded on *Columbus* since that fool, Dickenson, ran off. John, be at the companionway in ten minutes time with your dunnage, and you may return to *Columbus* with me."

Still in his state of elation, unable to make his smile vanish, Trevett acknowledged the order and left the room, followed closely by First Lieutenant Craig.

"I am sure the boys will find the energy to celebrate in Lewes, tonight," Whipple said as he rose to take his leave."

"No doubt, Abe, no doubt," Biddle responded.

"You are a good man, Fitz," Matthew Parke remarked, clapping a firm hand on the junior lieutenant's shoulder.

"You have all been more than kind to me, Mr. Parke."

"Nonsense, John. You are the key man in the company. You have something Sam and I do not. Your common heritage gives you a rapport with the company that we could never emulate. The men will follow you into hell—sailors as well. You are not only respected, Fitz. You are loved."

"You had best shove off, sir. You are delaying the boat."

Lieutenant John Fitzpatrick watched the boat disappear into the darkness. It would stop and pick up Marine officers on every ship in the fleet, taking them to celebrate the promotion of their newest colleague. Parke's comments warmed Fitz's heart.

John was thankful for his commission as a Marine lieutenant. He likely owed it to his acquaintance with Parke. The two met not long after Parke relocated to Philadelphia. John was a tanner, and Parke sold him hides imported from the Caribbean for tanning.

A widower with four children, Lieutenant Fitzpatrick was still giddy at having married the former Eleanor Pryor at Christ Church just days before the fleet sailed. She would watch after the young ones, and his officer's pay would provide for them all. He was proud to be part of this expedition but still looked forward to returning to his new bride and young family.

Fitz made no pretense of being a proper gentleman. His gregarious and genial demeanor, however, was neither affected nor learned. It was his genuine character.

"Any post, sir?" Private Owens asked. He and Dougherty were standing sentry in the bows, and Fitz strolled forward to check on them. He was dreaming of Eleanor. They had so little time together before the fleet sailed—married only the beginning of the second week in February. How he would love to feel her warmth tonight. Owens' question jerked him back into the present.

"Nothing today, Owens. It may take a day or two to come overland."

"'Spect it will be nice to have a letter from your new Missus, Lieutenant," Private Dougherty offered with a smile. He winked at Owens."

Fitz looked at him firmly.

"No disrespect intended, Mr. Fitzpatrick. Only passin' the time, sir."

"Of course, Dougherty," Fitz replied. "I will inform Mrs. Fitzpatrick that you inquired after her welfare when I write."

"Thank you, sir. And please send my respects."

The main commercial street in Lewes—the street that carried the commerce frequented by sailors—was called Front Street, likely because it fronted the creek that ended its travels in Delaware Bay. The first recorded European to visit the area was Henry Hudson, who traveled up the Delaware River in the late summer of 1609. Dutch settlers ultimately began building Lewes in 1631, making it the first European village in Delaware.

For decades its sheltered location just inside the protection of Cape Henlopen made it a valued anchorage and port, even attracting such notorious mariners and Captain Kidd. This night, the various taverns and public houses hosted men who were just as intrepid, though less infamous—men like Samuel Nicholas, Hoystead Hacker, John Trevett, William Hallock, and John Paul Jones.

The men, navy and Marines together, sat around several tables near one of the large fireplaces. They came right up the creek, stepped dry footed onto the Front Street boardwalk, and selected the most imposing tavern in town. A brick building, it boasted two large fireplaces, both of which blazed away with inviting warmth on this cold night.

Now they celebrated the fact that they were no longer bound by winter's ice in the gray depression of the Delaware River. They also celebrated the welcoming of their newest commissioned officer—Marine Second Lieutenant John Trevett.

"Welcome, John, to the brotherhood of the Marines. You are definitely a rare specimen, sir."

Lieutenant Trevett was not sure exactly how to take that remark, but he was not eager to take offense at his first social gathering of the commissioned officers.

"Thank you, Lieutenant Wilson." Trevett raised his glass to James Hood Wilson then took a sip. "And to what do I owe my rarity."

"Why, you are a New Englander, to be sure, sir. It seems that our service is generally populated with Pennsylvanians, and the naval ranks are more populated with New Englanders. I, for one, applaud the variety, sir."

"Why, I suppose you are correct in your assessment, Mr. Wilson. I will tell you this, however; I am only happy to be serving in this great endeavor."

"I, for one, am happy to welcome you aboard, Mr. Trevett."

"And I thank you, too, sir," John replied with a quizzical look."

"Robert Cummings, at your service, sir," the man responded with a nod. "I shall be pleased to ship with an officer who may be able to translate the good captain's wishes."

"How may I take your meaning, Mr. Cummings?"

"You may take it to mean that even though *Columbus* has not yet cleared The Capes, Captain Whipple has alienated himself from the Marine officers."

"I have known Captain Whipple these many years, sir. I have sailed into battle with him and found him to be a brave leader. He comes from among the finest lineages in Rhode Island. I have no doubt that I owe him my commission."

"I have no doubt if it, either. And is it not a commission of first lieutenant? A step that should rightfully have been mine after Dickenson disappeared. Have I not done the work these many weeks?"

Shoemaker caught a look from Nicholas and discerned the admonition from the senior Marine. Shoemaker, as Marine Captain on *Columbus*, understood Cummings' frustration. When the first lieutenant position became vacated, it was rational to believe that Cummings would be promoted from his position as second lieutenant.

More importantly, Shoemaker was also aware that a rift was forming between Captain Whipple and his Marine officers, but he could not account for it. Perhaps Trevett could help close the chasm.

"Let's have an end to this discussion, Robert—shall we? I should venture to say that we are thankful to have the help of a new officer."

Cummings clamped his jaw closed, then nodded. He held his mug aloft toward Trevett, then drank to his health.

John Paul Jones broke the awkward silence that followed. "Gentlemen, let us drink to the good health and future fortune of our shipmate who made this possible—Lieutenant Fitzpatrick! He stayed aboard Alfred this night so her officers could attend this celebration."

Fitz was well liked throughout the fleet, and everyone raised a glass to him.

Two doors to the east sat a humbler, but no less inviting public house. Many of the common sailors of more modest means were crowded in there. Ale and rum flowed in direct proportion to the gold and silver currencies from around the world that escaped the sailors' purses. The group from the flagship became loud as their tongues became lubricated with drink.

"I'll be glad when we're shed o' this freezin' weather," said a small man with smooth, ink-marked hands.

"'Tis still bleedin' winter in the Chesapeake, Mate," replied a larger man with a scar across his face and his slightly graying hair plaited into a long pigtail.

A local man sat alone in the far corner, away from the stone fireplace and the tables crowded around it. His weathered hands wrapped a stoneware mug that was still half filled with the first ale he ordered when he walked in an hour earlier. His head was bent over the table, and his eyes stared into his drink, but his ears were alert as they sifted through the disparate conversations in the room.

"I tell ye, we not be a goin' to no Chesapeake, there Shipmate."

The large man's voice rose, and the local man listened closer. "Every blessed man in this here fleet knows we be going 'round the Virginia Capes and clearin' ol' Lord Dunmore 'n 'is pirate fleet out 'o the Chesapeake."

"Keep yer voice down, ye big dumb bosun's mate." The large man stiffened, then relaxed when his smaller friend poured him another drink.

"I been copyin' orders fer all these here captains all day, haven't I? Now, I'm a tellin' ye we're a bound fer the Caribe, most likely New Providence. There's powder 'n stores there that the army fellers can shore 'nuf be usin'."

The local man slowly took a swallow from his mug and placed it carefully back on the table, not making eye contact with any of the other patrons.

The large man looked at his small friend and was quiet while he processed the new information. He knew his friend could read and write and often helped out the commodore's and the captains' clerks. He finally relented slightly.

"Well, we'll see. As long as we get's t' grips with the bloody British I'll be satisfied."

"I'll drink to that," his small friend said and hoisted his mug.

The local man quaffed the remainder of his ale and dropped three copper coins onto the table as he rose and buttoned his long coat. He smiled and winked at the man behind the bar as he left the tavern.

February 17, 1776
Delaware Capes
Atlantic Ocean

"I'll have two reefs in the fore and main tops'ls," Lieutenant Jones shouted through cupped hands. Then, impatiently, "Mr. Hopkins, shall I have my servant send some hammocks aloft? I desire that we slow the ship today!"

Ezek Hopkins Jr.'s booted feet swayed precariously many fathoms above the main deck. He stood on the foot rope and leaned over the main topsail yard just windward of the fat mainmast. The seamen about him strung from the maximum extent of the windward yardarm to that of the lee and wore no shoes, giving them a better feel for the rope on which they stood.

"Smartly men. Be quick about it!" Hopkins, a midshipman and the son of the commodore, shouted into the screaming wind to make his authority plain to the topmen of the fore and main masts. He was the officer in charge of the tops during sail handling. Each top—fore, main, and mizzen—also had a petty officer who acted as captain of that top.

Hopkins suffered Lieutenant Jones's sarcasm stoically. He knew that the first lieutenant would drive the crew to perfection, and beyond, through every activity. He also knew that Jones did not single him out because of his pedigree—the first lieutenant was equally severe with everyone who had not yet attained his standard of perfect seamanship.

A stiff, cold breeze came from the northeast. It built rollers so large that *Alfred's* main deck was level with the crest when she rested in the trough. *Alfred* led the windward column, nominally of four ships, and *Columbus* led the leeward. Nominally because the fleet was yet to be fully formed.

The glass near the wheel had been turned three times since Captain Saltonstall gave the signal to weigh. In the intervening ninety minutes, all ships had weighed their anchors, and *Alfred* led them through the Delaware Capes into the unfriendly, gray Atlantic.

The wind was fair for one long board to sea but just barely. *Alfred* set the pace under only jib, driver, and stays'ls as she crashed through the steep billows and into the strong wind coming six points off her larboard bow.

The slate-colored Atlantic, with foaming whitecaps torn from the crests of its waves by the steady wind, reflected an overcast sky of ashen gray. The schooners and sloops had no trouble keeping pace behind the larger square-rigged brigs and frigates.

Captain Nicholas and Lieutenant Parke stood near the lee bulwark of *Alfred's* quarterdeck. As was customary, they left the windward side to the commodore and captain.

It was also convenient for Lieutenant Parke whose stomach rebelled against the ship's violent motion. It was not as if he had never been to sea, but his travels had hitherto been as passenger rather than crew. His breakfast long ago mingled with the wake, and he was thankful that his seasickness was beginning to subside.

Parke's general experience was nausea for the first few hours at sea, and then his constitution settled into a more comfortable state. His leader, Marine Captain Samuel Nicholas, was not a seafaring man either, but he was fortunate to suffer no ill effects from the motion of the deck.

Parke looked over the starboard bulwark and saw only gray. *Alfred* was in the trough and at the furthest extent of her windward roll. From this vantage, Matthew was looking directly at a mountain of seawater. As his eyes climbed to the lead-colored sky, he saw only the foam at the top of the wave separating sky from sea. A moment later his stomach hit the fir deck planks as the next wave shoved the larboard quarter toward the clouds, drove the bows deep into the sea, and rolled the ship to leeward.

White water crashed up on either bow and through the windward hawsehole. Samuel and Matthew bent their left knees, extended their right, and swiveled their hips naturally to *Alfred's* motion. They had their sea legs.

Commodore Hopkins didn't even try to suppress the smile on his lips as he swung the long glass across the starboard quarter, scanning from Cape Henlopen to Cape May. He left his hat in his cabin, and the wind blew the hair around his ears and forehead while he watched his fleet form into two divisions of four vessels each.

The sloops and schooners were slicing through the waves without effort. They reminded him of sheep-herding dogs dashing around the flock keeping the sheep together. He knew they would be in position before the glass was turned again. Hopkins lowered the glass from his eye and turned to face the bow before addressing his flag captain.

"You may order more sail at your discretion, Captain Saltonstall. Make best course and speed consistent with safe navigation. The remainder of the fleet will have no trouble keeping station."

"Aye, Commodore," Dudley Saltonstall replied as Commodore Hopkins made his way down to his cabin.

February 18, 1776
Palace Green
Williamsburg, Virginia

The British Army captain was damp from sweat on the inside of his clothing and on the outside from the cold drizzle of rain that seemed to hang in the air since midnight. He wore no uniform. Rather, he was clad in faded and mud-spattered togs and could pass for a sailor, farmer, or none-too-prosperous trader.

During the past seventy-two hours, he stopped to sleep three times. The longest stretch amounted to a luxurious five hours. Other than those stops, and a few to change horses, he was in the saddle continually since slipping out of the sailors' tavern in Lewes.

The leading edge of the weather that was covering the Continental Fleet kept him cold and wet for the best part of the last day. The horse's hooves clattered along the cobbles of Palace Green Street until he stopped at the steps to the governor's mansion.

The captain executed a maneuver, somewhere between a slide and a fall, and managed to land on his feet at the side of his horse, letting the reins fall to the cobbles. A slave materialized from somewhere near the steps to the mansion's entrance and grabbed the reins. The captain neither spoke nor looked at the man. With his remaining energy, he mounted the broad stone steps and pounded on the front door.

Only a moment elapsed, and an impeccably dressed servant with a powdered wig and a heavy aristocratic accent open the door a foot.

"I will see the governor, immediately," the captain stated.

The doorman tilted his head back slightly and looked up and down the captain with only the movement of his eyes. "Perhaps you would care to go around the house. You will find the kitchen there, and you may wait until I see what can be arranged."

"Out of my way!" With his right forearm, he pushed the door open and used his left hand to shove the servant back a step as he barged into the ornate reception area. His spurs clattered, and his coat dripped on the polished floor. "I am here on the king's business."

"But sir?"

"Shut up you fool." He shouted, "Governor!"

Two men arrived simultaneously. One, a servant, came rushing in from a hall entrance. The other, Lord Dunmore, had a book in one hand a drink in another.

"Captain," Dunmore greeted, "how good of you to come. Finnestere, find the captain something warm to eat and bring it to the library."

The servant bowed and backed away toward the kitchen. Dunmore stood to the side of the library door and held his arms wide, a book in his right hand and a drink in his left. He inclined his head and shoulders in the faintest of bows.

"Won't you join me in the library, Captain?"

The captain walked into the book-lined room and sat, sinking deeply into the nearest chair. Lord Dunmore poured a glass of brandy and handed it to him. Then he poked the fire and tossed a fresh log onto it. The captain drained the glass in one gulp, and the governor filled it again nearly to the rim.

Taking a seat facing him, Governor Lord Dunmore said, "I trust you have news that justifies your arrival in such a state, Captain."

"New Providence, Governor. The rebel squadron is bound for New Providence."

"You are certain of this, Captain?"

"Yes, Your Lordship—that I am. Hopkins' orders are to make for the Chesapeake to contest your rule of the bay. But like most rebels, he does not excel in following orders. I am certain he will take his rabble and attack Fort Nassau for their military stores—ammunition and guns."

"Excellent Captain. You have done very well."

The captain finished his second glass as Finnestere returned with a steaming meal in a china bowl. He set it on the table at the captain's right elbow. Dunmore rose from his chair and slowly paced with his hand on his chin.

After several turns, he spoke. "Finnestere, show the captain to a room after he has eaten his fill and draw him a warm bath. Captain, you will rest here a few days."

"Yes, Your Lordship."

"Finnestere, send someone to Captain Law and show him to my private study in thirty minutes. I have a mission for him to undertake. I believe he will enjoy the warmer climate."

"As you say, your Lordship."

February 19, 1776
East of Virginia Capes
Atlantic Ocean

"Go 'round to each lookout," Lieutenant Hoystead Hacker, *Fly's* captain, ordered the boson's mate on watch, "and make sure they are all keeping a keen watch. Report any sighting immediately to the quarterdeck. And no singing out, have them bring the message on the double. I do not desire that we should be heard by sharp ears on any of Lord Dunmore's pirates!"

"Aye, Cap'n," the sailor replied quietly and padded silently forward. He was nearly lost to the muddy weather and darkness by the time he reached the forward lookout on the fo'c'sle.

Hacker knew there was little need for quiet with the wind bellowing through his rigging, but he suspected the warning might just give his lookouts a bit of extra vigilance. As near as his fifteen years of maritime experience could tell, Hacker had *Fly* at the rear of the leeward column of the Continental fleet, and the fleet was sailing south by east—under almost bare poles.

The near gale was coming in just abaft the larboard beam. With little more than a couple of handkerchiefs bent onto the mast, *Fly* was shipping green water each time the lee bulwarks rolled to starboard. By dead reckoning—they had not sighted land or star since sinking Cape Henlopen two days ago—he was three leagues due east of the mouth of the Chesapeake Bay.

Lieutenant John Strobagh hugged a brass spittoon as he lay on his side in his hammock, huddled in the fetal position. As the leading edge of each mountainous Atlantic roller assaulted the larboard side of *Hornet's* hull, the sloop rolled sickeningly to starboard, and Strobagh's rump grazed the canvas door to the tiny hutch that the Navy was so fond of calling an officer's cabin.

The sloop hesitated for the briefest moment, crested the mighty billow, began her slide into the trough before the next oncoming wave, and rolled on her larboard beam end. Strobagh's hammock lightly bumped the curve of the larboard hull at the maximum extent of that roll . . . and began again.

John Strobagh began his military career as a Marine lieutenant at the end of the preceding year, along with the rest of his brother officers. Assigned as senior marine on *Hornet*, he drilled his small detachment of private Marines and assigned them their duties. He found that he adapted well to the military life.

John had no quarrel with the cold and hardship . . . even the seeming lack of support from Congress. What did bother him was the sea itself. Everyone told him their particular trick to appease his land-loving stomach, but none of them worked. He made up his mind. He would resign his Marine commission the moment he could set foot on terra firma. He had options.

John's friend, Proctor, had urged him to take a commission in Pennsylvania's first artillery battalion. But John was persuaded by his acquaintance with others who favored the sea service. Well, they were wrong, and if he lived through this storm, he would find Proctor and devote his energy to ballistics and cosines and minutes of angles that referenced a stable surface.

THUMP. The muzzle of the four-pound brass gun ten inches from John's head rolled into the sealed gun port for the ten-thousandth time that night. Strobagh cursed the gun captain, one of ten aboard, who failed to make sure the beast was bowsed up tight against the port when the ship last secured from gun drill.

"Cap'n, there be a ship out there, I can smells it, sir." The lookout from midships on the larboard side was standing face to face with Hacker.

Hoystead could see the gray outline of his face. He could also smell what he had eaten for dinner . . . and what he had washed it down with.

"What do you see, man?"

"I don't sees it, exac'ly, Cap'n, I jes' knows it." The man could be Hacker's grandfather.

The light padding of bare feet hurrying across the deck could be heard. The larboard bow lookout now stood next to his shipmate and drew a breath. "There's a ship Captain. When we crest a wave in time with her, I can see 'er poles against the clouds. Can't say for sure, but I'd say she's about a cable off, just for'ard o' the larboard beam."

"Get back to your posts, and feel free to sing out if you see anything else!"

Hacker considered the situation. Given the position of the other ship, it was not likely to be a stranger. It was probable that one of the ships in the windward division had drifted down in the storm. What should he do? The wrong decision could cost Congress one of her precious few ships . . . perhaps two of them. It could also doom two crews to a relatively quick but frigid death.

He could bear up, pointing *Fly's* bow closer into the wind and slow his headway. This would hopefully allow the other ship to drift ahead of him and slide off downwind, avoiding a collision. But it would also increase the closing speed of the two vessels and increase the damage if there was a collision.

Else he could fall off the wind, reducing the relative speed of his ship to the other, and sail a wide circle around the place a collision might occur. But that would put him on a course toward a lee shore, driving *Fly* onto an unseen beach at any moment.

It was not really a decision. It was a guess. The best he could do with his experience, and the information available was to influence the chances a few percent, from fifty-fifty one way or the other.

What did he know for certain? There were seven other ships out there—somewhere, at least. One was probably close aboard to windward and drifting down on him. There was a lee shore somewhere, not over a handful of leagues to starboard. If a collision were imminent, it would probably happen somewhere dead ahead or a few points on his larboard bow at a spot that was continually moving south through a violent ocean he could barely see.

"Helmsman, when I give the order, we will fall off two points. All hands standby to slack the storm jib." His decision was made. He would risk the lee shore rather than a bow-to-bow collision.

"Bear up! Bear up blast your eyes for a lubber!"

Lieutenant Strobagh heard Captain Stone's muffled but authoritative voice pierce the passionate sounds of the sea and ship. Before the implications of the decisive order registered in Strobagh's muddled mind, his world was viciously jerked sideways. He heard sharp cracks, shouts, screams, and loud thumps of gear falling to the deck above him. He completely forgot his nausea when he dropped the spittoon and ripped open the fragile door to his canvas hutch.

On deck, Strobagh had only the split second of a lightning flash to take in the scene and ascertain the situation. The watch below was rushing up on deck. Parted lines, broken blocks, and bits of spars rolled around the main deck. Right forward he saw the jib boom fouled in the taffrail and backstay of another ship. Just as the lightning bolt extinguished itself, heavy rain filled the darkness.

A Marine clutched John's arm and shouted, "The boys is right for'ard, 'Tenant. What'll ye have us doin'?"

While John was forming a response, he heard Captain Stone over his shoulder. "Take the Marines forward, John. Use axes, cutlasses, whatever you can find and cut loose anything fouling us to that other ship."

Now John Strobagh had a purpose. Grabbing the corporal by his soaked sleeve, they both felt their way toward the fo'c'sle to gather their Marines and begin their task.

Captain William Stone maintained his calm and authoritative demeanor to mask the seething fury inside of him. *Who is that foolish lubber who fouled my hawse? I'll see him in Hell if I lose my Hornet.* Sure, *Hornet* was chartered to Congress; and yes, Congress indemnified William against all perils.

But William's fortune was tied up in the neat little sloop, and he knew Congress's indemnification would be paid in Continental paper dollars. Worse than that, if he could not get free of the other ship, or if he lost his jib boom, *Hornet* would likely blow up on the Virginia Capes before he saw another sunrise.

The decision to fall off the wind was made moot and never executed. While the hands were taking their places to slack the sheets, a huge wave broke over *Fly's* larboard quarter. As her stern rose up the leading edge of the roller, *Hornet's* jib lanced out of the foam at the crest. It smashed through *Fly's* taffrail, snagging her backstay and falls that were faked down along the larboard quarterdeck.

Hoystead's immediate concern was to free his schooner from the violent interloper. Just as urgent was the need to send up a preventer backstay; for with the wind abaft his beam, the mast could easily go by the board if the backstay parted. The latter concern was immediately relieved when the wind forced *Hornet* around, causing both vessels to weathervane into the wind.

"Back the storm jib!" Captain Hacker ordered the darkness. "Helmsman, hold her thus as if your life depends on it, for it surely does."

"Heave to, aye," replied the helmsman. A shipmate stepped up next to him to help hold *Fly's* head into the wind, keeping her steady and keeping the violent rolling to a minimum.

"What ship is that?" Hacker shouted into the dark rain above and behind him.

"*Hornet*," yelled Lieutenant Harbagh back through the torrential rain. "What ship is that?"

"*Fly*," the reply was crystal clear when the heavy squall ended as suddenly as it began.

Harbagh swung the ax again. He had no idea where he got it. It seemed to materialize from the darkness as it was thrust into his hands. One more blow and the iron-taught manila line would part.

It was not easy to chop at a line that was suspended in the air. Several times he had missed on the dark, pitching deck. Had he considered the possible consequence, he would have said a silent prayer of thanks that the blade had thus far not bitten into his foot or shin.

Twang, snap, CRACK! The line parted. Then another behind him. *Hornet* began to pick up sternway as she drifted downwind. But not before the extreme end of her jib boom tore free of the bowsprit and the broken end splashed down into the Atlantic. He heard orders shouted from the quarterdeck. He was jostled and shoved as seamen scurried around him.

Men were desperate to send up a jury forestay before the gale blew the only mast down across the vulnerable quarterdeck. Bowlines were tied in near blackness as men secured lines around their waists before climbing out to the jagged edge of the bowsprit to find purchase for the new forestay. Others were already scrambling up the ratlines in preparation for their shipmates to pass new lines aloft.

"I can hear breakers to leeward," came the cry from one of the lookouts as his shipmates raced to complete their impossible feats of seamanship before their home drove onto the beach.

They needed to make headway to windward, and to do that they needed a forestay. Other groups of sailors were wrestling canvas across the wind and water swept deck so it would be ready to soar aloft as soon as the jury-rigging was finished.

Captain Stone waited by the wheel. His stomach was churning, and his heart wanted to explode from his chest. But his countenance displayed only experienced confidence.

He could occasionally see snatches of foam over his right shoulder as the Atlantic broke onto the beach at the southern approach to Chesapeake Bay. He already knew the fleet would have at least one less sloop when it arrived in the Caribbean. What he didn't know was whether or not that sloop would be able to return to Philadelphia.

Hacker wanted to be furious at Stone, but with a burst of evenhanded fairness he truly did not want, he had to admit that *Fly* could as well have been out of station as *Hornet*. There was no time for recrimination or contrition. The fate of two ships and their crews still hung in the balance. His crew was nearly through the heavy line that connected *Fly* to *Hornet's* jib boom.

He heard a loud crack and saw a degree of slackness appear in the line. *Hornet* broke the end off her jib boom, and it now trailed *Fly* in the water. Two more hacks from an ax and it drifted away toward the nearing beach. *Fly* was under command again. She was still hove to but riding much easier.

"Helmsmen, let her head fall off three points. Standby to shift the storm jib!"

Hacker waited as the men at the helm put the wheel up, and *Fly's* bow began swinging to starboard. There was no point of reference in the dark tempest and pitching deck. The captain let his other senses do the work unconsciously. The feel of the wind on his face, the motion of the deck, and the predominant starboard heel told him what he needed to know.

"Breakers t' starboard," a lookout's voice, seasoned liberally with panic reported from the sodden night."

Hacker glanced quickly over his shoulder. No sign of *Hornet*. A silent prayer for her survival was sent heavenward quickly. Now!

"Let go and haul!"

Men forward slacked the storm jib's larboard sheet, and the wind quickly blew it over to the starboard side. Other men stood, often thigh deep in frigid seawater, along the starboard bulwark and heaved with all their might on the jib's starboard sheet. Slowly —inch-by-inch—the jib clew was drawn back until the sail had just the right belly to harness the gale. *Fly* was once again slicing through the huge waves. She was heading southeast away from the capes and toward—hopefully—the fleet.

Captain Stone looped his left arms around the larboard shrouds and ratlines. *Hornet's* motion was too savage and unpredictable for keeping his footing otherwise. Nevertheless, he occasionally still struggled to keep his feet as the seawater soaked his legs on many of the steep rolls to windward.

There was no need to ask for progress. His first lieutenant was aloft and would report the moment a secure forestay was rigged to the remaining stump of the jib boom. The lightning returned. Occasional flashes told him what he needed to know. He would be receiving the readiness report in a moment.

Fly had escaped to the southeast. He assumed it was southeast from the direction of the winds and the location of the breaking surf that was now much too close under his lee.

"Forestay jury rig is set up, and storm jib is bent on, Captain, Stone." His first lieutenant stood dripping in front of him. His left arm was immobilized inside his coat, and his right hand gripped a shroud.

"Very well," he replied. "Thank you." Then—louder—"Set the storm jib. Sheet in to larboard. Helmsman, meet her. Thus. Steady as she goes."

Steady as she goes, aye, sir." Pause. "Cap'n, the binnacle light is flooded. Can't see the course, sir."

"Keep the wind as far forward of the starboard beam as she can hold."

"For'ard o' the starboard beam, aye, sir."

Hornet was literally slicing diagonally across the most seaward waves that were beginning to crash on the shore, but she was making headway to the northeast and under control. Stone considered that a gift from the hand of Providence. Commodore Hopkins would just have to capture New Providence without *Hornet*. She was returning to Philadelphia—with all hands.

March 3, 1776
Fort Nassau
New Providence Island—British Colony

New Providence Island is a roughly oval-shaped island running five miles north to south and ten miles east to west. It lies about twenty leagues due east of the Florida Keys and forty northeast of

La Havana. The population is concentrated in the town of Nassau on the northeast coast.

New Providence's harbor, being protected by the three-mile-long narrow, Hog Island, may be entered at the west end through the Narrows or the east end through shallows near Fort Montagu. Fort Nassau commands the entrance through the Narrows.

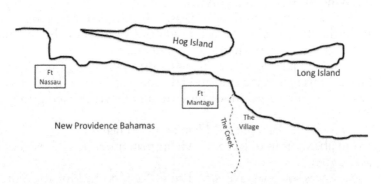

Governor Montfort Browne stopped and leaned against the stone wall before entering Fort Nassau. This was normally his favorite time of the day. The only pleasure—except for the fortune he was building—of this posting was the time he spent each morning sipping tea on his shaded veranda, enjoying the magnificent vista of deep azure seas breaking pure white across the reefs while the kitchen slaves prepared his breakfast. He savored the cooling breeze in the early mornings before the stifling sun rose high enough in the sky to turn the sodden air into a Turkish steam bath.

Today the vista was just as striking, and the breeze blew the same as always. But this morning was not restful—not enjoyable. Quite the opposite. This morning was a tragedy. That cooling breeze was blowing in a pile of trouble for him.

But Governor Browne could not even focus on the events that were spiraling out of his control. For the past two days, the gripes assaulted his bowels. He was not even dressed, standing now in his slippers and nightshirt.

Now his buttocks leaned against the rough but cool stone of the bastion while he leaned forward, bent double and clenching his stomach, praying for the wave of cramps to subside. Sweat beaded on his forehead, streamed into and between his eyes, and dripped from the tip of his nose.

The governor focused on the dark stains the sweaty drops made as they splashed on the crushed coral sand on which he stood. He counted the drops as the pain in his gut subsided. At last, he straightened his body, wiped his face with his handkerchief, and composed his mind.

The gates were thrown wide open, and he strolled through the palisade into Fort Nassau's quadrangle as if he had not a care in the world—as if he were clad in his finest suit of clothes and not a wrinkled nightshirt. He must maintain this persona as long as possible.

Browne saw them waiting in a small group, sheltered close to the far stone palisade, enjoying what shade there was at this early morning hour. Why didn't he tell them to meet him at the Assembly House? At least there would be shade, and he could sit down.

The fort was designed for cannons and soldiers, not for meetings of leading citizens. Therein lay the reason for meeting at the fort. It was time for him to demonstrate his martial leadership in a crisis. But was there a crisis? There was no need for this to be a crisis. These things could be worked out. Perhaps even now Parliament and the king had resolved this insurrection, and these rebels could be made to see reason.

But now was the time for him to show leadership and decisiveness. A handful of militia had arrived. Most were too dumbstruck to think on their own, but then, thinking was not encouraged in the rank and file. A corporal and sergeant organized them and began preparing three of the guns that bore on the Narrows.

"Sergeant,"—Browne spoke sharply, "load those guns and inform me when they are ready to fire!"

The man touched his forehead and replied, "Load the guns, it is, Guv'ner."

Browne gritted his teeth but remained erect as another wave of intestinal cramps assaulted him. People were watching now, and he could not let them see weakness. He walked as casually as he could toward the gentlemen in the shade. The drums continued to sound every sixty seconds as more militia, officers, and Council members trickled into the fort.

"Good morning, Governor," William Chambers and William Grant greeted Browne simultaneously. Browne nodded and looked around to see who else had arrived.

Chambers and Grant were careful to look him levelly in the eye and avoid noticing his state of undress. Both managed to dress and be rowed ashore from their respective ships before the governor arrived at the fort. Captain Chambers was the skipper of the *Mississippi Packet*, now swinging lazily to her hook in the harbor, still laden with the milled lumber she brought from North America.

Lieutenant William Grant captained His Majesty's Armed Schooner *St. John*, the only British naval vessel on the Bahamas Station. With six small guns and twelve one-pound swivels, she was currently engaged in much-needed repairs and cleaning in New Providence.

"What is the situation, Lieutenant?" Browne snapped.

Lieutenant Grant pressed his lips momentarily to compose his response. He smelled the acrid smoke from the slow matches that were burning above the water tubs placed between the guns in the embrasures. The aroma excited him.

"The situation, Governor," he finally replied, "is much as I warned you it would be yesterday. The report brought by the trading sloop has turned out to not only be accurate but quite precise, as it happens."

"So, Dorsett was correct as it turns out," Browne mused aloud.

"Dorsett! What do you mean, Dorsett was right, Browne? Who the Devil is Dorsett and what was he right about?" Captain Chambers asked accusingly.

Browne looked like a child discovered in a lie by his schoolmaster. "Dorsett, the captain of that whaler that came ashore two days ago. He reported much the same as the sloop's master."

"Are you telling me, sir, that you had advanced warning . . ." Grant began but was cut off by a militia officer standing on the wall with a long glass.

"Three guns ready to fire, sir. And three sloops approaching the harbor, Governor," the officer reported. "Two are local traders, the third—larger—I don't recognize."

Governor Brown was happy for the interruption. "Do your duty, Lieutenant. Let them know what we are about."

The militia officer looked dumbly at the governor.

"Fire the guns, Lieutenant!"

"Yes, Governor," he replied. Turning to the captain of each of the thirty-two-pound behemoths, he repeated the order to fire.

The gun captains stood holding their linstocks as the gun crews timidly backed away.

"Go ahead," the officer encouraged them, "fire the guns."

Finally, a slow match lowered to each of the three touchholes, and the guns roared out toward the approaching sloops. There was a great roar and much belching of fire and smoke as the three thirty-two-pound iron balls flew in a generally northern direction.

When the smoke cleared and commotion settled, one gun remained capable of being reloaded. The carriage of the second splintered and collapsed from the recoil. The third tore the ringbolts out of the ancient stone wall, and it recoiled off the landing onto the ground below. Thankfully, no one was severely injured.

DONT TREAD ON ME

Captain Samuel Nicholas of the Continental Marines skipped up the battens on *Alfred's* larboard side and paused at the top once both feet were planted on the main deck. His stormy countenance was at odds with the striking blue sky and dazzling sea. He just returned from being stuffed into *Providence* with nearly 100 Marines, all of whom expected to be ashore pillaging New Providence by this hour.

He and his staff spent the dog watches and evening watch of the previous night overseeing the transfer of all the fleet's 240 Marines into the three sloops—*Providence* and the two captured coastal trading sloops. All three vessels—in fact, the entire fleet, were now standing off and on just to windward of the harbor entrance.

The bulk of the men were stuffed below decks in the stifling air. He had lost enough Marines to fever already and didn't even want to think about how many more would be affected by these appalling conditions. He'd been discussing the situation with Lieutenants Parke and Fitzpatrick when the commander-in-chief recalled him to *Alfred*.

As Nicholas shook hands with Lieutenant Jones at the entry port, a concussion could be heard from the fort. Smoke billowed out, followed about two seconds later by three geysers erupting from the blue water. None of them was less than a cable's distance from any of the ships.

Scarcely noticing the shots from Fort Nassau, Captain Nicholas said, "Good Morning, John."

"Welcome back, Sam," *Alfred's* first lieutenant greeted his returning shipmate. The two men had gotten on well during the cruise from Philadelphia. This was a state of congeniality that did not exist between *Alfred's* first lieutenant and her captain, Dudley Saltonstall.

John Paul Jones explained the situation before leading his shipmate to the quarterdeck. "The big ships were too close when the sun came up. The lookout on Hog Island smoked us right away. There was no thought of a surprise landing after that."

"Standing off and on here is getting us nowhere," Nicholas replied. "Quite. I have interrogated both of the captured masters. It's clear that there is good holding ground three leagues to the east in the Hanover Sound. Of course, the captain tries to persuade the commodore that the prisoners lie. But he offers no better solution."

"It's common knowledge that there are many sympathizers with the Rebellion on this island—and what have we to lose? Perhaps the sloop's master is one. We can't simply wait here for the worms to eat our bottoms."

"Mr. Jones," Captain Saltonstall shouted from the quarterdeck, "If you are quite finished with Captain Nicholas, Commodore Hopkins and I would covet a moment of his time."

Both men went aft to attend their superiors.

Commodore Hopkins, the Continental Navy's commander-in-chief, looked at each of the three officers in turn, then he said, "Welcome back, Captain Nicholas."

"Thank you, sir." Nicholas was not in the mood for pleasantries. "May I ask, Commodore, what is the plan? My men are becoming less effective by the minute. As you know, fever already claimed several on the passage. One more died this morning. Being stuffed below decks on those filthy sloops is not helping the situation . . . sir."

"The town has seen our approach, Captain. We have lost the element of surprise and must reconsider our plan."

Nicholas struggled to keep his voice calm but firm. "May I beg to recommend, Commodore, that we reconsider faster? Captain Lowe has informed us, sir, that Nassau is as much as defenseless. We must strike before that can be rectified." Captain Gideon Lowe, from Green Turtle Cay, was master of one of the two sloops *Alfred* captured near Great Abaco Island on the first instant.

"We must not rashly gamble all that we have," Saltonstall countered heatedly. "Now, I have proposed that we sail to the west of the island and discover a suitable anchorage with a beach for landing."

There was a commotion at the entry port as a boat bumped alongside, and an officer sprang aboard, quickly stepping toward the group of officers. The smiling man extended his hand toward the commodore and said, "Thomas Weaver, Commodore, second of *Cabot*. I have known these waters, man and boy, sir. Captain Hopkins sent me over to see if I could be of help." He winked and continued, "Your brother said to bid you good morning, sir."

Commodore Hopkins was momentarily disarmed. Then he replied, "At last, someone I can trust with actual experience of the area. Captain Saltonstall was just proposing to take the fleet to the west to find a place suitable for landing, Lieutenant."

"Can't be done, Commodore. I was just telling your brother that just to the east of Hog Island, here, is the perfect site. Prettiest little anchorage you ever saw, Commodore, just north of the Rose Island Rocks. The Marines can just wade ashore at their leisure at The Creek."

"Much as Lieutenant Jones was telling me." The commodore continued, "I have decided the fleet will proceed to Hanover Sound. Upon arrival, Captain Nicholas will report his recommendation as to its suitability as a landing site for the Marines. *Alfred* will be in the van. Lieutenant Jones, you will take one of the prisoners to the foretop and con the ship to the, er, anchorage."

"Aye, Aye, Commodore."

"Have you any observations, Captain Saltonstall?"

Saltonstall stared in Jones's eyes for a moment before replying, "Perhaps you would like to leave part of the fleet to blockade the Narrows, Commodore."

"I will not divide my forces, Captain Saltonstall." He paused to consider. "No matter at any rate. They have no squadron, and I expect Captain Nicholas will have secured the port before noon. Have you any questions, Captain Nicholas?"

"None, Commodore."

"Very well, then. You are dismissed. Lieutenant Jones, before you go aloft, please be kind enough to signal the fleet to follow in the flag's wake."

"Aye, Commodore."

"Captain Saltonstall, you may get the frigate underway when it is convenient."

"Aye, Aye, Commodore."

"Lieutenant Weaver, you will stay with me in the event I require further local knowledge."

"Pleasure, Commodore."

A couple of dozen militiamen were present in Fort Nassau. A handful was just starting to gather up the splintered pieces of the gun carriage that recoiled into the parade area of the fort. The rest stood around watching or waiting for orders from their officers.

Some men were armed with various vintages of firearms and swords. They scattered from the middle of the parade to the edges when two gentlemen trotted their mounts through the gate that stood wide open. Both slowed to a walk and stared down at the fallen gun and broken carriage as they passed. They pulled reins and stopped in front of the governor and the other officers and notable citizens.

"Very impressive artillery display, Governor," Samuel Gambier observed dryly, looking down on his governor.

Samuel Gambier, former judge of the Admiralty Court in the Bahamas, was a prominent merchant and landowner, well respected by the local citizens, and brother to John Gambier, Lieutenant Governor of the Bahamas. He and Captain Law rode in together in answer to the governor's summons.

Lieutenant Governor John Gambier and council member William Bradford also rode in while Governor Browne was searching for a reply. While his council, assembly, and militia officers stood staring at him, another wave of cramps gripped the governor's bowels. In addition to the sharp pain, he could also sense a growing need to return to his privy.

"It would appear that Captain Law's intelligence has proven to be accurate," Samuel Gambier continued when he was satisfied that the governor had no suitable reply to his gibe.

"Intelligence?" Captain Chambers burst out! "What intelligence is this?"

"Captain Law was just confiding in me on the ride over that he delivered credible intelligence to the governor this week past from Delaware Bay. Lord Dunmore himself provided the good captain with news of a large rebel fleet preparing to plunder New Providence. And why have I just heard this news this morning, I asked him." He looked at Captain Law.

"The governor," Law replied, looking down at Browne, "told me to keep it to myself until he had occasion to call the Council."

"It would appear," Lieutenant Governor John Gambier broke in, "that the Council has been called—albeit about a week too late —to prepare a defense. Just what do you propose, Governor, now that the wolf is at our door."

"And it would appear to be quite a feeble door at that," Captain Law could not resist dropping an insulting comment.

Governor Browne attempted to think clearly while the sharp cramps subsided. The need to return to his privy continued to plague him, and he clenched appropriately. *I am not presenting the commanding demeanor that befits a king's governor. I must regain control of the situation. I must think of the crown and protect the king's interests.*

Major Robert Sterling, commander of the local militia, arrived while the governor was still considering his options.

"Thirty men and four officers present, Governor," he saluted his nightshirt-clad superior as he stood resplendent in his militia officer's uniform.

"Yes, very well Major," Browne replied absently, still lost in thought. "We must protect the king's stores," he finally announced decisively. Then he turned to Chambers. "We will transfer powder and other military supplies aboard *Mississippi Packet* and dispatch it to a suitable port on the mainland."

"I would be pleased to consign the cargo, Governor, but you forget that the packet is still laden with lumber which I am obliged to deliver to Jamaica," Captain Chambers replied. "It normally occupies several days to offload and then load a new cargo."

"That is not the point of the matter, Captain," Samuel Gambier broke in. "Have you considered, Governor, that the king would have us defend his possessions in the Caribbean rather than to divest ourselves of the means to do so and acquiesce to the rebels?"

"Our defenses are weak, and the enemy is strong Mr. Gambier. We must salvage what we can from the situation."

"We must save our own skins, you mean, Governor. Whose fault is it that we are weak? You have had plenty of warning, plenty of time to prepare our defenses, and instead, you chose to do nothing and hide the impending invasion from your closest advisors. This situation is unconscionable, and the ministry shall hear about it."

"Let us leave the ministry aside for the time being, shall we? The ministry cannot . . . " Browne broke off in mid-sentence as his midsection was assaulted by more cramps.

"Are you unwell, Governor?" Major Sterling asked with a concerned tone.

Governor Browne mustered his composure and replied, "I will be fine, Major. Thank you for your concern."

John Gambier and William Bradford both ignored the governor's malady and broke in to agree with Samuel. "We must hold the powder until we know the enemy's strength and intentions."

"Oh, very well. Captain Chambers, would you undertake to get your vessel underway and reconnoiter the enemy fleet. You are not to hazard the *Mississippi Packet*, however, as we will likely need her to evacuate the king's stores."

"I would be happy to, Governor." With that, he turned and hurried to the landing, calling out for any of his crew he encountered on the way to join him.

The governor was beginning to feel in command again. "Captain Grant, return to your schooner and bring her down to the town landing to bolster our defenses."

"Aye, aye, Governor. It'll take some time, sir, to get *St. John* in order, what with the refit underway and all, but I will make haste." He too left to join his schooner.

Satisfied that he had at last taken some decisive action, the governor motioned to a couple of his advisors, and the trio ascended the wall where he could look out toward the sea. He enjoyed the breeze that puffed at his nightshirt and cooled his skin. The three stood on the wall and talked among themselves for some time. Eventually, they returned to the ground level.

Very little shade was left in the fort's quadrangle. Morning was not yet very far advanced, but it was far enough that the sun had climbed above the bastion, yet the refreshing breeze did not explore below the top of the walls. Militiamen were standing loosely in ranks. Few had weapons, and the weapons present were ancient or filthy.

Hunting was rare in New Providence, pirates were something of a bygone era, and the Spanish had not attacked in years. So, the militia relied on government for military accouterments. However, Governor Browne was not one to require frequent military drills for his militia nor spend freely on their equipage.

"Your men don't appear to be very well turned out, Major," Browne accused Sterling.

Somewhat taken aback, the major cleared his throat and replied, "Well, yes Governor, but you will recall several conversations we have had on the subject and your final orders." His words were just slightly vague as he decided it was not in the Colony's best interest for him to share too many details of the governor's official penury publicly.

"That will be quite enough backing and filling Major. The king charged you with the island's defense, and I expect you to carry that out. Now then, suppose you attend to the armory and issue the proper turnout for your troops, eh?"

Major Sterling swallowed the first reply that came to his lips, as in fact, the king charged Governor Browne with the island's defense. Instead, he merely saluted and marched off toward the armory, gathering subordinates along the way.

Governor Browne paced slowly for a few moments. Considering the options open to him, he could not find a path that would resolve the situation with any sort of satisfaction. He eventually halted before a group of Councilmen and Assemblymen and engaged them in a hushed conversation.

The Gambier brothers and Captain Law formed their own private council, standing in a small circle and holding their horses' reins. Occasionally, one or another of the trio would glance at the governor or major.

Finally, "Would you excuse me please, gentlemen," asked Samuel of his two confederates. He handed the reins to his brother and walked over to speak to Major Sterling.

After a few moments of deliberation, he motioned for John and Captain Law to join him. The group, along with several militia officers, joined the governor and his advisors. Captain Law observed—to himself—that the island seemed to have more leaders than followers.

"An observation, Governor," Samuel Gambier began. The governor nodded, suspiciously. "You have ordered Lieutenant Grant to bring his schooner closer to the sally port to deepen our defenses. "While an admirable idea, it seems that it may leave us somewhat open to attack from the eastern end of the island."

The governor became defensive again. "I haven't the vessels at my disposal to cover the entirety of the Caribbean, sir."

"Of course, Governor," Samuel agreed with a conciliatory tone. "But perhaps you might consider ordering the major to dispatch a detachment of militia to Fort Montagu."

Fort Montagu was a small stone fort to the east of the town, sited to protect the narrow opening between the main island and the eastern end of Hog Island—the back door to New Providence as it was termed. Built more than thirty years earlier, of quarried limestone, Montagu mounted eight eighteen-pounders, three long nines, and six six-pound guns. The fort also included a cistern, capable of containing thirty tons of water, making it a difficult proposition to besiege.

Governor Browne swallowed his instinctive reply that he would command the military and decide the strategy. He had to admit that the Council and Assembly were in place to advise him. Further, it would not hurt to spread the responsibility around a little if things went awry.

"It is a sound recommendation, from a tactical standpoint," Captain Law interjected.

Advice from an active Army officer. That is good, the governor reasoned. *Let us follow that up.* "Major Sterling, what is your opinion, sir?"

"A very sound idea, Governor. The rebels could easily anchor in Hanover Sound and land any troops they might have at The Creek. It'd scare the Devil out of the mulattoes, no doubt. Probably think the Degos had landed to carry them off to slavery, ha!"

"Very well, Major. Attend to the details, but don't leave Fort Nassau defenseless."

The major saluted and addressed his subordinate officer. "Lieutenant Pratt, you will take thirty men, including two non-commissioned officers, and occupy Fort Montagu. Ensure that a dozen men are properly outfitted with a stand of arms each. The remainder will man the fort's guns."

Pratt saluted, "Thirty men, a dozen armed, occupy Fort Montagu, Sir!" He turned toward the troops and took a step before Samuel Gambier stopped him.

"Major, what are the lieutenant's orders, should he encounter the enemy?"

Pratt stopped and turned around. Sterling looked at Gambier, then at the governor. No one spoke.

"Lieutenant Pratt," Major Sterling ordered. "You will do your duty. You will not allow Fort Montagu or its stores to fall into the hands of the rebels."

Pratt thought about eight ships loaded with desperate and bloodthirsty rebels. Then he considered his thirty militiamen and twelve muskets. He swallowed. "Yes, sir," he said, turning to gather his detachment.

A few minutes later, footsteps on the sandy ground heralded the return of Captain Chambers. Sweat, or salt spray, or both, plastered his black hair to his forehead. Breathing hard he addressed the governor. "The wind is directly in our teeth, Governor. There's no getting out through th' Narrows. But I could see the rebel ships over Hog Island. They've hauled their wind and lit out due east. May be that they lost their stomach for it when you sent a little iron in their direction."

Several of the gentlemen looked at the militiamen still working to set the overturned guns to rights. John Gambier dryly stated the obviously shared sentiment, "That is not a likely scenario, Captain."

DONT TREAD ON ME

"In half a cable, bring the ship starboard one-and-a-half points," Lieutenant Jones shouted from *Alfred's* foretop. The officer of the deck shouted his understanding and glanced at the quartermaster on the helm, who nodded at him.

Alfred led eastward through the reefs and shoal waters. The fleet followed behind like docile ducklings on a pond. Lieutenant Weaver balanced easily and watched the familiar north coast of Hog Island glide by while he chatted unselfconsciously with the commodore and Captain Saltonstall.

"There be a mulatto village near The Creek, Commodore— mostly freed slaves, local Indians, and the like. Won't be no trouble, though."

Disinterested silence followed his comments, so he continued. "I reckon Fort Montagu will be the first real obstacle, that is if the addle-brained governor remembers he has a fort guarding his back door. And you'll probably want a couple of ships to cover the march along the coast road in case any of them British officers has the sense to set up an ambush." He had the commodore's attention now.

"Fort—what fort? You told me of no second fort!"

"Won't be no problem, Commodore. Those guns probably ain't been fired since she was built over thirty years ago. 'Sides, they's probably nobody on the island knows how to fire 'em. Army all pulled out and went up to Canada or Boston on account of the war, you know?"

"Someone certainly knew how to work the guns in Fort Nassau," Hopkins replied.

"Yes, well, there is that. I'll grant you."

"Well, Ezek, it seems you have now committed our enterprise to the whims of two lieutenants," Dudley Saltonstall replied.

"That is not necessary, Captain. A decision had to be made, and Congress chose me to make it. Washington needs powder, and I will obtain it for him."

"In any event, now that we are committed, we have to cover the advance or chance losing the entire expedition before they even reach the town. I shall detach *Cabot* and *Andrew Doria* to cover the advance along the coast road. Together, they mount a broadside of fifteen guns. That should be enough to discourage any interference from the militia."

"You will do no such thing, Captain. I will not hazard both of my brigs in unknown shoal water. *Wasp* will cover the landing, but she will not enter the lagoon. I have already lost contact with *Hornet* and *Fly*."

"As you say, Commodore," Hopkins spoke briefly to a lieutenant who began preparing the signal for *Wasp* to cover the landing.

"Lieutenant Weaver, I will order fifty sailors from the fleet to augment the Marines. You will command them. Offer Captain Nicholas what advice you can, but he is in command of the landing. Is that understood?"

"Perfectly, Commodore."

Seymour Sinclair, *Cabot's* sailing master, wiped sweat from his brow yet again and replaced his hat. It was hot, and there was no place to hide from the relentless sun on the brig's quarterdeck. He didn't even want to think about what it was like for the poor devils below decks. The marines would be fortunate if they could even breathe in the stiflingly humid atmosphere. The breeze faltered, and the foretopsail shivered then cracked.

"Mind your helm, you lubber!" Sinclair scolded the helmsman.

"It's the wind Mr. Sinclair," the helmsman defended himself.

Seymour was jumpy conning the ship through the shallow reefs and bars. He mistook the wind for the helmsman's inattention. Captain Hopkins looked over at him and grinned.

Sergeants Burke and Neilson stood on the companionway ladder just high enough that the tops of their heads occasionally felt the relative cool of the wind. They were allowing the privates about a minute each in the same position in the hopes that the brief breath of air would keep them conscious.

Hours below decks had taken their toll on the Marines. *Cabot's* first lieutenant of Marines, James Wilson, could have taken advantage of his status as an officer and stood on deck, but he chose to remain below to encourage his men.

"How much longer we gotta stay down here, Mr. Wilson," Private Kaine asked his lieutenant.

"Don't bother the lieutenant," George Kennedy chided his shipmate. "He's stuck in this same hole we is." We'll gets there when we gets there."

Patrick Kaine and George Kennedy were both Marine privates assigned to *Cabot*. They had signed on together in Philadelphia with adventure and prize money in their heads.

"It's okay Kennedy," Lieutenant Wilson responded. He took a shallow breath and wiped his face with his sleeve. "Last I saw we are about four cables off from the anchorage. Shouldn't be long now.

The Spring day on New Providence was well advanced. A breeze still blew in from the lagoon, but its efforts at cooling the tropical island grew less effective as the sun climbed higher into the sky. The crowd in the fort was growing as more and more militiamen arrived.

Major Sterling's discipline was not rigid, but he did manage to keep some semblance of organization, and his subordinate officers and sergeants tracked the men as they arrived.

Judging that he had done all that was possible for the present, Governor Browne decided it was time he dressed. When he looked around, it was apparent that he was the only man present still in his nightshirt.

"Muster your men and ensure they are ready to defend the colony, Major," Browne gave the unnecessary order.

Sterling looked coolly at the governor and let several silent seconds elapse before responding flatly, "Of course, Governor."

"And find me a messenger."

Sterling found a corporal and sent him to see the governor for messenger duty.

"Corporal," Governor Browne addressed the local farmhand who now served as a corporal, "Hurry down to the landing and go onboard *St. John*. Tell Captain Grant my orders are for him to take his command to the east end of the lagoon. He is to prevent the rebel fleet from entering between Hog Island and Fort Montagu."

"As you say, Governor."

"At the double, man," the Governor ordered sharply!"

The corporal trotted out the gate toward the town's sally port.

To the group in general, Browne announced, "I believe I'll just go home and make myself a little decent. My health is not all that it could be this morning, you know." Inwardly, he wanted to run to

his own privy, but he settled for a fast walk to maintain what
decorum he had remaining.

After he left, John Gambier looked at his brother and Major
Sterling and said dryly, "No, I don't imagine that it is."

Captain Law smiled grimly to himself.

DON'T TREAD ON ME

The bell on the quarterdeck chimed four times, Ding-ding,
ding-ding. The same brass tones floated across the Hanover Sound
from several other vessels of the fleet.

Ten A.M., Samuel Nicholas translated silently to himself. *Four
bells in the forenoon watch. I wonder if I will ever get used to the
nautical way of keeping time.* As he stood looking around at the
dazzling blue water, the azure sky, and the foamy waves breaking
on the distant beach, he couldn't deny the beauty of creation.

He prayed silently for a bloodless assault but steeled himself for
the opposite. Facing forward, Sam felt the breeze shift from behind
his left ear, across his cheek, and settle on his face as *Providence*
swung into the wind.

"Back the tops'l," came the order from Captain John Hazard.
Braces were hauled aft, and the yard squared itself. The square
topsail laid back against the mast as the sloop faced into the wind.
Her headway quickly stopped, then she began to slide astern.

"Let go," the next order from Hazard. A powerful bosun's mate
swung his mallet against the stopper. The anchor cable was
unleashed, and the huge iron anchor splashed into the translucent
blue Caribbean, sending up a white geyser.

In only a second, the anchor hit bottom in fifteen fathoms of
water. Smoke rose from the hempen cable as it flew through the
hawse. When it slowed, the men on the anchor detail threw a
stopper around it, snubbing the great hawser.

The sternway on the sloop dragged the anchor across the sandy
bottom until the fluke dug in and held. The cable lifted out of the
water and grew taught, squeezing itself dry as it stretched.

"Clew up the topsails." The sheets on the lower corners of the
sail slackened, taking the pressure off as the wind spilled. The
sloop's sternway ended, and she reversed course, sliding forward
slightly as the cable relaxed.

She finally settled to her anchorage, loosened the stoppers to slip a little more scope of cable through the hawse, and seemed to exhale a sigh while the anchor detail secured the cable.

It was time for Captain Samuel Nicholas, America's senior Marine officer, to earn his pay. The Marine drew breath preparatory to issuing orders to get the debarkation and amphibious landing underway before the anchor crew was even finished.

Before he gave the order, an explosion of activity erupted around him. Falls were bent onto boats that were then lifted to the end of the booms, swung over the side, and launched into the water. The crews tumbled over the bulwarks and quickly took their places on the thwarts, ready to follow the orders of their cox'ns.

Lieutenants Parke and Fitzpatrick were seemingly everywhere, receiving muster reports, checking weapons and kits, issuing orders and directing squads of Marines into the waiting boats. Sergeants and corporals were mustering their platoons, shoving and cuffing the private Marines into place, making sure muskets and rifles were not left on the sloop or dropped over side, and settling disputes before they flashed into physical fights.

Nicholas marveled. It had actually worked. The planning and organizing, and arranging details with the sailors, were actually resulting in an orderly operation. If pressed, he would have to admit that he was slightly surprised.

A young boy, James Edgar, stood at the foot of the mast. A drum was slung over his shoulders, and he held drumsticks in his left hand. He was the drummer from *Alfred's* marine company.

"Jim, what are ye doin', boy?" Sergeant Neilson asked. "I done told you you're s'posed to be in the third boat. Lieutenant Parke wants you ashore to help form up the fellas." He grabbed Edgar gently by the shoulder and led him to the bulwark.

"Thanks, Sergeant"

Privates Owens, Dougherty, Cogan, and Richey were already there waiting to debark with the remainder of their platoon.

"We'll keep an eye on the boy, Sarge," said Private Owens.

"You better do a better job of it than you have been, Tom. I just found the young scamp skylarkin' at the foot o' the mast."

"Hey Lubbers," Lieutenant Rathbun jibed as he walked up, "If you ladies are done with your tea, it's time to get into the boat. Lieutenant Parke give me a schedule to keep, and you all are gonna be swimmin' ashore if I don't keep to it."

"You men heard the Navy lieutenant," Neilson ordered. "Now get over the side with you and into the boat!"

Captain Nicholas took in this exchange as well as all the other activity unfolding around him.

"Good luck, Sam."

Nicholas was startled to see Captain Hazard standing next to him extending his hand. They did not know each other well, having only spent a couple of days together.

"Thank you, John," Sam replied as he shook the hand of *Providence's* captain.

"The boat is waiting, sir," Corporal Tom Anderson, from Shoemaker's company, was now standing in front of Nicholas.

"Yes, Corporal. I will be there directly." Nicholas had told Lieutenant Parke that he wanted to go to the beach in the first boat. Parke and Fitzpatrick both tried to talk him out of it during the planning meetings, but he would not be dissuaded. *It was his place*, he insisted.

"Right, then—Judkin—I think you had better wait here with the men. And for Heaven's sake, keep them quiet!" Lieutenant Burke, of the New Providence Militia, glared at his neighbor as he waved his hand in front of his face in a vain attempt to drive the cloud of mosquitoes away.

Both officers, small landholders on New Providence, arrived at Fort Montagu half an hour earlier with thirty reinforcements for the new garrison. Through some vagary of fate, Burke was senior to Judkin, so Pratt put him in charge of the reconnaissance detail.

Reconnaissance detail—more like a street mob. *Why did Pratt believe thirty men were required to watch what must be a thousand invaders come ashore? And a good one in three were armed only with a cudgel or rusted bayonet.*

"As you say, Lieutenant," Judkin replied. "We'll just wait here in the trees for you to take a peek at what our Yankee cousins have sent along. Then he hissed at the troops, "Everyone find some cover and stay low."

The men spread out and sat or lay in whatever shade they could find. Burke motioned at two men who worked his farm regularly and bid them to accompany him. Moving behind cover provided by the thick bushes, the three set off toward the Marine's landing beach.

Occasionally, the trio came across residents of the free black village of New Guinea spying on the growing group of men on the beach. Burke sent them home with assurances that the invaders were not the Spanish come to take them away and enslave them again.

They finally lay down behind a thick, scrubby bush growing out of a sandy hump of the island's north shore and set about counting the Americans on the beach. A handful of boats were slid up onto the sand, but no more seemed to be ferrying invaders ashore. Not very clever at arithmetic or memory, Burke stopped counting at two hundred, guessed there were about one hundred more, and sent one of the militia privates back to inform Judkin and Lieutenant Pratt.

DONT TREAD ON ME

Captain Nicholas stood on the highest dune he could find, swinging his glass from the sparse collection of shacks or huts in the southeast, to the trail leading away to the west along the lagoon. Shoemaker and Welsh, the two other Marine captains, were likewise employed.

Lieutenant Weaver trudged up the small slope to the three men. A cheerful smile showed in the middle of his beet red face that he was mopping with a huge white handkerchief.

"All the sailors are ashore, Sam," Lieutenant Weaver said with his usual friendly tone. "Took about six to eight off each ship. Not all the captains were eager to comply, I can tell you that—'specially the ones have lost several crewmen t' fever already."

Captain Shoemaker flinched inwardly when Weaver addressed their senior officer as "Sam." Shoemaker knew Nicholas for years—rode with him in the Fox Hunting Club. *If he could show military courtesy, surely the Navy could as well.* John Welsh was not surprised by the address. Having sailed with Weaver on *Cabot* since January, he was very used to the man's informal demeanor—even appreciated his habit of diffusing tense situations.

"Thank you, Lieutenant," Nicholas replied. He took his glass from his eye and used it like a baton, waving it to the southeast. "I don't like the looks of that village, Thomas. I imagine we will need to post a rear guard there to prevent any mischief on their account."

"What, New Guinea, sir? Oh, Lordy no. They won't be botherin' nobody, Captain Nicholas. That's just where the free blacks and the mulattos settled. They're close enough to the town to get work, but far enough away, so they don't mix with the white settlers."

"I think Lieutenant Weaver's right, Captain," Joseph Shoemaker said with his glass still focused on the village. "I don't see much of anything in the way of activity over there.

Sweat streamed down Shoemaker's cheeks and the back of his neck. His shirt was plastered to his skin under his linen coat. The weather in New Providence was hot, even in early spring, but he was glad to be away from *Columbus*. He did not get on well with Captain Whipple on the voyage south. There was no particular rubbing point. It was more that the easy Philadelphia gentleman did not fit well with the New England merchant.

It could also be that Whipple seemed to prefer Trevett to him. Joseph could not fault Trevett for that. He did nothing to curry the favor of his patron. It was just a natural state of affairs. All of that was neither here nor there at this point. There was a job to do, and they must all pull together to see it accomplished.

Marine lieutenants began to gather at the foot of the dune. They talked in quiet voices, joking and boasting to one another while they waited for their captains to grant them recognition. Eventually, Nicholas addressed them.

"I imagine that you are here to make your reports, gentlemen."

First Lieutenant Matthew Parke was Nicholas's direct subordinate, so the others deferred to him. "The company from *Alfred* is all present, Captain. The sergeants are checking their weapons and ammunition. There were no casualties coming ashore, sir."

"Excellent, Matthew."

Each company made similar reports right down to Lieutenant William Huddle, of *Wasp*, who only mustered five marines. While all the men were safely ashore, most were stretching out in whatever shade they could find to rest their cramped muscles. Their forced sequestration in the small sloops was exhausting to most of them.

"Very well, gentlemen—superb work getting the men ashore. Form them in companies by their ships. Form the Marines from *Providence* and *Wasp* along with the sailors. They shall constitute the rear guard. *Alfred* will lead. Ensure that everyone has a good drink. I don't want to lose any casualties to thirst."

The lieutenants were quiet. Feet shuffled, and glances were taken at one another.

"What is the problem," Captain Welsh asked?

John Trevett spoke up. "There is no water, Captain—nor victuals, either."

"We've plenty of shot and powder," Lieutenant Craig, from *Andrew Doria*, added.

Shoemaker summed it up. "It would appear, Samuel, that the landing was a complete success with the sole proviso that we neglected to provision the men for the campaign."

"Come now, Joseph, it is hardly a campaign. Look, here is a creek for our services."

"I do not think that would be a good idea, Captain," Lieutenant Weaver warned. "That creek flows right past New Guinea—and it is likely to be fouled at this point. No sir, I should not drink that water."

"There is nothing else for it, we shall have to send to the fleet for water butts," Huddle put in.

"We shall do no such thing," Nicholas answered. "We squandered our surprise at dawn. I do not intend that the enemy should have time to redeploy and repulse our advance. Surely there will be water and stores at Fort Montagu."

"I would wager that to be true, Captain," Weaver agreed.

"That is good," Cummings murmured to Trevett, "because he is wagering all of our lives on it." Robert Cummings was the Marine second lieutenant on the Continental Frigate *Columbus*, under First Lieutenant Trevett and Captain Shoemaker.

"A suggestion, Captain," Trevett addressed Nicholas during a pause in the discussion. Nicholas nodded. "The track is narrow, sir. Bordered on the north by the sea and on the south by the forest. It would be advisable to throw out pickets on our left flank to seek out possible ambush. There are, no doubt, ample opportunities for the enemy to deploy along our line of advance."

Nicholas discussed the suggestion with the other two captains. It took them some time to reach a final conclusion.

"That is tactically a sound recommendation, John," Nicholas replied at last. "In this particular instance, I believe that our sudden appearance and swift advance will serve as surer protection than flankers." Nicholas looked around the officers' faces. None offered further comment. "Very well, then. Gentlemen, join your companies. We move out in five minutes time."

Governor Browne stood in the entry of his residence admiring his image in the tall mirror as his valet smoothed the linen riding coat over his shoulders and set his tricorn firmly atop the freshly powdered wig. *This is much more fitting for a king's representative,* he thought. He turned to face the door and waited for his man to open it. He squinted so the bright morning sun would not blind him as the door opened. His groom awaited him at the bottom of the steps.

"The nails you asked for, Your Honor," the groom said when he handed the governor several small spikes. Governor Brown grabbed them from the man and stuffed them in his pocket. Then he gathered the reins and mounted his horse while the groom held the stirrup for him. He clucked the horse to a trot and set off for the short ride down to Fort Nassau.

Two minutes later, Governor Browne pulled rein just inside the fort and studied the scene. Eighty militia troops were formed into two companies in marching order. Major Sterling was at the head of the column in discussion with the leading Assembly members. Browne walked his horse over and looked down at the group.

"You may make your report, Major," Browne ordered.

"We are ready to march to Fort Montagu, Governor. The Assembly has just ordered me to lead the militia to the fort and defend against the invasion."

"You will take your orders from me, Major," Browne spoke to Sterling, but his eyes addressed the Gambier brothers.

"As you say, Governor," the major replied. "What are your orders?"

"You will remain here, Major. Garrison Fort Nassau with whatever stragglers arrive and any other volunteers you can gather. I shall lead the companies to Montagu and drive the rebels back into the sea."

Major Sterling saluted and stood aside while the column set out for Fort Montagu with the governor riding his horse at their head.

Lieutenant Grant stood at the foot of the schooner's foremast. The anchor was set, the main and foresails were loosely furled along their booms, and the wind was from the north-northeast. He could easily see the rebel fleet ferrying troops ashore at The Creek. Even though his crew was tired from the tedious beat into the wind, making very short boards through the narrow channel, William had put them to work immediately casting loose the guns and filling powder charges.

With little to employ him at the moment, Grant walked aft toward the quarterdeck. As he walked along, his eye was caught by a boat rowed by two men putting off from the beach near Fort Montagu. He stopped near the tiller and rested his right hand on the smooth, hot wood.

The boat made straight for *St. John*. The craft thumped alongside, and a militia sergeant—a local fisherman most of the time—spryly hopped from the stern thwart and over the schooner's bulwark. Taking a couple of steps, the man handed Grant a letter. It was not even sealed.

"This is from the governor," he said, touching the brim of his hat.

William opened the letter and read it quickly. A storm cloud drifted across his face, leaving a darkened and disturbed countenance.

"The governor gave you this himself?"

"He did, Cap'n. Told me to bring it to you straight away."

Grant crumpled the paper and threw it over the taffrail. "Stations for weighing anchor," he shouted at his crew. Men scrambled to their positions and took up various lines for heaving or loosing.

How in Heaven's name did that man ever become a royal governor? This is the third contradictory order I have received this day, and it is not even noon yet. Lord help us if it ever comes on to a real fight.

"You may return to the governor and tell him his orders will be carried out."

The sergeant touched his hat again and slipped over the side to begin the short pull back to the beach.

Lieutenant Grant prepared to move his *St. John* back to town—again.

Captain Nicholas handed his telescope to a private who was accompanying him. The Marine put it into a leather satchel that slung over his shoulder. The Marines were formed by companies in a relatively flat and open stretch of beach. Ahead of them was a thick line of brush and scrubby trees extending to the water's edge. A small opening a few yards inland from the waterline revealed the start of the road—track—to the main town.

"Move out," Samuel ordered and began trudging through the sand toward the west.

Alfred's marines were separated loosely into three groups of twenty men. Calling the disposition a *formation* would be generous. Sergeant Neilson marched at the head of the second group. Corporal Marshall occupied the "guide on" position in the group. Marine privates Tom Owens, Richard Evitt, Sam Mickery, John Dougherty, and John McLocken were in the first two rows. They had formed a close group on the voyage.

Even before facing combat, the deprivations of service and sea instilled a firm camaraderie of association. They were all reared in the environs of Philadelphia. They were of the same generation of restless patriots, and all typically bounded from one to another menial labor jobs.

"What now, Corporal?" McLocken asked.

"It's like this here, McLocken. Captain Nicholas comes to me when we gets ashore this morning. 'Jim he says'—cause he calls me Jim—'Jim, he says; when all the men gets ashore, how do you advise me to proceed?' Well, Captain, says me, this here track headin' off to the west is the only road I sees on this piece o' rock. So, I thinks Captain, that you should have the men follow this here road down to the town."

"You sure 'nough is a martial genius, ain't you, Jim?" Owens jibed the corporal. He jabbed Dougherty with his elbow, and all the men in the two leading rows burst into laughter.

"All right, ladies, pipe down! That's enough 'skylarkin'," Neilson bawled at the men.

The thumping of military accouterments, whispers and chuckles, and feet shuffling through the sand marked the beginning of the march. Nicholas, Parke, and the private entered the road at the head of the column. Coming around the first bend, Nicholas was startled to see an officer and a private militia soldier standing and facing them about fifteen yards away. The private held his musket aloft with a large white handkerchief tied to the ramrod that was protruding from the muzzle.

Nicholas held up his arm and shouted, "Marines, halt."

The companies shuffled to a stop. Most were unable to see around the bend to realize the reason for the stop. Nicholas sent the private back to collect the senior officer from each company and bring them to him.

A good distance back in the column, Captain Welsh and Lieutenant Wilson had just got *Cabot's* Marines moving down the road when the halt was called.

"What's going on, Lieutenant?" Private Kennedy asked.

"What's going on is we halted before we got going good, private. You're right behind me, Kennedy. For crying out loud, you know as much about what is going on as I do."

"I think you win the shilling this morning for asking dumb questions," Pat Kaine whispered to his friend, Kennedy. Both men grinned.

"John," Captain Welsh ordered Lieutenant Wilson, "Wait with the men while I go forward to see what's going on."

Lieutenant Burke was sweating; he was also shaking. He walked forward deliberately, covering half of the space between him and Nicholas. Captain Nicholas followed suit, stopping two paces in front of Burke. He saluted, and Burke returned the compliment.

"I am Lieutenant Burke of the New Providence Militia. In the name of the King, sir, and Governor Montfort Browne, would you please identify yourself and state your business?"

"I am Captain Samuel Nicholas of the Continental Marines of the United Colonies. I am here under the orders of Congress to take possession of the warlike stores on the island belonging to the crown."

"You are not intent on piracy and plunder?"

"I can assure you, sir, that I have no designs on touching the property or the persons of the local inhabitants—save in our own defense."

"By your leave then, Captain Nicholas, I will make my report to the governor."

Nicholas saluted again and said, "Good day to you Lieutenant."

Burke returned the salute and rejoined the private. Both men disappeared at a quick walk to the westward on the road.

Governor Browne stood on the wall of Fort Montagu staring through his telescope at the approaching rebels. He was flanked on either hand by various militia officers likewise engaged.

"Captain-Lieutenant Walker," the governor said to an officer on his right.

"Sir," Walker replied.

"Take your company and reinforce the scouting party. They will not be able to hold the rebels, else."

"Sir," he obeyed. He and his ensign descended the stone steps and were shortly seen leading his troops out the gate and down the road to the east.

Walker's company covered about two hundred yards before they rounded a bend in the road and came face-to-face with Burke, Judkin, and their thirty scouts.

There were several thumps, yelps, and curses as the two groups came to an undignified halt with men bumping into each other and treading on heels and toes.

"What are you doing here?" Lieutenant Burke asked Captain-Lieutenant Walker.

"The governor has sent us to reinforce you."

"The governor? Where is Major Sterling?"

"Governor Browne left him at Nassau and brought eighty more troops to Montagu himself."

"How gallant of him," Lieutenant Judkin interjected. Burke silenced him with a scowl.

"That is neither here nor there. Reinforcements are a vain gesture. We cannot hope to hold off three hundred well-equipped and disciplined troops with a handful of shopkeepers, farmhands, and fishermen. One in three of our men carry cudgels and fowling pieces. I have spoken with the enemy, man to man. They carry muskets, bayonets, and cartridge belts."

"Do they have artillery, Lieutenant . . . do they have scaling ladders? How are they provisioned Lieutenant Burke?"

Burke did not like arguing in front of the militia troops. He took Walker by the elbow and led him off the road a few paces toward the water. He then hissed in a loud whisper.

"I think we can dispense with the 'Lieutenant' talk, Walker. I am a planter, and you are a shopkeeper. You know nothing more about raising a siege than I—and we certainly don't need to argue in front of the others."

"Today, Burke, we are soldiers. What do you think those men are who landed on the beach today? A few weeks ago, they were planters, shopkeepers, and ne'er-do-wells. They know nothing more about soldiering than we. And we have a stone fortress with seventeen cannon."

Burke stared at him and said nothing.

"Very well then," Walker continued, "we will return to the fort and make our report to the Governor."

Walker left Burke standing on the beach and made his way through the column from what had been the lead to what had been the rear. He ordered the men to turn about and follow him back to Fort Montagu.

It lacks fifteen minutes of three o'clock, John Trevett said to himself as he trudged along the hard-packed track. He snapped his watch closed, returned it to his pocket, removed his hat and drew his arm across his forehead to wipe away the perspiration.

Very rarely, but occasionally, the Marines would march under the brief shade of a lone tree to be teased for just a moment. Just as often they encountered a patch of deep sand that was not packed, making their march that much more difficult for a few steps. Insects buzzed loudly from the thick bushes on their left, and the surf lapped quietly, nearly to their feet on the right. They knew a stone fort awaited their arrival, but they had yet to see it.

"John," Captain Joseph Shoemaker's voice startled Trevett out of his thoughts.

"Yes, sir."

"Hurry on to the front of the column. I've Robert as a second." Lieutenant Robert Cummings was second lieutenant of *Columbus's* sixty-three Marines. "I suspect Captain Nicholas would be glad of an aide de camp."

"Aye, Joe," Trevett responded. He touched his hat and stepped out, lengthening and quickening his pace to pass *Alfred's* company and join Nicholas at the head of the column. Trevett did not hesitate and run the risk of losing his opportunity to be in the thick of any impending action.

"Hello John," Nicholas said when Trevett fell in step beside him.

"Afternoon Captain. Captain Shoemaker said you might be able to use an aide de camp."

Nicholas looked sideways at Trevett; then he said, "And I imagine you volunteered."

"It seems *Columbus* has and extra Lieutenant of Marines."

"Well, not at present."

The governor and his officers saw the dust cloud growing thicker and closer as the invaders continued to advance. The sun beat down on them as they faced southeast. The north coast of New Providence Island was generally a straight line running nearly due east and west. Fort Montagu, however, stood at the northwest promontory of a small U-shaped bay that dug into the normally straight coastline.

Across the narrow lagoon to the north was the eastern end of Hog Island that also ran east and west, protecting the town and the harbor. The track that the Marines followed ran along the edge of the small bay so that the final leg carried them along a route to the northwest.

Governor Browne looked along the top of the fort's walls, then down to the ground inside the fort. It was a sturdy stone structure several feet thick with a very strong gate. Most of the guns were sited to prevent ships from forcing the channel, but three faced the rebels' line of approach.

Less that 150 men stood about on the walls or lounged below in whatever shade they could find. About half of them had some type of musket or fouling piece. A crew stood ready at each of the guns facing the enemy's advance. Browne considered his options. Eventually, he stuck his hand in his pocket and withdrew the nails he brought. He thought some more, shoved them back in his pocket and said, "Lieutenant Burke."

"Governor?" the officer replied.

"Take a detachment and parley with the rebels. I demand to know their intentions."

"Governor, I did that already. I conveyed their intentions to your person."

"I want you to go again as my direct representative. I especially require specific assurances that they will do no harm to the populace nor abscond with personal property and wealth."

"Sir, I spoke with their commander. He has already given those assurances."

"Do . . . not . . . question . . . my orders, Lieutenant," Governor Browne spoke slowly and distinctly.

"As you say, Governor," Burke replied and skipped down the stone steps to collect a detachment.

Slowmatches were burning in the linstocks held by the three gun captains. As there was almost no breeze, a light cloud of smoke formed along the top of the wall. All the men present could smell the acrid aroma that hung around them. It accentuated the atmosphere of confused expectation.

"Captain-Lieutenant Walker," was the next thing the governor said.

"Yes, Governor." The man already stood by the governor.

Governor Browne retrieved the nails from his pocket and extended them to Walker with his fingers open and his palm facing upward. "Take these and spike the fort's guns." . . . . Walker gazed at the nails in Governor Browne's hand, then looked up and stared into his eyes. He could see sweat running down the man's face in rivulets.

"Go on, Man, take them!"

"But sir—Governor—the guns are already loaded and ready to fire."

"Not those guns, you ninny--the rest of them! Will none of my officers obey my orders?"

Walker stretched out his arm and gingerly collected the nails from Browne's sweaty palm. He curled his fingers around them and looked into the eyes of the other officers in turn. No one spoke. No one offered encouragement or disagreement.

"Right then," Walker finally said. "Sergeant."

"Sir," said his leading non-commissioned officer.

"Take these nails and carry out the governor's order."

"Yes, sir," the sergeant said, grabbing the nails and distributing them to several militia soldiers with specific instructions.

"Open the gate!" Burke said from below. Men moved to obey his command.

"One moment, Lieutenant," the Governor countered. "Are your men ready to fire?" he asked the gun captains.

"We are, sir," they responded.

"Very well, then. Take careful aim at the dust cloud to the southeast and fire when you are ready."

The officers on the wall stared at the governor in silence as the gun crews set about making final adjustments to their aim. One by one the gun captains lowered the glowing match to the touchholes, firing their guns.

Marines dove for cover as a six-pound iron ball screamed over their heads. Some sought protection in the thorny bushes to their left. Others rolled over the low embankment and hugged the sandy beach to the right. Many just fell prostrate into the middle of the road.

Moments later, a second ball splashed into the bay then made several more splashes as it skipped along the gentle waves. A third was heard crashing through the brush to the left. Nicholas, Parke, Fitzpatrick, and Trevett were all crouched on one knee at the head of the column.

Lieutenant John Fitzpatrick turned to check on the troops while the other officers watched for an enemy advance.

"Everyone, take cover behind the road. Watch the bushes for an ambush," Fitzpatrick ordered the Marines of *Alfred's* company.

Neilson poked his nose up over the edge of the road. Owens was on his left hand, and several more men stretched along to the east, finally ending with Private McLocken and Corporal Marshall. One by one they checked the priming in their pans and ensured that their muskets were on half-cock.

"Do you still desire that we should parley, Governor?"

"Of course, I do. Now get moving."

Lieutenant Burke nodded toward the gate, and the men began opening it.

"Very good. Now then, Captain-Lieutenant Walker, form up the rest of your men to march back to Fort Nassau."

Again, Walker could only stare at the governor.

"What is the matter with you, Mr. Walker? Cannot you follow the most basic orders?"

"But Governor, this is our strongest position. You have just provoked the enemy. They cannot possibly hope to reduce the fort."

"I do not intend that myself or the bulk of my militia be besieged in the fortress, Captain-Lieutenant. We will leave two men to inform Lieutenant Burke of our actions when he returns."

"Governor Browne. We have plenty of water here. The rebels have landed no artillery. None of their ships have made any movement indicating a bombardment. We can hold here until they tire of the whole project and slink off back north."

The two men stared at each other for a full minute in silence.

Eventually, Walker shouted at the man who had spiked the guns, "Sergeant, form the men for march."

Governor Browne smiled and descended the steps . . . followed slowly by the other officers. A private stood at the bottom of the steps holding the reins to Browne's horse. Without a word, the Governor mounted the animal and accepted the reins. He jerked the horse's head, prodded his heals into his flanks and trotted out the still-open gate. Once through, he turned down the road toward the town and accelerated into a canter.

"We have to pull back to a more defensible position," Lieutenant Dayton argued.

"I am inclined to agree with Henry," First Lieutenant Wilson agreed. "We are strung out for nearly a cable along this track and fully exposed to artillery and a flank attack from the brush."

Although Lieutenant Huddle represented only the five marines from *Wasp*, he was neither shy nor timid. "Gentlemen, we must not forfeit the ground we have captured. I am for continuing the advance and laying siege to Fort Montagu."

After the brief barrage of three shots ended, all the officers made their way along the road to express their opinions and concerns to Captain Nicholas. Not being completely sure what to do next, he was glad to hold the brief council of war.

"Sir . . . Captain Nicholas," Trevett spoke.

"What is it, John?"

"Down the road, sir."

Heads swiveled to the northwest. At the farthest extent of their vision along the road, the officers saw a small party of men approaching under a flag of truce.

"It seems the English want to parley again. Perhaps we will learn more of the governor's intentions."

"It might be a trap, Captain," Lieutenant Dayton stated.

"Well, we will just have to find out, Lieutenant. Ensure that the companies are vigilant and prepared to repulse an attack from the bush," Nicholas ordered. Looking around he noticed that Lieutenant Craig from *Andrew Doria* had brought Sergeant Turner to the council with him. "Turner, find a suitable flag of truce and select a detail of two men to accompany Lieutenant Trevett."

"Aye, Cap'n."

"John, meet the party and find out what you can about their intentions. You may repeat my terms of their peaceful capitulation."

"Yes, sir, Captain."

"Be careful; it is probably a trick," Wilson added. Nicholas scowled at the man.

Minutes later, the two parties stood facing each other in the midst of the dusty road. Burke removed his hat and bowed, followed by Trevett.

"I have come to talk with Captain Nicholas again," Burke spoke. "I see you are surprised. I met him earlier this afternoon."

"I am authorized by Captain Nicholas to parley with you."

"I am ordered by Governor Browne to parley with your commander."

Trevett considered his situation. He did not want to relinquish the authority he'd been given, but neither did he want to delay the discussion while the Marines were in such an exposed position. He looked down the road toward the fort; then studied the brush. He was trying to discern any type of trap or trickery.

"Do you parley under the cover of artillery, Lieutenant?"

"The governor ordered the firing of the guns," Burke countered.

Trevett considered his answer and finally submitted, saying, "Follow me, Lieutenant."

"Lieutenant Burke," Nicholas addressed the man when he stopped in front of him. "To what do I owe the pleasure of your second visit this day?"

"The governor sends to ask your intentions, Captain Nicholas."

"My intentions and my terms have not changed, Lieutenant Burke. But I cannot say I am convinced that the governor intends to comply with them."

"It is my belief that he fired the guns only to appease some trivial sense of personal honor or pride. He has subsequently spiked all the guns in the fort and abandoned it with all his militia."

"I only wish I could have confidence in your assertion, sir."

"Follow me to the fort, Captain. You will see the gates standing open and the wall devoid of life."

Nicholas turned his face and stared across the lagoon toward Hog Island. He considered his options, finally deciding he had nothing to lose and everything to gain. If there were a trap, he would eventually have to discover it no matter what course he pursued—short of returning to the fleet and abandoning the enterprise.

"Very well, Lieutenant Burke. You may go. We will follow you shortly and occupy Fort Montagu. If nothing untoward occurs this evening, I shall wait on the governor in the morning."

Both officers bowed. Burke turned and led his detachment back up the road while Nicholas ordered his officers to prepare to resume the march.

Commodore Hopkins held the scrap of paper at arm's length and high enough that the fading light from the setting sun illuminated the writing. He sat in the great cabin with his back to the stern windows. Captain Saltonstall sat across the desk in an armchair waiting impatiently for his commander-in-chief to finish reading the report from Captain Nicholas. Hopkins came to the end and scanned the document quickly again.

Marines and seamen in complete command of Fort Montagu . . . too exhausted to continue . . . no provisions . . . I estimate over 200 militia under arms . . . no opposition to this point but have had two parleys with subalterns . . . have assured Governor Browne no harm to populace if the garrison cooperates . . . intend to occupy town and Fort Nassau on the morrow.

"Read this Dudley," Hopkins said and handed the report to his flag captain. "Then call my captains. I will draft a reply to Captain Nicholas while I await their arrival.

Twenty-five minutes later, Lieutenant Jones slipped quietly into *Alfred's* crowded great cabin and stifled a cough when his nose was assaulted by the aroma of the humanity packed into the cramped, humid space.

Closing the cabin door, Jones whispered in his captain's ear, "The message has been dispatched to Captain Nicholas, and all the captains have assembled, sir."

"I can see that, First Lieutenant," Saltonstall gave the unnecessary and testy reply.

Commodore Hopkins frowned at Jones and Saltonstall, then said with a raised voice, "Gentlemen, thank you for joining me. This island is ours . . . or nearly so, at any rate."

"Bravo," said Captain Biddle, of *Andrew Doria*.

"Give you joy of your victory, Brother," Captain John Hopkins congratulated.

"I am in receipt of Captain Nicholas's dispatch informing me of the capitulation of Fort Montagu and his intention to add Fort Nassau to his victories when the sun rises."

He paused to let the assembled captains absorb the news.

"Further, in order to ensure there is no senseless violence, I have issued a manifesto to the governor and the inhabitants of New Providence. It is at this moment being borne ashore."

"And what have you decreed in your manifesto?" Captain Whipple asked.

An oil lamp, suspended in gimbals from the overhead, illumined the cabin. Hopkins picked up the rough notes from the document he sent ashore and held it close to the lamp. "I shall read the salient parts."

It is the intention of the Continental Forces to take possession of the powder and warlike stores belonging to the Crown, and if I am not opposed in putting my design in execution, the persons and property of the inhabitants shall be safe; neither shall they be suffered to be hurt in case they make no resistance.

"If I may, Commodore," John Hazard of *Providence* Sloop replied, "it might be prudent to consider that a good number of the hands in this war and the late war with France have sailed letters of marque, sir. No doubt many will be set on a store of private plunders."

A couple of the other captains nodded their agreement. Hopkins laid his notes down on his desk and looked around the room, locking eyes briefly with each captain.

When the commodore replied, his voice was firm, and the cadence of his words was measured. "I too sailed letters of marque in the late war, gentlemen. Hear me now. This fleet is composed of government ships, not privateers—and certainly not pirates. War is waged according to accepted convention, and this navy will conduct itself as befits a sovereign state. There will be no private plunder, and any attempts to the contrary will be dealt with in a decided fashion. Are there any questions on that point?"

No one replied.

"Excellent."

"One point if I may, Commodore."

"Yes, Dudley; what is it?"

"Now that the governor can have no doubt of our intentions," Hopkins frowned at the preamble, "Perhaps we can dispatch *Cabot* and *Andrew Doria* to blockade the Narrows."

Hopkins replied condescendingly, "I commend your zeal, Captain, but the sun is ready to set at any moment." He waved his arm across the great stern windows. "The governor hasn't the shipping available at his disposal to remove his stores. And further, would he intentionally deprive himself of the means to defend his colony?"

"But sir, it would cost us little to add surety to your wise observations."

Hopkins turned and stared at the setting sun while considering the suggestion. The cabin was quiet except the creaking of a ship at anchor and the collective breathing of the gathered officers. The air was still stifling. Finally, the commodore turned back to face his flag captain.

"The men are tired, Dudley. A night of rest will do them good. I won't have two ships standing off and on all night."

Saltonstall opened his mouth to utter another argument, but Hopkins held up his hand to forestall it.

"No Captain. Now, there is an end to it. Gentlemen, the fleet will weigh one hour before dawn. You are dismissed."

Captain William Chambers rested his right hand on a spoke of the *Mississippi Packet's* wheel. The meeting in the fort was concluded, and he was glad to be back on his ship. He was a loyal subject of King George. Further, he had no beef with Parliament.

English law was very favorable to his trade, while any taxes and tariffs he might be associated with were only passed on to his clientele. And, truth be told, the high tariffs might even make it possible for him or his crew to profit by the occasional personal trade transaction.

So, there was little remorse in his heart as he watched his crew, augmented by a dozen militiamen, tossing the valuable lumber overboard into the harbor. Even though he agreed voluntarily with the order, he still asked Governor Browne to sign an order for the act. Chambers would present that order to his consignee in Jamaica and let him battle with the Crown for satisfaction. He had little doubt that much of the cargo would eventually be salvaged and its value somehow find its way into the governor's purse. But that was no longer his concern.

Watching the progress of the men jettisoning his deck cargo by the light of oil lamps hanging from the rigging, Captain Chambers considered the events of the day. Before sunset, Governor Browne came riding back into town alone. After deciding that his militia was insufficient to protect the colony, he published a notice to recruit more volunteers.

Browne's order even included the enlistment of free blacks, offering a free pistol as bounty to any who would accept his offer. A few more recruits came to the fort, joined shortly by the main body returning from Fort Montagu.

During the short period when the governor was thinking with a clear tactical mind, he ordered Captain Hogdon and Lieutenant Barrett to take forty men and secure the high ground around government house with two four pounders.

After sunset, the rebel admiral's manifest began to circulate. Not long after, the militia—private soldiers, officers, and new recruits—began to melt into the shadows and evaporate into the night. It was believed by some that a handful even walked to Fort Montagu to join the rebels. It was then that the governor called for a vote of the Assembly, officers, and leading citizens.

Popular vote, rather than military assessment, determined that the Colony's position was indefensible. And this decision led Captain Chambers to be involved in his present activity. Although there was considerable fear of retribution from the rebels, the Assembly nevertheless, decided to ship the powder to St. Augustine consigned to Governor Tonyn.

Ding-ding, ding-ding, ding-ding, ding-ding. Midnight. Chambers glanced across the water at the only other ship in harbor. He could see Grant's silhouette under the single lantern. A boat was alongside, and powder was already being swayed up and loaded aboard His Majesty's schooner. Grant's own men were nearly finished offloading that boat, and not a moment too soon. Another, dangerously overloaded with powder barrels, was just coming alongside.

They wouldn't take it all. They would leave a small quantity of powder and all the materiel. They would leave the powder in hopes of appeasing the rebels and the materiel because there was no hope of loading everything in the two small vessels. Everyone was working with a will to finish and clear the Narrows before daylight. No one knew whether the rebel fleet would be waiting to capture them and render all their effort naught.

March 4, 1776
Nassau Harbor Sally Port
New Providence Island–British Colony

Lieutenants Trevett and Parke stood together at the top of the steps leading down to the New Providence sally port. Having been ordered by Captain Nicholas to meet the commodore and escort

him to Fort Nassau, they watched the barge pull away from
Alfred's starboard chains.

Only a minute earlier, the frigate had splashed her bow anchor
into the translucent azure of the Caribbean harbor. Men were
scurrying around the ship now, securing the anchor, passing
gaskets over the neatly furled courses and topsails, and squaring the
yards.

"Good afternoon, Commodore," Trevett said, raising his hat
slightly and greeting Hopkins as he hopped out of the boat onto
the hewn coral steps of the sally port.

"Hello, Lieutenant. Take me to Captain Nicholas forthwith."

"Aye, sir. Right this way."

The group of men walked a few paces in silence. Then Trevett
broke it. "The governor has surrendered the island, sir. The local
militia has disbursed, and the Marines control both forts.
Governor Browne awaits you at Fort Nassau, and Captain
Nicholas has ordered an inventory of Crown stores."

He paused and drew a breath. Hopkins made no reply. "Forty
guns there were, sir. Forty guns mounted in embrasures of Fort
Nassau—every last one charged with ball, langrage, or canister.
Forty guns and the fort deserted. Governor Browne as much as says
'how do you do' and hands over the key to a deserted fort."

Commodore Hopkins halted in mid-stride, turning to look
Trevett straight in the eye. "You don't say, Lieutenant. Well, I'll be.
You have my congratulations, sir—and so does Captain Nicholas.
Well done—well done to you and the whole landing party." A
wide grin broke out on his face. The fleet had lost many to fever.
He was thankful for a bloodless victory ashore at least. They
resumed their short walk.

Walking through the gate of Fort Nassau, Commodore
Hopkins was greeted by the sight of several men sitting around a
table shaded from the fierce tropical sun by a temporarily erected
canvas awning. At his appearance, they all stood, and Captain
Nicholas walked around the table to greet him. "Good afternoon,
Commodore. The island of New Providence is yours to command,
sir." They shook hands.

"I give you joy of your victory, Captain. You have my heartiest
congratulations and strong thanks for a superb job."

"Thank you, Commodore. May I present Governor Montfort
Browne, Sir." Browne stepped forward and bowed. "Governor
Browne, this is Commodore Ezek Hopkins." Hopkins extended
his hand, and the two men shook.

"Commodore, I thank you for your gracious offer of kind
treatment of His Majesty's subjects."

"Conditional, Governor, upon satisfaction of the terms of the offer."

The governor made no reply, and several of the other men looked grimly at one another.

Nicholas interjected, "If you will have a seat, sir; I have prepared an inventory of Crown stores for your review."

Hopkins took a seat in the shade and picked up the inventory. He read the first few lines, scanned the rest, flipped the page over, and turned it face up again. Then he looked up at Captain Nicholas.

"Is this all?" he asked quietly.

"Yes, sir, it is," Nicholas answered in the same level tone. Governor Browne was pale, and sweat beaded on his forehead.

"Thirty-eight barrels of powder?" Hopkins' voice was quite loud now, and he said each word to a slow cadence. His eyes locked those of the senior marine, silently demanding an answer. Nicholas blinked, swirled his tongue around inside his mouth in a vain attempt to moisten it, and then swallowed.

"I have discussed that point with the governor, Commodore. He has assiduously avoided providing any information as to the scant quantity of powder stores. However, sir, it seems to be common knowledge that two ships, *St. John* and the *Mississippi Packet*, were loaded with powder after dark last night. I am told that the loading was completed at four bells in the middle watch, and before dawn, both vessels had cleared soundings and were bound with orders to the governor in St. Augustine."

The tops of Hopkins' ears reddened, and he laid the paper on the table. A faint breeze lifted one corner but was of insufficient force to dislodge the entire page. Saltonstall's admonition to blockade the harbor troubled his mind for a moment. Placing his hands flat on the table he pushed himself to a standing position. His face swiveled from Nicholas to that of the governor. Browne shrunk back half a step.

"Is this true, Governor?"

There was no answer. Browne wiped his hand across his face then dried it on his coat.

"Did you violate the terms of surrender even before I came ashore?" Hopkins' voice was loud and forceful—even angry. Their attention aroused, several men standing around in the fort looked at their leaders.

"Well?"

Browne lowered his head and looked at his feet. He raised his eyes but kept his head bowed. "There was no formal surrender, sir," he said sheepishly. "We had no agreement."

"You ungrateful, treacherous, dishonorable scoundrel!"

"Now you see her, Mr. Hopkins. There can be no question of honor with a treasonous pirate." The governor stood erect again, jutting his chin out slightly.

"Governor Browne, you disreputable carrion. You will learn some manners, sir." To his captain of Marines, the commodore went on, "Nicholas."

"Sir?"

"Confine this man under guard until I decide what is to become of him."

"Mr. Trevett," Nicholas relayed the order, "Assemble a guard and confine the governor in solitary in the fort."

"Aye, aye, Captain," Trevett responded, turned on his heal, and began issuing orders to Marines.

Moments later Governor Browne found himself alone in a room with a stone floor, bare of any furniture. Diffused light from greased parchment windows supplied the only illumination. He was furious but knew he had only himself to blame. His consolation—and it was considerably satisfying—was that he had done his duty for the king.

Later in the afternoon, he rose from the cool stone floor when the door opened abruptly. He blinked when led out into the bright sunlight and found himself surrounded by more than two dozen rough-looking rebels. He recognized Trevett.

"Let's go, Governor," Trevett ordered. "The commodore has ordered us to arrest you in Government House until further orders." With that, the group set off up the hill toward Governor Browne's home.

March 16, 1776
Continental Frigate Alfred
New Providence Island–British Colony

The heat had moderated some, but not the humidity. Cotton and flax togs were the norm, although woolens were being aired. Everyone knew the fleet would be sailing toward New England soon, and it was still late winter—or early spring at the very best—in those waters. Wind sails were rigged, gun ports stood open, and the movement of air they permitted made life below decks bearable.

Bearable, perhaps, but not truly healthy. The fleet carried fever —the pox—with them from the continent. Scores of the sailors and Marines were stricken with the disease. Many died, and dozens still languished in their hammocks wishing they were dead. As in all wars throughout history, disease and ill health claimed many more victims than battle.

Sergeant Turner on *Andrew Doria* made a name for himself. With no regard for his personal health, he continued to care for his stricken Marines. A goodly number of Marines and sailors owed a great deal to his care.

There were other infirmities as well. The normal social diseases associated with seaports and sailors claimed their victims. The fleet's losses were somewhat mitigated by a few local residents who decided to throw in their lot with the Continentals.

A number of the Continental sailors and Marines accepted the ministrations of the ships' surgeons after suffering the consequences of naval justice. Commodore Hopkins established a triangle in the fort to punish any under his command convicted of molesting or plundering the populace.

The temptation for many was too strong and they paid the consequence with well-administered stripes across their bare backs. This order did not sit well with many, even some of the officers. Many—perhaps most—had sailed as privateers and were very used to claiming any plunder that Providence presented. But the commodore was determined to conduct his fleet under the customs of international maritime law.

It was mid-afternoon in *Alfred's* wardroom—the hottest part of the day. Several officers sat around the table in knee breeches with their sleeves rolled above the elbow and chests bare to catch any merciful movement of air.

The head of the table, rightful place of the first lieutenant, was vacant. Captain Nicholas sat in the first seat to the right of the vacant chair. Across from him was Lieutenant Parke. Both men sipped warm wine in a vain effort to satisfy their thirst.

The Marine second lieutenant, John Fitzpatrick, was ashore seeing to the collection of the remaining Marines. The plunder was all loaded, and Governor Browne and his secretary, Lieutenant James Babbidge, were under guard in one of *Alfred's* cramped and airless storerooms.

The plunder was considerable. Ballast in the fleet's holds was replaced with captured round shot. Two more ships, one local and one recently arrived from America were chartered by the commodore to load the remaining materiel and transport it back to the government on the continent. *Fly*, recovered from her encounter with *Hornet*, finally rejoined the fleet five days earlier.

Lieutenant Jones walked in and took his place at the head of the table. He slid a one-page document across the worn fir table to Nicholas. "Your rough notes, Sam. Thank you for the loan of them. They were very valuable in preparing the final report for the captain, which I am just returned from delivering to him and I am confident he is now delivering to the commodore."

Nicholas nodded and looked down at the document—his inventory of captured stores. He scanned it silently. Eighty-eight cannons, ranging from nine to thirty-six pounders, fifteen mortars, 5,458 mortar shells, 11,071 shot, thirty-eight barrels of powder. It continued to list much more military weaponry from the British arsenal. The two forts captured did not even make it on the list.

Jones sat silently while a sailor, who worked as servant in the wardroom, placed a glass of wine in front of him. Swallowing the entire contents, he held the glass aloft to be refilled. "We'll sail in the morning. Your troops should be settled before dark. I can't say I'll be sorry to sink this island."

"All in all, I would not say the expedition was unsuccessful," Parke added.

Both of his senior officers looked at him.

"What you say is fair, Matthew. We've more ships than we sailed with—and each and every one is fully laden with captured stores—all valuable."

"What then?" Parke asked.

"Powder," Jones answered. "The commodore surely applied the broadest interpretation possible to his orders from Congress when he brought the fleet to the Caribbean. He gambled on being a hero to the army by taking back shiploads of powder. He has some, but certainly not what he had hoped."

The space became silent again. Not exactly silent—thumps and scrapes and creaks and splashes penetrated from the outer world—but no talking.

Parke changed the subject. "The scuttlebutt is that Hinman is to have the sloop."

"A good man, he," Nicholas answered. "Commanded his first brig at nineteen. 'Tis a fair appointment."

"What of his vacancy?"

"I am sure the commodore will find a deserving cousin to be first lieutenant in *Cabot*," Jones said. "Any word of the deserters?" It was Jones's turn to change the subject.

"None," Parke said. "Hard to blame them. They only want to avoid the pox. Probably hiding in New Guinea."

Three of *Alfred's* sailors and one Marine deserted the frigate.

Nicholas took a swallow. Jones quaffed another glass and stood.

"I am off, gentlemen. Time and tide await no man. We shall see each other again at dinner." He walked out.

DECK LOG 1776

- April

The year in summary

*T*here was war in North America as Winter melted into Spring. At sea, the fledgling states battled the most powerful navy in the world with their infant navy in the first fleet action of the war.

Across a continent, Spanish were founding the Presidio at the mission of San Francisco, other Spanish explorers probed deep into the continent's southwest, and Mozart was composing music in Europe. In the autumn, General-come-Admiral Benedict Arnold would lose the Battle of Valcour Island on Lake Champlain, but in so doing stalled the British invasion of New York. The year ended with George Washington's famous crossing of the Delaware River, resulting in the capture of nearly a thousand Hessian troops during the Battle of Trenton.

Hessian troops reinforced the British ranks late in the summer and Washington was ultimately forced to abandon New York by the end of the year. The end of the year witnessed the Hessian's surrendering to General Washington in Trenton on the Delaware River.

April 3, 1776
Block Island Sound
Continental Frigate *Columbus*

Their garb marked them more as nautical than military—the small knot of somber men gathered in the waist. But for all that, they were Marines. Their ship, *Columbus*, as was the entire fleet, was hove to.

The faint wind blew out of the north-northwest over her starboard bow. The men unconsciously adjusted their bodies to the slow roll and pitch, bending one knee then flexing another as they leaned their shoulders first one way then another.

Three of the men wore well-tailored green coats, and one of them held a telescope trained on the brig, *Andrew Doria*. These three, Shoemaker, Trevett, and Cummings, were the officers of the Marines on *Columbus*. Their coats, designed by the fleet's senior Marine, Captain Nicholas, were the only attempt at anything approaching a uniform.

Ribbons of mist and amorphous banks of fog floated through the fleet, coming together then ripping apart as they concealed one ship then revealed another. A shape splashed down the side of *Andrew Doria* just as one of the small patches of fog ghosted between her and *Columbus*. Another life given over to the fever.

"Isaac will miss that one, I'm bound," Lieutenant Fitzpatrick commented to the gathered Marines. Sergeant Turner as much as ran the Marines on *Andrew Doria*.

"As well he should, Lieutenant," Sergeant Nielson replied. "The men fairly worshiped Tom."

"Aye, right you are, Alex," Fitzpatrick agreed with his sergeant. "Many of them worked for him in Philadelphia. He's watched over them since we left the docks in the winter. Now, here we are almost home and safe from the fever, but he still visited his sick men daily and looked after their needs, even after *Andrew Doria's* surgeon succumbed."

"Jones and I were reviewing the fleet's muster, yesterday," Trevett spoke. "One in four men in the fleet are still down with the fever. Fifteen years, he told me, sailing in and out of the Caribbean, and he's never seen the like of it."

"The cooler weather certainly makes the difference," Captain Nicholas stated.

"Yes, sir. The men recover quicker, and there have been no new cases reported in three days."

Since arriving in northern waters, there were fewer burials at sea. The ceremonies now involved but one or two men at a time. The gale that scattered the fleet for several days finally abated, and when it did, the tropical weather was days to the south. New England Spring times were pleasant and temperate. The winds around Montauk were steady but light. The ships were open to the air and finally beginning to dry out. Morale was improving.

"It is just as well; the commodore intends to cruise a few more days for prizes before we go to New London."

"God bless the man," a private Marine spoke. "We'm barely 'nough men t' work the ships, let alone the guns."

"It will have to be enough," Nicholas countered. "It's all we have."

April 4, 1776
Jamestown, Rhode Island
Conanicut Island

Lieutenant William Jones stood in the trees of Bull Point on Conanicut Island. He was an officer in the Rhode Island Militia. Colonel Henry Babcock himself gave him the oath. The parchment of his commission felt strong tucked inside his breast pocket. Jones was fighting this war since before it was a war, but the events of last December caused him to reevaluate his position.

Two weeks before Christmas, Wallace (Jones knew in his bones it must have been Wallace) somehow scrounged up some Hessians and Lobster-backs to punish the local residents. Not smugglers or Sons-of-Liberty mind you, but peaceful farmers and shopkeepers in Jamestown, on Conanicut Island.

It happened on a quiet morning like this one, only cold. Smoke curled out of the scattered chimneys into the frozen air as the locals tossed the first wood of the morning onto the previous night's banked coals. At first, the wood sent wisps of smoke floating up the stone flues; then the wood popped; then the wood crackled.

Moments later, flames made their appearance and drove the chill from the modest homes. The local people felt a moment of cheer standing before the hearth, thinking of the Christmas holiday approaching while absorbing the warmth of the new day's fire.

Then a crash; before the entire household was even out of bed, the black boots of the Hessian's and British redcoats crashed their doors in, breaking furniture, smashing crockery, and terrorizing the sleepy residents. They landed at East Ferry and marched across the island to West Ferry in less than half an hour.

The landing and a few small structures of West Ferry were already in flames when the troops reversed course and started back to the east. They took more time moving east, destroying a score or more buildings, including fourteen homes which were burned. Little, if any, distinction was made between loyal Tory, Revolutionary Patriot, and those merely working to survive in the colony.

This was the justice meted out by the sovereign George III to his colonial subjects. By the time they were back aboard their transports, over a third of the islands five hundred some odd residents had no choice but to gather their meager belongs and relocate to the mainland.

That was the event that made up William's mind. Shortly after the New Year began—January fifteenth if truth be told—he accepted his first lieutenant's commission in Colonel Babcock's Regiment. That was the day the Colony stood up the regiment. That is how he came to be here on Bull Point. His assignment was to watch the British squadron and gain intelligence.

The nearest vessel was anchored less than half a mile from him. He used a large glass and watched the activities on the various ships. Jones knew that with the sun rising directly in his face, there was every likelihood that men on the vessels would see a flash from his lens. That was not an issue. The colonel wanted the British to know they were under close surveillance. Twice a day he sent reports to the militia headquarters via clandestine couriers. Often, they were women.

Jones read over his first report of the day. All of the known ships in Wallace's squadron were riding to anchor. He scanned the list; *Rose*-20, *Glasgow*-20, *Bolton*-12, *Nautilus*-16, *Swan*-14, *Hawke*-6— and the two frigates had a tender apiece. The tenders were important. They were local prizes Captain Wallace decided to keep and use. They carried messages to his ships when out of visual range and also raided outlying farms or traded with Tories to keep his squadron in supply.

Jones turned pensive—six ships plus the tenders; over four score guns and about a thousand men to point them—trained men. A very formidable squadron indeed. He further noted a significant amount of activity, indicating that they were likely to put to sea within the next twenty-four hours.

Lieutenant Jones added more details about the activities and preparations of the squadron, folded the report, and stuffed it in a leather satchel. He handed it to the first courier for its journey who then departed without a word.

Mounting twenty nine-pound guns on her main gun deck, *HMS Rose* was one of the most imposing warships on the

American station. She was certainly the nemesis of smugglers as well as legal trading ships—few though they were—in Rhode Island.

As the sun began its daily circuit, climbing over the spires and warehouses of Newport, *Rose* and her consort, *HMS Glasgow* swung gently to their anchors in Newport Roads near the mouth of Narragansett Bay.

To the eyes of a landsman, and few of those there were in Newport, the two frigates might be twins, right down to the number and position of their gun ports. Neither vessel was idle during the colonial revolt. While *Rose*, under Captain Wallace, was suppressing smuggling and bringing Newport's economy to its knees, Captain Howe had *Glasgow* in Boston harbor supporting the British Army at their capture of Breed's Hill. The two ships now worked in concert with their smaller consorts to keep the Block Island Sound clear of rebel shipping.

Captain Tyringham Howe hailed from a prestigious Royal Navy family. His uncle currently served as First Lord of the Admiralty. Howe's senior naval officer on the station, Captain James Wallace, was the same James Wallace who was outfoxed by, and lost his tender *Diana*, to Commodore Whipple and the Rhode Island Navy in the prior year.

Both men were enjoying their breakfast tea. Greasy residue on the plates and platters was the only evidence of the fried eggs, bacon, root vegetables, lamb chops, and soft tack they had enjoyed.

Howe put the cup on its saucer and waited while Wallace's servant refilled it. "Your mind is far away this morning, James."

Wallace frowned at the interruption then replaced the image with a smile. "I do apologize, Tyringham. I am afraid you caught me gathering wool like some ninny schoolgirl."

"No doubt you were thinking of home."

"Quite. I confess I had much rather be in Georgia overseeing the planting."

"Aye—and no doubt enjoying the companionship of your lady rather than that of a broken-down sea captain."

"No doubt, my friend, no doubt."

Both men chuckled. A year earlier, Wallace married Anne Wright—twenty years his junior—on his plantation in Georgia. Wallace had been at sea since he was fifteen, but since marrying, he found himself longing more and more for a solid home. His service to the crown on the American station was highly successful. If there were any justice in the world, he would be knighted when this commission was paid off.

Wallace shifted the course of the subject. "But we have a job to do yet. The rebels grow bolder by the day. Every colony is issuing letters of marque—even commissioning paper navies under the spurious authority of their illegal legislatures."

"*Glasgow* is ready. We finished with watering last night."

"That is well, Tyringham. I intend that we will sweep the sound for another week. Pass the word for my first lieutenant." The last to his servant.

A moment later the door to the dining cabin opened. "Yes sir," his first lieutenant said as he entered with his hat under his arm.

"Signal *Bolton* and *Hawke* to weigh and proceed to sea as ordered."

"Aye, aye, Captain," the first lieutenant replied and withdrew.

As the door closed, both captains heard the brass notes of the bosun of the watch striking eight bells. Eight o'clock in the morning and time for the men who had been standing the anchor watch since four o'clock to be relieved.

Captain Howe pushed his chair back and stood, stooping slightly to avoid the overhead beams. "I am afraid I must bid you good day and thank you for breakfast, sir. I will await your signal to weigh."

Captain Wallace also stood and shook his companion's hand. "Do not you leave yourself at short stay, Tyringham. It is likely I will dispatch only *Bolton* and *Hawke* today. I will expect them to screen our departure—most likely on the morrow. No breakfast for us tomorrow, I am afraid. I intend the rest of us will sail at dawn."

Captain Howe nodded and disappeared through the cabin door, calling for his gig.

Lieutenant Edward Sneyd, commander of the bomb brig, *HMS Bolton*, rested a hand on each hip and allowed his weight to swing fore and aft as his new command pitched through the gentle swell of the Block Island Sound. Crossing that imaginary demarcation between Narragansett Bay and the sound, he allowed himself a quick glance over his shoulder at the two frigates and their smaller consorts riding peacefully to their anchors in Newport Roads.

Patches of fog floated around the sound to the south, but a bright yellow sun hung in a blue sky over the town and anchorage. Edward twisted his body farther and saw the schooner, *Hawke*, following obediently in his wake half a cable astern.

He knew the master's mate commanding *Hawke* would obey his orders. Edward allowed himself to relish the moment. *Twenty years old this December past. Nine years ago I was a mere captain's servant on Katherine, the royal yacht. Nine years I served—sloop, two frigates, and a third rate. Well Eddie ol' boy, you passed for lieutenant and here you are commanding a King's ship.*

Coming back to his duty, Edward faced forward and took in his command with a glance. "Mr. Coggins," he shouted at a man who seemed to be everywhere directing the work of several small groups of men.

"Sir," John Coggins replied as he hurried aft toward his commander.

As the only commissioned officer aboard, Sneyd had no first lieutenant. He gave orders directly to the warrant officers. Coggins was the bosun, responsible for the decks, hull, cordage, brass, and all the rigging, canvas, and spars that made up the brig-sloop's two masts.

Bolton was an awkward rig. She was rated a sloop by the Royal Navy because she was smaller than a frigate and only rated a lieutenant as a commander. With two square-rigged masts, she was, in fact, a brig by design. *Bolton's* oddity came from the fact that she was a bomb—a brig designed for shore bombardment. Her masts were widely separated to allow deck room for two twenty-four inch mortars mounted along the centerline of the main deck.

These mortars lobbed huge exploding shells over defensive walls and other obstructions to wreak havoc within shore fortifications. She also had twelve standard naval cannon for battles at sea; but with only four score sailors and marines aboard, Sneyd was hard pressed to sail the brig and work the guns together.

Sneyd looked into his bosun's open face. "Find the Gunner, Mr. Coggins. We shall have an hour's exercise running the guns in and out. One never knows when one of the local pirates will try us."

"Aye, sir," Coggins replied, then ducked below to go to the powder magazine—the place he knew his shipmate would be working.

DONT TREAD ON ME

The breeze rippled the mouth of Narragansett Bay, creating millions of prisms and mirrors that invited the morning sun to play on them capriciously. The effect was a dazzling display of brilliant and often colorful reflections.

William Jones lowered his telescope and watched as the two small vessels—*Bolton* and *Hawke*—disappear around Castle Hill to begin their sweep of Block Island Sound. He was making a note of this for his next report when a sound caught his attention. He looked up and saw one of his couriers approaching.

"Morn' 'Tenant."

"You are very early."

"Come from the colonel, 'Tenent."

"Is that so?"

"He wants to see you . . . right away . . . at headquarters."

William knew that headquarters was a tavern in Narragansett, an easy two-hour ride from the colonel's home near the border with Connecticut.

"You will man the lookout?"

"Someone will be along directly. I am to return with you, 'Tenant."

Jones stuffed his notes in a satchel slung over his shoulder and said, "Let's be about it."

If it could be possible, the morning was growing in magnificence. The last vapors of early fog had melted into the azure sea, and the sun continued to climb its daily circuit. The wind held steady at about six knots as the two English ships separated for their assigned duties.

Bolton rounded up and spread her canvas for New London. *Hawke* spread her wings to patrol the area around Block Island. Both had orders to rendezvous with the entire squadron at noon the next day.

It seemed as if *Columbus's* entire crew was topside. The frigate ghosted north under staysails alone just faster than steerageway.

Marines lounged in the foretop, sailors in the maintop, and the Marine officers and sergeants in the mizzen top. Each group staked out this territory over the months at sea without actually discussing the subject.

The sun was warm, the fog was gone, and many of the men savored the aroma of sailing in their home waters. Captain Whipple stood alone at the rail with his thoughts. His head was bare, and he also enjoyed the Spring sea air as he thought about home. This was his water, and Abraham Whipple gloried in it. He sailed here when he was first learning to read.

I could be home on the next tide if Ezek would make up his mind. But that is not what I want right now. His mind was active even if his body was stationary. *Wallace is here; I can feel it like I feel Columbus's easy roll and pitch—like I smell that salt air and tar. He is still here. We are well matched now. Columbus and Rose could hardly be better matched for a duel at sea. How I would love to send that scoundrel to the bottom of the sound.*

"The captain is pensive this morning," Trevett whispered to Grinnell, Whipple's clerk.

The two were standing near the taffrail where Grinnell was bringing *Columbus's* smooth deck log up to date.

Grinnell looked up from his writing and stared into his friend's eyes. "He is torn between going home and laying alongside *Rose.* He has thought of little else, John, since the anchor broke ground in Nassau," William Grinnell replied in a hushed voice.

Not having met before, Grinnell and Trevett had grown close during the cruise. This was not by design—rather they assumed the unenviable position of liaison between Whipple and the Marine officers. Trevett knew he owed his commission, and therefore his allegiance, to his patron, Whipple.

Captain Shoemaker and Lieutenant Cummings did not, and relations were strained at best. Whipple maintained unrelenting discipline and demanded decorum. Shoemaker was somewhat more relaxed with the Marine company. Their different stations in life and the disparate regions of their rearing did not aid their relationship.

A tradesman from the Northern Liberties of Philadelphia had little in common—other than dislike of the English overlords—with a wealthy sea captain from New England. Whipple had, as a privateer in the late war with France, partaken in the capture of prizes worth literally millions.

The strained relations were now at the point that discourse only occurred on the strictest matters of administering the ship's routine.

"Mr. Trevett, a word please," Whipple called to John.

Trevett ended his conversation with Joseph and walked quickly forward to the rail at the break of the poop. "Yes, sir, Captain?"

"She's out there, John. Can you smell her?"

"*Rose*, Captain?"

"Yes, *Rose*, my boy. Of course, I mean *Rose*."

"I pray God you are allowed to lay her alongside, Captain. It would bring a fitting closure to the bloody nose you delivered to Wallace with *Katy*, sir. That it would."

Whipple thought momentarily of *Katy*, now renamed *Providence* by Congress and sailing somewhere just over the horizon under John Hazard.

"It is my destiny, John—my right—if there is a just God in heaven."

Trevett did not answer but looked curiously at his benefactor.

"Sail ho. On deck there, sail t' the north'rd," came the familiar hail from the main crosstrees.

Whipple turned and faced Trevett, their eyes locking. A smug, satisfied look came over his face.

"Sail to the south, sir," *Hawke's* lookout shouted to the tiny quarterdeck below. Clinging to the top part of the schooner's main mast, the lookout swayed comfortably to and fro as *Hawke* rolled and pitched through the Block Island sound.

Lieutenant John James Wallace, captain of *Hawke* and nephew to the squadron's senior officer, waited about five seconds before replying, "Finish your report, blast your eyes!"

"Ship rigged, sir—sailing due north."

A fat prize. A merchant laden with contraband from the Caribbean or perhaps France. Bound for Connecticut more than likely, Wallace thought. He began estimating prize money even as he shouted, "Make all sail. Cast loose the guns!"

The men, also figuring prize money, scrambled to their stations, some slackening lines or extending spars to carry more canvas, others untying the breechings of the six four-pounders and removing tompions from the muzzles. In most minds, their share was already being spent in the taverns and brothels of Boston—or perhaps New York if the rumors were true.

Hawke's commander waited for the activity to subside before ordering, "Hoist the colors."

The British naval ensign flashed out at the head of the main mast. Being a schooner, *Hawke's* taller main mast was aft. The bright patch of red, floating against the sky's blue background, cheered the excited crew even more.

DON'T TREAD ON ME

First Lieutenant Jones (the one in the Rhode Island Militia, not the one on *Alfred*) stood inside the front door of the dimly lit tavern. Most tables were crowded about with men he knew to be militia officers by their faces alone. For none wore anything approaching a uniform. None, save an older man at a table in the corner who sported a uniform coat of his own design. William approached the man and stood waiting to be recognized.

A moment . . . then Babcock looked up from the maps and charts spread before him. "William?" he said. "What are you doing here? Who is watching Wallace?"

Jones was puzzled for a moment, but he was familiar with the older man's eccentricities. "You sent for me, sir."

It was Colonel Babcock's turn to look puzzled. He recovered quickly enough. "Yes, of course I did my boy. Come closer. Look here." He slid a tallow candle across the chart of Narragansett Bay and stabbed a weathered forefinger first at Coddington Point, north of Newport, and then at Brenton's Point on the southeast headland of the bay. "Here—and here," he announced.

"Sir?" William replied to his regimental commander.

"Batteries, boy, batteries."

"There are no batteries there, Colonel."

"Not yet, son. That is your job. I want you to get there as quickly as you can and site batteries at these two locations to our best advantage. It is high time that Wallace and his scourge is driven from the bay once and for all."

Jones looked closely at the chart. He pictured the locations in his mind; he had been to both many times—seen them from landward and seaward. He raised his eyes to meet those of his commanding officer. *At last, a real job, not just counting sailors and rowing boats. People say that the old man is losing control of his faculties. But I'll not second guess this order.*

"Don't dawdle, boy," Babcock scolded. "I want those batteries sited and ready for use tomorrow! You may begin using them at your discretion."

"The worst performance yet, gentlemen," Captain Whipple returned his watch to his vest pocket and glared at the two men—his own first lieutenant and Marine Captain Shoemaker.

Both junior officers were silent, but the similarity ended there. The first lieutenant looked sheepish and stared aft over his captain's shoulder. Captain Shoemaker returned Whipple's glare and directed his own into his commander's eyes.

The rift between Whipple and the Marine officers was more than unpleasant. It now affected the efficient operation of the ship. It took over twenty minutes to bring the ship to action stations after the lookout's hail as, naturally, the sailors sided with their captain and the resentment of the Marine officers spread to the rank and file as well.

"The schooner approaching from the north may be of little consequence, but I can assure you she portends the proximity of her larger consort, *Rose*. Return to your stations and ensure that your men's accuracy and rate of fire exceeds their efficiency in clearing the frigate for action."

The first lieutenant touched his hat, said, "Aye, Captain," and scurried away.

Shoemaker spun silently on his heel and strode into the waist to confer with Lieutenant Cummings.

Only two years old, *Columbus* was formerly Willing and Morris's merchant ship, *Sally*. As such, it was not too difficult for her to transform her appearance from that of warship to merchant. All that was required was for her crew to crouch below the bulwarks and refrain from opening the gun ports.

Whipple had the yellow flag, emblazoned with a rattlesnake, bent on to a halyard, but it waited on deck until the order to break it out should be given.

"You may fire when ready, Gunner," Lieutenant Wallace ordered. *Hawke's* gunner carefully sighted along the barrel of the forward four-pounder on the schooner's starboard side. The muzzle began to rise, and the big ship filled his vision in the open port. He stabbed the linstock down into the touchhole, and primer sparks spurted both upward and downward. The gunner could actually see a dark gray streak as the orange-sized iron ball flew true on its intended path.

Lieutenant Wallace smiled broadly as the prize clewed up her courses. *I would have backed my topsails too, but at least she is stopping*, he thought, again estimating prize money in his head. Something did not look quite right, though, as the fat merchant ship lost way and *Hawke* came alongside.

DONT TREAD ON ME

"By Jupiter. That was too close by half!" Whipple expostulated as the English shot splashed under his bowsprit and ricocheted away toward the Atlantic. "Clew the courses. Hoist the colors. Open your ports!"

Men hauled away on the clew lines as the lower corners of the great sails climbed up to their yards and lost all their wind. The bright yellow flag broke out at the masthead, and the larboard gun ports opened up when the second captains pulled on the lanyards. Officers and men looked down into the astonished faces aboard the schooner that was coming alongside.

"Lower your colors, if you please, Captain," Whipple shouted to the officer on *Hawke's* tiny quarterdeck. You may consider yourself a prisoner of the Continental Navy Frigate *Columbus*."

Lieutenant Jones was exhausted. *Just past eleven o'clock*, was his last thought as he drifted to sleep. He made three ferry passages and several aboard borrowed horses. He contacted enough troops, horses, and equipment to move the guns. He even found two second lieutenants to command each battery. His last act was to procure a blanket and roll up in it on a pile of straw before losing consciousness. Tomorrow the heavy work would begin.

April 5, 1776
Near Block Island, Rhode Island
HMS Bolton

"Fire!" Sneyd shouted.

All six of the four-pounders on *Bolton's* starboard broadside discharged fire, smoke, and iron simultaneously. The iron crossed the cable-and-a-half of water in about a second. One struck in the big ship's larboard quarter, causing a thump and minor shudder but nothing more. Another pierced the mizzen topsail, and the rest splashed into the sound or were not seen.

DON'T TREAD ON ME

"I'll have the colors now," Captain Saltonstall ordered the midshipman standing near him with the deck log.

The midshipman nodded to a seaman who jerked on the halyard. The slipknot came loose, and the continental colors broke out to the breeze at the masthead.

"As they bear, Mr. Jones," Dudley Saltonstall shouted down on the gun deck to his first lieutenant. Jones was standing behind the forward most nine-pounder of the larboard broadside.

John Paul Jones crouched to see the British brig through the open gun port. When he was satisfied, he stood erect.

"You may fire when you are ready," he ordered the first gun captain.

The gun boomed and recoiled violently on its tackles as Jones strode aft toward the next cannon. The ball splashed about three fathoms ahead of the brig, *Bolton.*

The ball from the second gun tore through *Bolton's* foretopsail. Jones continued aft. The fall of balls three and four could not be discerned from *Alfred's* deck. By the time Lieutenant Jones directed the fire of all ten of the nine-pounders on the main gun deck, one more ball struck the target.

That ball pierced the bulwark amidships, dismounted one of *Bolton's* guns and wounded two men. Ricocheting off the gun, it smashed into several belaying pins securing braces and sheets for the mainmast. With no control of the sails on her aft mast, the brig slowed, and her head began to fall off—swinging toward the American frigate.

"Get 'hold o' that there line you infernal lubber! Where's the carpenter? I needs the carpenter!" John Coggins was shouting orders to his mates in a vain effort to restore control to the sails on *Bolton's* main mast.

Lieutenant Sneyd watched his bosun's frantic motions. The antics on deck appeared to be pandemonium, but he knew that Coggins was a professional who knew what he was about. Sneyd equally knew that it was all to no avail.

"Larboard your helm," Sneyd ordered. Then, "Back the foretopsail."

He swiveled his eyes from his own deck to the south. Barely fifty yards of Block Island Sound now separated *Bolton* from *Alfred*. The big frigate was heaving to with all her guns reloaded and trained on the brig.

Sneyd freed the halyard and lowered the naval ensign himself.

DONT TREAD ON ME

Captain Saltonstall watched the rectangular patch of red flutter to the brig's deck. He glanced at Commodore Hopkins, and both men shared a satisfied look.

"Captain Nicholas," was all Saltonstall said to the Marine commander.

"Sir," was the one-word reply. Then Samuel said to the lieutenant next to him, "John, take a dozen marines with muskets, pistols, and cutlasses and wait at the entry port."

"Aye, sir," Lieutenant Trevett responded.

"Lieutenant Jones, secure the prize," Dudley Saltonstall ordered John Paul Jones.

Jones touched his hat and began giving orders to put a boat over the side.

Saltonstall cupped his hands around his mouth and shouted to *Bolton*, "You may come under my lee, sir."

He then gave the orders that caused *Alfred* to slide forward through the waves, making it easier for the stricken brig to come around and heave to just downwind of the frigate.

The master's mate standing anchor watch on *Rose* ordered the seaman to strike three bells. What sounded like echoes were actually the bells ringing on the frigate's consorts, all within seconds of each other. Another Spring day made its magnificent appearance in southern New England.

Rose's freshly scrubbed white oak decks were nearly dry where the two captains stood near the larboard entry. Captain Howe ordered his gig along the larboard side to dispense with the ceremony normally required for a post captain joining or debarking a warship. Howe and Wallace shook hands.

"Thank you, James, for another magnificent breakfast. I shall have to do my bit and host you tomorrow."

"I would be delighted, Tyringham, if this weather holds."

"It shows every sign of doing so."

"Perhaps we shall be celebrating a brace of prizes by sunrise. I have no doubt that *Bolton* and *Hawke* already have a string of Yankee smugglers trailing out behind them." They both chuckled.

"That would suit me well. I would consider it a fine parting gift. I must be off for the Carolina's, you know."

"You are pleading those infernal dispatches no doubt. It is just as well. I am ordered to gather the squadron and sail for Boston. I believe there is to be some sort of combined operation with the Army."

"Then let us be about it, what?" Howe ended the conversation. He saluted his senior captain and skipped down the side into his waiting gig.

DONT TREAD ON ME

Lieutenant William Jones stood taking deep breaths. His shoulders and chest felt grimy from the dust and salt of the dried sweat. The evening breeze was picking up, and he gave a slight shiver. Pulling his shirt over his head, William surveyed the day's work.

The two heavy pieces of artillery were mounted in a pit hidden in the trees. A firm decking of planks supported them, and they could be trained nearly forty degrees in either direction. An open but shielded magazine was sited twenty yards deeper in the forest.

Satisfied with their handiwork, Jones smoothed his hair back with his fingers and turned to look out over Narragansett Bay. The afternoon sun was hanging over Gould Island. William raised his right hand to shield it from the bright glow and was surprised at what he saw.

What in the Devil's name are they doing here? Must have had some sort of trouble. That's Rose, but no sign of Glasgow or her tender. Nautilus, Swan—well now, here is an opportunity if ever there was one. It is a shame we didn't have more wagons. But Wallace always stays at least a week when he sorties.

Other men began to gather around William and point.

"Here then," William said to a second lieutenant, "take some men and go on back. Tell them not to wait until morning, but to bring the powder and shot up tonight."

"Sure enough it is, William. We will make it a special night for our English cousins, eh?"

Marine Lieutenant Henry Dayton was positioned perfectly to observe the fleet. His heart was full of emotion. As the first lieutenant of twenty marines on *Providence*, he felt pride in what they accomplished. He was also grateful his Creator spared him from the storms and fever of the past several months.

The gentle following breeze was coming in over the larboard quarter. Henry stood a fathom or so above the windward bulwark and hung from the shrouds. He was comfortable in his shirtsleeves, and with the breeze behind the sloop, there was almost no relative wind to ruffle his hair. The sun was still above the western horizon but would be setting soon enough.

Henry looked down and saw Captain Hazard chatting with the helmsman. Both men chuckled from time to time. Letting his eyes wander fore and aft along *Providence's* deck, he saw several groups of men sitting or leaning on rails, smoking, talking, and enjoying the delightful evening. Raising his eyes, Henry looked forward. *The bulk of the Congress's Navy*, he thought. *Two frigates and two brigs.* He looked carefully at each—courses furled and topsails full on all four.

They were snugged down for the night. Commodore Hopkins put his main ships in two columns of two. The windward column, to the larboard, was led by *Cabot* with *Alfred* following about half a cable astern. The other column was two cables downwind. It was led by *Andrew Doria*, and *Columbus* brought up the rear.

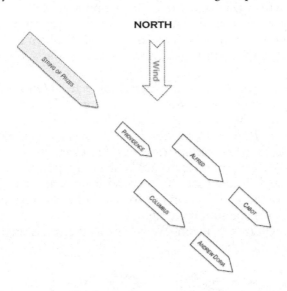

With nearly two-tenths of a sea mile between the columns, there was little risk of separation or collision during the darkness. *Providence* was the link between the main body of the fleet and the prizes. Henry spun his head aft and looked them over.

Quite a string of them, he thought. *The folks in New London should appreciate them. Now we are all assembled, we should be making port soon. It will be good to see my family after all these months.* Lieutenant Dayton looked over the half-dozen prizes then squinted to see *Fly* bringing up the rear of the column. *Twelve ships. That will make an impression on the good people of the town.*

Captain Wallace sat brooding in his cabin, barely able to control his anger. Darkness was settling in over Narragansett Bay as evidenced by the darkening sky in the great window behind him. His last opportunity to sweep the sound with a powerful squadron had set behind the horizon with the sun.

When there was a knock at his door, he did not rise. He barely moved his head, in fact, choosing rather to merely raise his eyes and bore them into the three men who entered. His first lieutenant escorted Mason and Ayscough into the cabin. Wallace was so angry he had not even greeted the two captains when they came aboard—at his order.

Wallace looked at his first lieutenant, "You may leave us."

The man nodded, touched his forehead with his right index finger, and backed out of the cabin without a word.

Wallace said nothing else for several moments. He just stared venomously at the two men who stood side by side with their heads slightly bowed under the overhead beams.

"Well then, gentlemen," Wallace finally began, "The rebels hereabouts owe you a deal of gratitude. Thanks to your abominable lack of seamanship, a goodly number of them will sleep safe and secure this night—and much more to come."

"I protest, sir," Captain Ayscough began. "There was a wind shadow . . ."

"Enough! I have not asked a question, and you will be silent. I have no doubt the admiral will not be pleased with any of us. Until this afternoon my squadron has supplied his purse with a steady flow of the flag's share of prize money."

Lieutenant Mason, Captain of *Nautilus*, glared sidelong at Ayscough. "Captain Wallace, surely you cannot assign blame to my crew."

"There you are right, Lieutenant. I assign all the blame to the two of you."

When clearing the bay at midday, *Nautilus* was momentarily becalmed. Following her—likely too close—*Swan* ran afoul her quarter. What at first seemed only an annoyance, turned out to have caused stays to part on both ships, requiring a quiet anchorage to splice and set up new standing rigging.

"I expect both watches will be working continually until the damage is put to rights. Tell my first lieutenant if you require support. That is all, gentlemen."

Second Lieutenant John Fitzpatrick inhaled deeply on his cigar causing the end to glow brightly in the night air. He savored the moment, not so much for the soothing tobacco in his lungs as for the anticipation he created. Fitz was much loved for his storytelling by the officers and the rank and file.

He judged the moment and delivered his next line in the story. "We settled ourselves there in his office, and the vicar said, 'I am surprised you kept our appointment, Mr. Fitzpatrick, in view of the fact that you have a *prior* engagement.'"

After a very short moment of silence—the Marine officers and First Lieutenant Jones laughed heartily. Captain Saltonstall and Commodore Hopkins smiled politely but looked puzzled.

First Lieutenant Parke brought them into the joke. "You see," he said to the two naval officers, "just before we sailed, Fitz married the former Miss Eleanor *Prior*."

After several moments of laughter—and Hopkins wiping the tears from his eyes—the men settled into silence.

Fitz covered his relief with a broad grin. He always felt a little out of place in what he considered the officer class—especially Hopkins and Saltonstall. They were all polite enough, but he knew they were bred to a higher station in life. Regardless, he considered himself blessed to be among them.

Eleanor will be thrilled when I return and recount our exploits on this mission. Perhaps even, she may meet Captain Nicholas. It would give her great joy to count such people among her acquaintances.

"May we expect a son awaiting your return when next we moor in Philadelphia, Fitz?" Lieutenant Jones asked, smiling.

The darkening covered Fitz's blush. "I do hope for a son, John. With all my heart I do. But please, God, may it not be that long before we return home."

"War and the sea, my boy. War and the sea—two things that combine to keep a man long from his home and loved ones," the commodore contributed sagely. "Who can say when next I will take my fleet to the nation's seat of government?"

Captain Nicholas held his tumbler of rum and cigar in the same hand. He raised the hand aloft. "Gentlemen," he said. "I give you

Commodore Ezek Hopkins. He built a navy from raw material and bloodied the king's nose."

"Here, here," was the universal reply followed by deep swallows.

"I thank you, sir," Hopkins replied, raising his glass to Nicholas. "I only regret that we have not had the opportunity to come to grips with more of His Majesty's Navy ships."

"It promises to be a long war," said Jones. "The opportunity may, no doubt, present itself soon enough."

A half cable forward of the knot of officers, Sergeant Neilson was engaged in his second favorite pastime—regaling the troops with his exploits (real and imagined).

"So ya' sees, then, some o' those officers thinks there better than the likes o' us. But's not true. We was shop keepers 'n cobblers 'n parish clerks right alongside 'em."

"Go on, then Sergeant. Who wants to be an officer anyway? We're right happy without having to figure stuff out and be on our toes all the time around the commodore and the captain."

"Well, I'm tellin' ya boys. I intends that this here war is my chance to make life better for my Mary and me. With the prize money we already got, I'm gonna find her better lodgings and buy her some dress makin's from Paris. She'll have a dress better 'n her sisters. You can count on that."

No one had anything to say for a spell after that. The men could hear the muffled conversation floating on the night from the quarterdeck. It also mixed with voices drifting across the sound from *Cabot*, half a cable ahead of *Alfred*.

"How can he sleep, Seymour?" Lieutenant Wilson asked *Cabot's* sailing master.

"A clean conscience, John, a clean conscience. That and too much French claret and Rhode Island rum."

The officers on *Cabot's* quarterdeck chuckled quietly with their captain sleeping only a few feet below the deck on which they stood. Expecting to drop their hook in Connecticut in the next day or two, Captain Hopkins entertained his wardroom in high fashion for dinner. He and his first lieutenant were sleeping off the night's celebration in their respective cabins.

Second Lieutenant Weaver, who had the deck watch, Seymour Sinclair, and Marine officers John Welsh and James Hood Wilson were enjoying the fresh sea air on the quarterdeck. John Hopkins seemed to have a better than average talent for building camaraderie among his officers. The officers, in turn, capitalized on the good morale in the brig to instill a fighting spirit and proficient seamanship in the sailors and Marines.

"I hasn't never been to New England," Private Kennedy told his shipmates after exhaling.

The mixed group of sailors and Marines sat on the deck in the vessel's waist. Even though most were assigned to the watch below, it was too early for them to turn in. The master-at-arms would extinguish the smoking lamp at the next turn of the glass, and they wanted to fortify their lungs with enough tobacco smoke to see them through the smokeless hours until dawn.

"What are you goin' t' do when we drops the 'ook in Connetykut," a foretopman asked his friend, a bosun's mate?"

"Don't be a askin' me stupid questions, ye silly bugger. I intends on doin' what sailors is bred t' do when they gets into port."

The men laughed, then fell quiet. Many were thinking of past shipmates. So many lost. Many still teetering on the brink.

"Surgeon told me t'day he's pretty certain the boys that still got the fever will make it t' port so's we can get 'em to a proper hospital," Private Kaine pronounce to the group.

"You're a good man, Kaine," Kennedy told his shipmate. "Takin' care o' the fellas like you do.

"No different than our Lord woulda done; that's what my ma always says. Can't wait till I see her again. You fellas know you're all invited to Ma's house for the best meal in Pennsylvania when we anchors in the Delaware again."

Kaine's shipmates viewed his simple ways as naïve, but they liked him a lot—and many of them owed their lives to his caring for them through their battles with the fever.

"We'll be holding you to that, Kaine."

"I'll be standing good for your first drink in New England, Kaine," Private Kennedy promised his friend. "And your second one, too."

Kaine blushed. He didn't drink spirits, but he knew Kennedy was being kind to him. The two men had become like brothers, and Kennedy looked out for Kaine when necessary, during the cruise.

The ship's bell rang out of the darkness. "The smoking lamp is out. Relieve the watch. Relieve the wheel. Relieve the lookouts . . ."

HMS Glasgow slipped silently through the dark waters. A faint glow from the binnacle aided the compass rose in revealing her course of east by north a half north. She was slowly patrolling an area four leagues southeast of Block Island and had been since the second dogwatch.

Below the poop, in the master's tiny chartroom, another faint glow showed the pinprick the master made again on the worn chart.

"It's not like them, Captain. The dead reckoning confirms the stars. I know this is the rendezvous."

"I agree," Tyringham replied. He knew from long practice there was no need to second-guess his sailing master's navigation. *Something is definitely wrong,* he thought. *Sneyd and Young Wallace know what they are about, well enough. I don't like this, and James will like it even less when he finally brings Rose and the others out tomorrow.*

"What are your orders, Captain?"

Tyringham pursed his lips and rubbed his chin. Stubble made a rasping noise. "We'll keep on. The weather is pleasant enough. Wear ship every glass using only the watch on deck. We will find them by sunrise, I'm thinking."

"Aye, sir. I'll inform the officer of the deck."

April 6, 1776
Seven Leagues South of Newport, Rhode Island
HMS Glasgow

"Sir?"

The third lieutenant approached the lookout standing at the starboard end of *Glasgow's* taffrail. "What is it?"

"I think it might be the ol' *Bolton*, Lieutenant."

The third lieutenant generally enjoyed the midnight watch. He was typically the senior officer awake, and so, felt greater authority and responsibility for the frigate. He brought the night glass up to his eye and scanned the blackness to the north. *There*, he thought. *It's a brig all right. And . . . more lights beyond. Looks like Bolton and Hawke have had a successful day.* He smiled to himself in the darkness. *Those lucky fools. Just the two of them and no one else to share the prize money with.*

"Midshipman of the watch."

"Yes, sir."

"Tell the captain we have a brig in sight to the northwest. And there are other lights beyond."

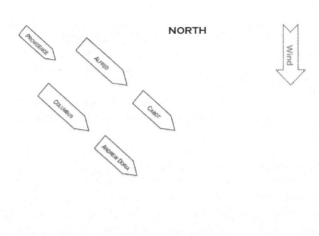

The boy was excited. "Shall I tell him it may be *Bolton* and *Hawke*, sir?"

"There is no call for conjecture in your report. Captain Howe has been acquainted with the sailing rig of *Bolton* and the composition of Captain Wallace's squadron for quite some time now. Allow him the leisure of arriving at his own conclusions."

"Aye, sir," the midshipman replied glumly and faded quickly into the dark night.

A forty-two foot sloop-rigged tender shadowed *Glasgow* like a bird dog healing at its master's side—fifty yards on the frigate's larboard quarter. The master's mate at the tiller stretched his foot and nudged a man sleeping on deck near the lee scupper. With only three men in the crew, one or two were able to catch a quick nap when duties permitted.

"Hey Mate, wake up. Somethin's afoot onboard. I kin see lights up t' the north'rd."

The man snorted and growled; then rolled over and pulled himself up by the bulwark. "Where away, mate?"

"Out there," he pointed.

The lookout on the bow called back at the same time, "Lights to the north. I can hear more noise on the frigate, too. No signals."

DONT TREAD ON ME

Captain Hopkins emerged into the night on *Cabot's* main deck. His breeches were pulled on but the nightshirt he still wore covered them. He padded forward in his stocking feet to the scuttlebutt secured on the forward side of the main mast.

John took up the ladle and plunged it into the fresh water, then poured the contents over his head. His palms rubbed the refreshing cool dampness across his face, and his fingers combed his wet hair back over his collar. Now refreshed and alert, he walked forward to visit the lookout.

"Good morning to you, Eb."

"G'mornin', Cap'n."

John shivered when the breeze blew across the wet hair on his head and back of his neck but still enjoyed the fresh feeling that poured through him.

"I kin feel somethin', Cap'n. Like I know somethin's about t' happen."

"I got the same feelin', Eb."

Both men stared into the night on the starboard bow. Then they saw it. At the same time, both sets of eyes saw the top light to the south.

The lookout pointed, "You see it too, don't ya', Cap'n?"

"Yes, I do. I can see the dim shape under the light as well. About a mile and a half—maybe two. It's big, I'd say big as *Columbus* or *Alfred*. Keep an eye on her, Eb." Then he was gone.

Moments later Captain Hopkins materialized on the quarterdeck dressed and wearing his sword.

"The captain's on deck, sir," Midshipman Richards whispered to the first lieutenant, who had the deck during the midwatch this day.

Nicholas Biddle slung the heavy cutlass belt on his shoulder as he arrived on *Andrew Doria's* quarterdeck. The brig, leading the leeward column was standing south by southwest under single reefed topsails on fore and main. Captain Biddle vaguely remembered hearing two bells struck at one a.m., but he didn't think it was one thirty yet.

"Good morning, Captain," the officer of the deck greeted Biddle.

"Morning, Lieutenant. Where away?"

The lieutenant pointed to the south. "There, sir, just over a mile. Looks like a ship and a smaller sloop beyond." He handed Captain Biddle the night glass.

"Mr. Patten . . . Mr. Patten! For the love of Heaven, where is Mr. Patten?" Biddle demanded.

"He is indisposed, sir," Midshipman Bevan answered. "I have taken his watch."

"Oh, very well, Mr. Bevan," Biddle said turning to look the young man in the eye. "Make a signal to the flag—Enemy to south. Two vessels."

"Enemy to south, two vessels, aye, Captain." Bevan flipped through his list of signals by the dubious glow of the binnacle until he found the proper combination of lights to hoist aloft.

"Take the brig to action stations, if you please," Captain Biddle ordered the officer of the deck. "Clear away the guns and load with round shot."

Men began scurrying about, waking their shipmates, casting loose guns, spreading sand on the deck, and a thousand and one other things that transform a peaceful floating village into a weapon of war. The master finished buckling his sword belt as he came on the quarterdeck.

"Good morning, Mr. Dunn."

"Good morning, Captain. Bit of excitement this morning, I'm given to believe."

"May be, sir, may be. For now, I'll have the reefs out of the foretopsail, if you please."

"Shake the reefs out of the foretopsail, it is, sir."

Below deck, Marine Lieutenant Craig was bemoaning the loss of his sergeant as he went through the hammocks and packed humanity, ensuring his remaining two and a half dozen marines were awake, shod, and properly armed for battle. All of this by the dim glow of a couple of dirty battle lanterns.

Captain Whipple snapped his watch closed. The fire from his eyes was all he needed to illuminate the dial. He was furious at the pandemonium around him. It was taking far too long to bring the ship to quarters.

"Mr. Arnold," Whipple shouted. "Will those guns be loaded before sunrise?"

Arnold was trying to be everywhere, pushing men into place, deciding replacements, answering questions from his various heads of departments, and ensuring that every man was assigned most profitably. But he stopped to answer his captain's question.

"It will be soon, sir."

"Soon is not five minutes ago, sir!"

"I am aware, Captain. But sir, sixteen men—and their officers—are away in prizes. We have lost over a score to the fever and near a dozen are still on the surgeon's report."

"Result, Lieutenant Arnold, not excuse. That is all I require."

"Yes, sir," the harried first lieutenant replied and then resumed his work.

Captain Shoemaker stood behind Whipple during his discussion with Arnold. As soon as Arnold left, Shoemaker touched his hat and said loudly, "Marines at action stations, Captain."

Whipple spun around and looked at his subordinate. "That is well, Captain. Perhaps you can spare some of your men to aid the first lieutenant in filling out the main battery."

"As you wish, Captain." He dropped his salute. "Mr. Trevett?"

"Captain Shoemaker?"

"Find Lieutenant Arnold and provide whatever men he needs to fill out his gun crews."

"Aye, sir."

Lieutenant Jones bobbed up and down as he strode the length of the gun deck ducking under each overhead beam. Two rows of ten nine-pounder cannon were arrayed on either hand. Their crews stood to the ready at each gun, bearing their rammers, sponges, and linstocks, awaiting his command. Nine-pound iron shot was arranged in garlands ready for instant use. Powder boys scurried about delivering powder charges to each gun crew.

John knew that there were ten more guns—six-pounders—arranged topside on the fo'c'sle and quarterdeck, but these twenty were his domain. As first lieutenant, John Paul Jones would direct the fire of the flagship's main battery during its first major engagement with a British man or war.

"Cast loose your guns. Load with round shot."

The breechings came off, and the trucks squeaked as the carriages rumbled inboard. Powder bags, shot, and wadding were rammed in each muzzle. Jones had drilled these men, and they knew what they were about.

"Open the ports," the order seemed to float down the main hatchway to the gun deck."

"Open your ports," Jones shouted.

As one, twenty 2nd gun captains tugged on the lanyards, and the gun ports swung up and out on their hinges.

"Run out your guns."

The men pulled on the tackles, and again the trucks squeaked and rumbled across the deck to poke their menacing muzzles into the darkness.

At the extreme aft of the quarterdeck, Captain Nicholas stood with about a dozen Marines. They were lining the taffrail in an effort to stay out the way of the officers and gun crews until their marksmanship was called for. Nicholas was overseeing the loading of their muskets to make sure each was done properly. Lieutenant Fitzpatrick walked up to him holding his own rifle in his right hand.

"Is everything in readiness, Fitz?"

"Yes, sir. I just came from the barge. Matthew is there with most of the company. Sergeant Neilson is in the main top with half a dozen men. They have their muskets and two swivels."

"Excellent, Fitz. Go ahead and load up that rifle of yours, and we'll see what we are about tonight."

"Aye, Captain. I'm thinking another prize or two will be nice. I plan to buy my bride a wedding gift. Didn't have the time or the funds to do a proper gift before we left Philadelphia. I don't doubt I will find something real nice in Connecticut. She will like that, what with it being imported and all."

This while he was ramming a ball down the muzzle of his rifle. The rifle was slower to load than a musket but much more accurate at long ranges.

"That's a nice idea, Fitz, but keep your wits about you tonight."

Lieutenant Henry Dayton finished counting his Marines. There were just over a dozen left after fever finished its winter assault on the men of the fleet. Eight of those were augmenting the sailors on *Providence's* gun crews. Even with them, Captain Hazard was hard-pressed to fire one broadside of six four-pounders.

Dayton was now standing in the fighting top with the rest of his men. He didn't think he would remain aloft during the battle, but it gave him some time to joke with the men and gauge their mood. It was also a good viewing platform.

Even though it was dark, the moon and the top lights of the ships allowed him to discern the relative dispositions. Henry could see that the continental fleet did a creditable job of maintaining their formation through the hours of darkness.

He had enough years at sea to know that if you want to see something at night, you can't look directly at it, so he forced his mind to scan the darkness but to focus on areas around the center of his vision. He had no idea why this worked, but it did.

I will discuss it with Captain Nicholas at some time, he thought. *I believe he is conversant with Dr. Franklin, and perhaps they have discussed the topic.* At any rate, the method paid dividends when he spotted a frigate several cables just east of south from *Andrew Doria*.

A few more shillings for my purse. Twill be a nice bit for my wife and daughter that might help balance the scales some for my long absence. I will take leave in New London and find a way to reach Newport without tipping the British squadron. It will be good to hug my wife and daughter, and that's no mistake.

Tyringham Howe did not lower the night glass as he continued to study the lights and silhouettes of the ships to the north. *Glasgow* was still sailing just south of west, and the strangers were standing southeast as near as he could tell.

"Tack the ship," he said to the officer of the deck who immediately put the order into action. Men scrambled from their positions of repose to their stations for swinging the frigate's bow through the wind.

Sheets, tacks, and braces were loosed on the larboard side and then pulled home to the starboard causing the topsail booms to swing and the foresails to first back then blow through the stays. Eventually, the jib boom swam clockwise through the wind from east through north toward the west.

"Just so," Howe commanded. "As close to the wind as she will bear." *Glasgow* steadied on north northwest, causing the leading edges of her canvas to shiver occasionally in the light breeze.

"Beat to quarters."

"Beat to quarters!" the officer of the deck repeated.

The sleepy drummer, only ten years old, raised his sticks and began the rhythm that was so familiar to him and all his shipmates. The watch on deck secured the final lines from tacking the frigate and ran to their combat stations.

Bosun's mates strode through the ranks of swinging hammocks shouting, "out or down" and emphasizing their words with generous jabs and kicks, urging the crew to stow their hammocks and hurry to their places on the guns and in the tops.

Tubs were set on deck and filled with water. Slow matches were lighted while rammers, swabs, prickers, and other tools were sorted out. The gunner unlocked the magazine, and his mates began filling powder charges and sending them to the gundeck via the powder monkeys. This ship, a machine of war that was but a speck in the greatest navy of the world, came to life, ready to defend or attack on a moment's notice at the will of her brain, Captain Tyringham Howe, Royal Navy.

DONT TREAD ON ME

Hopkins, Saltonstall, and Nicholas stood aft of *Alfred's* helm.

"General signal, Lieutenant," Hopkins ordered the signals officer, "Engage the enemy!"

The lieutenant already had the signals ready, and at his nod, the men assigned to the task hoisted them aloft.

"This will be a feather in our cap, gentlemen," Hopkins stated. "We'll lead two British men of war into New London. The army will notice that, I can tell you for sure."

"It will be a fitting end to a profitable expedition, sir," Saltonstall replied.

Nicholas absentmindedly touched the butt of one of the pistols in his belt and walked forward. Looking aloft, he could see the vague impression of the men in the top. Occasional sounds from their muted conversation drifted down to the deck.

When he arrived amidships, he stepped up on a boom and reached for the barge's larboard gunnel. Grabbing hold of it to steady himself, he peered in at the Marines. There were a lot of them. Parke noticed his commander and picked his way through the packed men, steadying himself by placing hands on their shoulders as he made his way over.

"Is this going to work, Matthew?"

"Not a lot of choice, sir. It keeps them out of the way of the gunners and gives us a little elevation to pick our targets better."

"What bothers me is that one round shot through the middle would scatter limbs and splinters through the whole lot of 'em."

"It's what we signed up for, Captain."

"You've come a long way from Alexandria, Matthew."

"Even farther from England, Sam."

"Any regrets?"

"Not a one—though Grandfather would not be pleased. No doubt of that." He took a breath and continued. "I've thrown in my lot with my new country, Sam. John invited me to move to Philadelphia, and the hand of Providence put you and me together when I arrived. It is not like I have turned my back on my old country, Sam."

"The King would likely see it differently, Matthew."

"Sure—the King. But the people are not in favor of this war. Besides, now the Marines are my family."

"Befriending you was certainly no sacrifice on my part, Matthew."

"You have been a good friend, Sam, and Fitz like a little brother. Lord, how he loves that Lizzie. And she's a right pistol, that lass is." He smiled.

Nicholas smiled up into his subordinate's face. "Be alert tonight, Matthew. Watch the men and make sure they keep their heads about them." He looked at the massed Marines again. "How do they have room to load and shoot?"

"We've a plan, sir. Half the men will load, and the others will shoot. 'Twill allow us to keep up a steady fire and give each group room to perform their function."

"It's a good plan. Stick with it."

"One would hardly think a hundred men could take up so much room, Kaine."

"A job for every man and every man does his job, Kennedy."

"You been a listening to the captain, I'd say."

"Best way to stay alive is to do what we been taught." He nodded forward. "That's a mighty big ship over there."

The two men, along with a couple of other Marines, were crowded along *Cabot's* bulwark at the extreme after end of the starboard quarter. In their minds, it looked like they could reach out and touch the British frigate as she slid through the dark water.

"She's not so big as you think. No bigger 'n *Alfred* is what I'm thinking'."

"Well, that's plenty big enough to suit me, Kennedy. And you'll mind what your about if ya' know what's good fer ya'."

"You men pipe down!" Lieutenant Wilson hissed. "You're on the quarterdeck, and the ship is cleared for action. This ain't no French bawdy house."

Both men held their tongues. Several other Marines and some sailors manning the aftermost six-pounder stifled the guffaws. Wilson commanded the Marine squad on the quarterdeck while Captain Welsh and the sergeant led those amidships and in the fo'c'sle. Fewer than three-dozen privates survived the ravages of fever.

Wilson stood by Captain Hopkins and the master. They watched as the British frigate slid through the water, menacing, like a Leviathan. A Marine from the sergeant's squad walked up to Lieutenant Wilson. He had no musket, and a canvas bag was slung over his shoulder. A smoking slow match was gripped in one hand.

"Got some grenades, Lieutenant. Sergeant thinks they might come in handy up in the top. Cap'n thinks it's a might crowded on the quarterdeck, and maybe one o' your fellas wants to come aloft with me."

Wilson nodded and looked over at his squad. They were shoulder to shoulder. His eyes settled on Archibald Edmonson who was wedged in between Kaine and Kennedy.

"Ed, get aloft with you, and take your gear."

"Aye, 'tenant."

"So long, Archie. See you when it's over, mate," Kennedy said. Edmonson clapped his friend on the shoulder then left to follow the order. The two men swung out on the larboard rigging and scrambled up to the main top. They were mostly lost in the darkness above.

"Wind is backin', Captain," *Glasgow's* sailing master reported to Howe.

"Stand by to tack the ship!" Captain Howe's lungs forced the air across his vocal chords and out past his lips. No speaking trumpet was required for him to be heard throughout the frigate. In fact, the order was heard by some of the sharper ears in the American fleet. For all of that, there was no need. Men were already at their stations with the appropriate lines in hand ready to cast loose or heave around on. "Tack the ship."

Down went the helm. *Glasgow's* great jib boom curved gracefully through stays. The men with the jib sheets allowed the wind to give her just enough push over to the northeast. Then, they let go on the larboard sheets and heaved around on the starboard. The main and fore topsail yards creaked around clockwise, and sheets, tacks, and braces were adjusted to the frigate's new course.

The enemy ships were momentarily masked by *Glasgow's* foresails as her head swung through the north. Howe watched as one by one the curtain of sails opened, and stars and moon dimly illuminated the enemy fleet.

The four closest would be enough to challenge even a British frigate. He silently cursed Wallace and the remainder of his squadron for sending him out alone. *Where are they, blast them? Well, at least now I know why Bolton and Hawke were not at the rendezvous.*

"'Pears the wind has backed to north northwest, Captain. I can lay the ship just a bit north of northeast, sir."

"Very well. Keep her thus."

"Aye, Captain," the master replied.

DON'T TREAD ON ME

"Wind has backed, Captain Hopkins," Sinclair reported. "Right under our coat tails, sir."

"Thank you, Seymour. Quartermaster, put down your helm!"

The helmsman spun the brig's wheel, and her bow swung to the larboard.

"Mr. Sinclair, lay me alongside yon frigate—within pistol shot if you please."

The master looked at the captain, then at the compass card, then at the big frigate—and finally at the ten nine-pounders pointed from her ports. *Cabot's* bow continued to swing through the points of the compass.

"Captain, that ship will throw over twice our weight of metal. She'll blow us to matchwood, sir."

"Then I suggest you look sharp and carry out my commands instantaneously. This is, after all, Mr. Sinclair, what our countrymen are paying us to do."

Sinclair looked at the frigate, then at the compass card again. "Steady on northeast, quartermaster."

"Northeast it is, Mr. Sinclair."

"Peter," Hopkins put his hand on the young man's shoulder. "Cut along and tell Lieutenant Weaver that I intend to lay alongside the frigate as close as I dare. Make sure all guns are ready to fire together when I give the word. Then report back here."

"Aye, aye, Captain," Midshipman Richards replied and hurried forward to find the second lieutenant.

John Welsh rested a cutlass on his shoulder and paced nervously along *Cabot's* centerline. Not frightened but nervous.

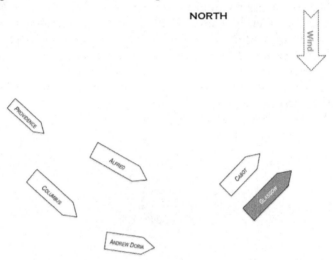

Well Johnny lad, this is what ye come for. Go to America Dad said. Fight the Lobsters, and when ye've whipped 'em, make a home there in the new world. Good enough, says I. Now here I am ready to fight 'em for real. This isn't going to be any la dee da walk into the fort and get the key from the governor. No sir, Johnny lad, you got a real honest to goodness fight on your hands now.

Welsh arrived in the brig's fo'c'sle where a handful of Marines crouched behind the bulwark. Half were resting on the deck with their backs to the larboard bulwark while the other half knelt behind the starboard bulwark training their muskets and rifles on the frigate. John started to speak to the Marines but stopped when he heard a voice carry across the narrow gap of the sound.

"On the brig—this is His Majesty's Frigate *Glasgow*. In the king's name, what ship is that?"

No response from the quarterdeck. *Cabot's* jib popped over his head as the wind left it momentarily then filled again quickly. The two vessels continued to draw closer. John could see dim squares of light from the open gun ports. Menacing shadows occluded the center of each where the powerful nine-pounder guns protruded. He occasionally saw the flash of British Marine cross belts or a white face illuminated by the moon or a battle lantern.

"Steady now, me lads," his Irish brogue was more pronounce when he was stressed. "Wait for the captain's order."

"Steady thus," Captain Hopkins whispered to the men on the helm."

It was as if *Cabot* was holding her breath. Every musket and six-pounder was trained on the enemy. The Marines in the top held their grenades at the ready and puffed on the slow match to keep it glowing.

"On the brig—what ship is that? Answer or I will fire into you."

Hopkins judged that his opponent was in earnest. He glanced quickly over his shoulder and was rewarded with the view of *Alfred* and *Andrew Doria* swinging close behind into his wake. He thought he could discern *Providence* and *Columbus* also swinging toward the east. He cupped his hands around his mouth and drew a deep breath.

"The *Columbus* and *Alfred*, a two and twenty gun frigate." He drew another breath and shouted, "Fire!"

The violence of *Cabot's* broadside caused the two Marines in the top to stagger and bobble the slow match as they were lighting the fuse. Archibald dropped his grenade before it was lit. The other man managed to hold his steady long enough to light it then hurl it across the narrow strip of water.

It landed on the frigate's larboard gangway seconds after the seven six-pound iron balls arrived. One smashed into the bulwark, another passed through the foretopsail yard brace. The rest passed harmlessly through the air and splash beyond, unseen.

James Hood Wilson stood behind his small squad of Marines. They lined the bulwark along the extreme after end of the starboard quarter, shoulder-to-shoulder. From the six-pound carriage gun to the taffrail was their station. Each man rested an elbow on the cap of the bulwark and sighted along his barrel toward the frigate's quarterdeck.

Hood stood with his arm extended, pointing his hanger unnecessarily toward *Glasgow*. He jerked involuntarily when the six-pounder on his left side fired and recoiled inboard on its tackles. He recovered quickly and knew this was the signal for him to take action. This was the decisive moment. He had been placed in the vanguard of a sea battle with a seasoned British frigate and years of resentment and pride would now be unleashed on the English oppressor.

"Commence firing!" Lieutenant Wilson ordered his small squad of marines.

Private Kennedy was ready. He felt the warmth of his shipmates on either shoulder. There was a camaraderie approaching kinship he sensed as Kaine's shoulder pressed his. Both men—all the privates, in fact—sighted along their barrels. Moonlight glinted along the oiled steel as they aimed their fire at the officers on the frigate's quarterdeck.

At less than thirty yards, this would be an easy shot. Kaine heard the lieutenant's order and tightened his trigger finger, squeezing gently just as his father taught him in the forest all those years ago. Then his eyes were dazzled by the brilliant flames erupting from the side of the frigate.

Glasgow's broadside, weighing over twice that of *Cabot's*, was immediate in its response and shocking in its brutality. Ten iron balls covered the short distance in less than a blink, each weighing nine pounds.

They delivered mayhem on *Cabot*. Sheets and braces ran free to the wind as iron shattered belaying pin racks. The foremast shook as one ball glanced off it and sent splinters showering into men nearby.

But much of the fire was concentrated on the brig's small quarterdeck. Several balls crashed into the bulwark and hull. One came through the open gun port and plowed a furrow of splinters across the grain of the deck.

The nine-pound cannon ball discharged from *Glasgow's* number ten gun impacted *Cabot's* bulwark just under the rail cap between Privates Kaine and Kennedy. Neither man completed their trigger squeeze before the chunks of wood and metal mangled the flesh of their chests, arms, and necks. They flew back, thumping into their lieutenant.

Having been shoved back by the privates' dead bodies, Lieutenant Wilson's forehead absorbed only a glancing blow from the ricocheted cannon ball rather than catching it fully in the face. He lay in a mangled heap on the quarterdeck with his squad of Marines.

Glasgow's first lieutenant swiveled his head forward then aft along the frigate's gun deck. By the murky light of the battle lanterns swinging overhead, he counted the right fists of ten gun captains raised in the smoke-filled air.

His second broadside was loaded, and the guns were run out, and the rebel brig had still only fired her first broadside. He stooped and peered through the square port of number eight nine-pounder. The men on the after train tackle scooted out of the way for him to see through the gap between the carriage and the frame.

She's close, he thought. *There'll be no missing at this range.*

The lieutenant backed away, and the men resumed their positions, bracing to check the gun's recoil. Weighing nearly a ton, the gun's inertia would absorb most of it. His internal senses told him when the deck reached the bottom of the roll and paused momentarily before beginning its rise from the trough.

"Fire," he shouted.

Sparks spurted like roman candles from the touch holes, and half a second later the guns discharged, recoiling to the extent of their tackles and blowing the four-inch diameter iron balls from their muzzles. The noise was deafening. Acrid gray smoke choked the sailors and made their eyes run as it occluded all but faint outlines in their Hades-like world.

Self-important midshipmen shouted gratuitous orders to men who could perform the required duties in their sleep. Sponge, powder, shot, wad, prick, prime, run out. Five minutes thirty-nine seconds. Still no response from the rebel.

Midshipman Hopkins was practically hopping with excitement.

"Sir . . . Sir . . . Mr. Jones," he nearly shouted.

"What is it, Mr. Hopkins?" Jones asked testily after pulling his head back in through the open port. He was generally impressed with the seamanship and professional demeanor of the commodore's son, but right at this moment, the tension of waiting was severely trying the first lieutenant's patience.

"Sir, the captain sends his compliments and desires that you should be ready to fire at your discretion the moment that you have a clear range to the enemy."

Jones chewed his lip and searched his mind for a suitable reply that would not be insubordinate but would display frustration. While he knew that he could not, in justice, fully blame Captain Saltonstall for the *Cabot* being between his guns and the enemy frigate, he was nevertheless beside himself with eagerness to bring his guns into action. Finally, he put a sea-weathered hand on each of the midshipman's shoulders and drilled his eyes into those of the youth.

"You may convey my duty to the captain, sir; tell him that my guns have been in readiness this past glass and more. I will join the action the moment I can do so without striking *Cabot*."

Esek Junior twisted free of the lieutenant's hands, bobbed his head, and disappeared into the gloom to deliver the message.

"Harden up that jib sheet. Four more men to the main brace. Now!" Master Earle issued these commands as Captain Saltonstall brought *Alfred* into the wind. "Put your backs into it."

"Mr. Varrel, I'll have more men on all the sheets and braces, if you please," Saltonstall shouted to the bosun who was on the fo'c'sle.

He waited too long to haul his wind and cut off *Glasgow's* escape to the north. All that remained now was to follow in *Cabot's* wake and try to get into position where his guns would take a toll on the enemy. Even without his night glass, he could see that the small brig was taking a beating from the British frigate. The seasoned Englishmen were firing almost twice as fast as the American and throwing over twice the weight of iron with each broadside.

"Mr. Parke," the captain shouted.

"Yes, sir, Captain," came the reply from the barge.

"When we come alongside concentrate your fire on the quarterdeck."

"Fire on the quarterdeck, aye."

Aft, on the quarterdeck, Fitz moved to the larboard side to get a better view of the battle. *Alfred* continued southeast while *Cabot* and the frigate were now moving northeast. The fight was not only leaving *Alfred* to the south, but worse, it was leaving her downwind.

At last—Fitz watched *Alfred's* bow beginning to swing around to the north. When the battle slid from his view, he paced back to stand with his men.

Trevett and Olney stood at the foot of *Columbus's* foremast. Lieutenant Olney just finished overseeing the securing of the forestaysail and jib sheets. Trevett was making the rounds of his Marines' positions. *Columbus* was sailing northeast by east. She could probably go two points closer, but Whipple was not anxious to run afoul of *Cabot* or *Alfred*.

"Cap'n's bound and determined not to be left out of this fight," John said quietly to Joseph.

"Got me runnin' all o'er the ship trimmin' sails and encouraging the men."

"There is no faulting the man's seamanship. Every sail is drawing to perfection. I know the boys are itching to use those muskets Congress procured for them."

"If there is any justice in this ocean, we will be alongside in just over a glass."

"Olney—Mr. Olney! Where is Lieutenant Olney?" Captain Whipple's voice came forward from the quarterdeck.

"I am here, sir."

"If you and Mr. Trevett have finished your chat, I would trouble you to give some notice to the foretopsail brace. I would desire that we come to grips with the enemy sometime before the sun makes its appearance and the offending sail is beginning to shiver."

Trevett met Olney's eyes in the dark and offered a rueful grin.

"Aye, Captain," Olney shouted and moved off to gather men and harden up the brace.

"You should really come below to the cockpit, John, where I can see what I am doing." *Cabot's* surgeon was the only man aboard who called Captain Hopkins by his first name, having treated his ailments since he was an infant.

"Nonsense, Doctor. You no doubt recall that Lieutenant Hinman is away commanding the *Endeavour*. I cannot leave the deck in the midst of this great battle."

Hopkins' left bicep had stopped a particularly nasty decking splinter. The surgeon could not remove it in the darkness. The

best he could do was sling the arm and make it fast against the
captain's chest with bandages.

"If I cannot talk any sense into you, then I will return to the
cockpit where I may be of some real benefit. When you regain your
wits, give the deck to Mr. Sinclair, and come below before you
bleed to death."

"Then go below, old man, where you may render some actual
assistance. Before you go, tell me, how is Mr. Wilson?"

"The cranial contusion is severe, and his condition is dire I am
afraid. The constant din of battle is not conducive to recovery."

"Doctor!" Midshipman Richards was tugging at the doctor's
sleeve. "Come quickly, sir, if you please."

"What is it, young man?" The surgeon asked yanking his sleeve
free of the youth's grasp.

Before he could respond, another broadside crashed out from
Cabot's guns, and it received an instantaneous reply from *Glasgow*.
The noise and confusion were shattering. Splinters cartwheeled
through the air. Bits of rigging, blocks, and chunks of spars, rained
down on the men's unprotected heads and shoulders.

Captain Hopkins cried out with pain and blanched white when
a chunk of wood bounced off his wounded arm. Midshipman
Richards helped the captain up using his uninjured arm, and
together they helped the surgeon to his feet, attempting vainly to
dust him off. Then, the captain noticed the crumpled heap of the
master's form lying amidships a few feet forward of the main mast.

"That is what I was trying to tell the doctor," Richards said.

The three men hurried over, and Richards and the surgeon laid
Master Sinclair on his back. Blood, black in the darkness, soaked
his torso from neck to midriff. The surgeon knelt beside his
shipmate and listened for his breathing. After a moment he looked
at Hopkins and shook his head.

Peter Richards grabbed the lifeless master's wrists and dragged
him over to the scuppers on the unengaged side where his body
would hopefully be out of the way until the action was completed.
Captain Welsh strode out of the darkness and saw the surgeon. His
questioning glance was answered with a shake of the surgeon's
head. He didn't break his stride until he reached the taffrail and the
small group of Marines still there.

"Keep pouring the fire into 'em boys," he encouraged them.

Their faces, almost black with powder smoke stains, were nearly
indistinguishable in the night.

"How be Mr. Wilson?" one of the men asked before he bit the
end from his paper cartridge, pouring the charge down the muzzle
of his musket.

"It is too soon to tell, but the surgeon is watching him closely."

The Marine nodded grimly and rested his musket across the bulwark. He never flinched when the six-pounder four feet away fired at the enemy. He took a bead on a moving figure and squeezed the trigger. Momentarily dazzled by his own muzzle flash, he had no idea if his ball found its target.

Crash—splinters—screams! Another ragged broadside from *Glasgow* came aboard *Cabot*. The brig rolled to larboard from the impact. Welsh staggered then looked forward. The scene that presented itself was truly frightening.

The helmsman lay on the deck, and the wheel was spinning on its own. The jib was in tatters streaming to leeward with its sheets parted by a nine-pound ball. The forestaysail had several shot holes but was still drawing. He looked back at her Marine captain.

"Stop your gob and belay your gawkin', John," Captain Hopkins shouted through clenched teeth, the pain in his upper arm throbbing.

Welsh looked at the captain.

"Get over to the wheel, and help Peter get her under control." When he saw that Welsh and Richards grabbed the spinning wheel, Hopkins turned toward the fo'c'sle to sort out the headsails. The second lieutenant blocked his path.

"Stay on the quarterdeck, Captain—'Tis where you belong. I'll go forward."

Hopkins relaxed slightly, watching Lieutenant Weaver begin ordering men to knot the critical lines and wrestle a new jib up to the foredeck. His relief was not long lived. *Cabot* was not yet under control, and her head was swinging toward the formidable frigate. He needed to sheer off so his exhausted crew could plug holes and repair the rigging.

A quick glance at the helm showed Welsh and Richards spinning the spokes to bring the brig's head to wind, but it was by no means a sure thing. Her shattered bow was falling off the wind, and her forward speed bled away like the blood running from the scuppers. Then the rudder started to bite, and the clockwise swing stopped.

"Harden the forestaysail, Mr. Weaver. Stand by to back it. I am going to tack. Put down your helm."

Richards and Welsh turned the spokes. *Cabot* began to turn into the northerly wind. Would she make stays? Hopkins held his breath. She teetered on the brink. Would she come about? Her vulnerable stern presented itself to *Glasgow's* full broadside.

"Rake her. Fire, blast your eyes, FIRE!" an extremely frustrated Captain Howe screamed through the break of the quarterdeck down to the gun crews.

But the moment was lost. The rebel brig achieved her turn through the northwest wind and sailed off to the south. *Glasgow* continued sailing to the northeast.

In less than a minute *Cabot's* shattered hull was disappearing into the darkening wake of the frigate. The guns had just fired the broadside that disabled the brig, and even the crack British gun crews could not reload with enough speed to finish the helpless enemy.

Howe took a moment to survey his command. She did not come through the engagement unscathed. Skilled hands were on deck and aloft knotting standing rigging and splicing what running rigging they could during the respite. The first lieutenant was standing before him.

"Two and a half feet in the well, Captain . . . and rising."

"Very well. Put some men on the pumps."

"I have already taken the liberty, sir. A dozen hands from the mizzen top and the afterguard have been assigned to pump. The carpenter is setting plugs twixt wind and water."

"Very well. Carry on, Lieutenant."

DONT TREAD ON ME

John Trevett stood several feet above the bulwark cap in the larboard foremast rigging. His booted feet rested on the ratlines with his arms woven through the shrouds. His naked eyes were augmented only by the moon, stars, and cannon flashes. His heart sank as he watched the stricken brig sheer off from the battle.

The heroes aboard her gave their best, taking no thought of their own safety as they charged ahead to engage the powerful frigate. All guns now silent, he watched as a new drama took center stage. Captain Saltonstall was clearly intent on bringing the English frigate to battle and neglected to allow for *Cabot's* barely controlled tack toward the west.

Neither officer apparently noticed that Captain Biddle in *Andrew Doria* was just as intent on sailing through the same piece of the Block Island Sound. *Alfred* continued her turn to the east, gliding through the dark water, and quickly overtaking the slightly damaged frigate.

Biddle was impressed. His time in the Royal Navy taught him the importance of discipline and gunnery. He could well appreciate the hell that was wrought on the decks of the valiant brig.

He was also well educated in close quarters seamanship. His seasoned seafaring eye expertly gauged the relative movements of *Andrew Doria* and *Cabot*. Undamaged and with a fresh crew, his brig could much more easily maneuver than Hopkins' *Cabot*. He would have to tack—at least haul his wind and bear up. It would probably take him out of the battle, at least for several turns of the glass.

"Mr. Dunn, prepare to back the jib. We may need to tack the ship. I am going to bear up to avoid *Cabot*."

The master waved back from the fo'c'sle and began ordering men to the proper lines.

"Put down your helm, quartermaster," Captain Biddle ordered.

The bow swung counterclockwise toward the wind's eye. Sheets were hardened, and yards swung to keep the sails trimmed for the varying wind.

"Captain, the *Alfred*!" Midshipman Patten shouted and pointed to the north.

Alfred was making no motion to avoid *Cabot* or *Andrew Doria*. She stood on in her single-minded pursuit of *Glasgow*. To Biddle, it was obvious that he would have to react, or all three ships would possibly run afoul of each other.

"What in the name of all that's holy . . ." Biddle stopped himself mid-sentence. "Mr. Bevan, throw your weight on the wheel. Bring her through the wind NOW! Mr. Dunn, back the jib and the forestaysail."

Midshipman Bevan was watching over the helm. He immediately added his strength to that of the helmsman, and the two of them spun the wheel as quickly as they could until the rudder reached its stop—hard over to larboard.

The brig easily swung through stays and began to steady on a new course of north by northwest. Then Captain Biddle saw *Columbus* coming out of the night with a fine bow wave foaming down either side.

"Captain Whipple?"

"I see, Mr. Olney." Whipple watched the four ships dancing across the dark water in front of him. The enemy frigate was obviously leading. *Cabot's* feet had been stepped on too many times, so *Alfred* was cutting in. It was evident that *Andrew Doria* was frantically executing a series of pirouettes to avoid the other dancers.

"Fall off two points, Mr. Olney."

"Aye, sir," the second lieutenant complied with obvious relief in his voice.

"Lieutenant Grinnell, Whipple said, "When you have a moment from scratching away with your quill, pray be so good as to go below and tell Mr. Arnold that it will be some time yet before his guns are required."

"Aye, sir."

Whipple was frustrated. *I should have been in the van. What in the devil was Hopkins thinking, putting his largest ships in the rear? I need to be in this fight. It is our first trial with a true man o' war, and I will not be left out.*

At least Biddle knows what he is about, Whipple conceded to himself as he watched *Andrew Doria* tack back through the wind to widen the space between her and his frigate. Passing downwind of *Cabot*, he was close enough to see the men frantically effecting repairs and to hear the orders being given aboard.

Whipple saw young Hopkins had one arm in a sling when he used the other to raise his hat to Whipple as they passed. Suddenly the men on *Columbus* sent up a cheer as they passed the stricken brig.

"Mr. Olney, I believe we have cleared the congestion, and the men have had their cheer. Please be so good as to put the helm down and pursue the enemy frigate. All sail she will bear."

"Steady as you go, quartermaster."

"Steady she goes, Captain," *Alfred's* quartermaster replied.

The frigate stood on, sliding through the water with *Cabot* a bare biscuit toss to leeward. The commodore breathed a tentative sigh of relief as he exchanged salutes with his wounded son on the smaller ship's quarterdeck.

"You have done well, John," Commodore Hopkins shouted across the water.

Captain Hopkins clenched his teeth from the pain, smiling and waving at his father. And then they were past.

Saltonstall strolled forward and bent over the main hatch. "Lieutenant Jones?"

"Captain?" Jones replied, turning his face up to see his captain."

"In a moment you will have opportunity to demonstrate the worth of all that training you have drilled into your gun crews. You will rake the enemy with your larboard broadside. I will then tack, and you will engage her on our starboard side. You will keep up a steady fire until she sinks or strikes."

"That we will, sir." Pause. "Is there anything else, Captain?"

"No, Lieutenant Jones. You may carry on."

Jones raised his hat and turned away.

"Stations to larboard," Jones ordered. Numerous men ran across the deck to the larboard guns. Like all warships—especially those ravaged by fever—*Alfred* did not ship enough men to fight both sides at once.

"Most of you heard the captain. We will engage to larboard first. You will fire fore to aft as each gun bears. A few of you have served the King, so you know what to expect. The rest will learn soon enough. Perform as you have drilled. Gun captains, listen to your division officers. As soon as you have fired once, reload and run up your guns. Then those of you who are designated, report to your starboard guns."

Parke stepped over each thwart as he picked his way down the length of the barge. He squeezed shoulders and patted backs as he leaned on various men to keep his balance.

"You men heard Captain Saltonstall giving his orders to Lieutenant Jones. So, stay in your positions, but those along the larboard gunnel will fire into the stern as we rake. The first ball should smash the stern window and give you some targets along the gun deck. Steady and accurate. You men on the starboard side be ready to pass over a fresh musket, and each Marine should be able to make two shots before we pass. Any questions?"

No one spoke.

Lieutenant Fitzpatrick moved his dozen marines to the larboard bulwark. They all had their rifles and muskets leaning on the cap, waiting the moment to fire. Fitz looked down the line. No need to give any orders. They knew what they were about.

He pulled his hammer back to half cock. When the privates heard the metallic click, they followed suit. Nicholas stood near Commodore Hopkins, but he was watching Fitz. That young man is not even aware, he thought, that he is a natural-born leader. He will go far in this war.

"Steady boys—steady," Sergeant Neilson directed his Marines in the main top. He watched from his perch one hundred feet above the water as *Alfred* swam across *Glasgow's* unprotected stern. Then the air split with a loud crack as fire and smoke billowed from the forward six-pounder on the fo'c'sle.

Neilson's order—"Fire!"—was swallowed by the noise as the main battery nine-pounders began their rolling broadside from stem to stern.

The Marines on the swivels yanked their lanyards, and one pound of lead balls screamed from each muzzle, speeding toward the enemy's quarterdeck. Noise and smoke and fire boomed out, walking down the frigate's side until they were past, and no guns would bear on the enemy's stern. The window was smashed in, and there were black marks on the transom where Lieutenant Jones's nine-pound balls went home. Then it was quiet—for an instant.

Captain Saltonstall's voice filled the silence, dashing it back into the night. "Put down your helm. Tacks and braces. Heave—put your backs into it there! Steady as you go. Mr. Seabury, the forebrace if you please. Lieutenant Maltbie, standby to clew up the forecourse."

Men ran, men heaved, men hauled, and men jostled together. There was a patter of bare feet from the gun deck, and then there was the squeal of trucks as guns were cast loose and readied to fire.

Marines shifted and reloaded. Sheets, tack, and braces were belayed, while clew lines were readied to draw up the corners of the lowest square sail on the foremast—the course. This would reduce speed when *Alfred* came alongside *Glasgow* and also keep the canvas above the sparks and embers of the main guns.

"Think those Marines of yours can hit anything, Matthew?" Seabury quipped as he walked past the barge on his way to the quarterdeck.

"You boys just keep the canvas out of our eyes, Ben, and keep your head down. The Marines will see you get through this."

Several men chuckled, sailors and Marines. Parke stood looking forward watching *Alfred* overtake *Glasgow*. He saw water running from the scuppers. *Glasgow* was pumping.

Corporal Marshall was wedged into the tight corner formed by the starboard bulwark intersecting with the taffrail. Private Marines, Owens, Evitt, Mickery, Dougherty, McLocken, and several others lined the rail forward of him until the line ended with Lieutenant Fitzpatrick. *Alfred* was near enough now that the corporal could see around her chains to the stern light on *Glasgow*. The ships were still drawing closer together—less than a cable— perhaps only a hundred yards.

"Twenty inches in the well, Captain. We'm gaining on it," the carpenter reported to Captain Howe.

"Very well. Carry on."

Howe turned his attention back to *Alfred* on his weather quarter.

"As your guns bear," he said to the midshipman who commanded the six-pounders on the quarterdeck.

The men were ready. They had been plying their handspikes this past half glass traversing the black muzzles as far aft on the larboard side as possible. The young officer crouched above the last one and sighted along the barrel. Ten more yards of relative distance and *Alfred's* jib boom would be in his sight picture. He moved out of the way to allow the gun captain to do his job.

"When you can hit the fo'c'sle squarely."

"Aye, sir," the gun captain replied to the midshipman.

"Mister," Howe said to another midshipman. "Cut along to the gun deck and tell the first lieutenant to hold his fire until the whole broadside can fire together.

The youth saluted and started to run below.

"Walk, Mister. You are a King's officer."

The midshipman skidded to a stop and began walking toward the companion. That was when the first six-pounder fired, recoiling with a twang on its tackles.

DONT TREAD ON ME

The first six-pound ball pierced the forestaysail and continued harmlessly into the darkness.

"Hold your fire," Lieutenant Parke ordered the men in the barge. "Don't fire till I give the order."

Pop, pop, bang. The Marines with Sergeant Neilson in the top were not waiting. They were already marking targets in the enemy's mizzen top. It sounded like bees buzzing the Marines' ears as British musket shot started zinging past them. Buzz, zip, or thwap, when the round slammed into a plank or spar behind them.

Then their world exploded. Both frigates fired their first broadsides together. Twenty nine-pounders and a half dozen throwing six-pound shot. Two hundred forty pounds of iron bent on tearing flesh and destroying oak, canvas, and rigging. Flames, smoke, embers, splinters, and oven-hot air blasts mingled together in a space of thirty by forty yards.

The black water between the frigates flashed orange and crimson. Men choked, cursed, screamed, and sweated, but their training took over, and without pause, they went into the highly regimented routine of reloading their guns.

From all corners on both ships, Marine marksmen selected targets on their opposite number and squeezed the triggers on their muskets and rifles. Hammers dropped, and flints scraped frizzens. Sparks flooded in the primed pans and ignited the powder charges in the breech. Small lead balls flew across the water and impacted oak, fir, and flesh, or splashed unseen into the water beyond.

Lieutenant Fitzpatrick set the butt of his rifle on the deck. He had no idea if his first round went home. He was determined to reload and follow it up with another one as fast as he could.

Fitz never got that chance. In one of the million and one vagaries that make up a war, the British Marine in *Glasgow's* mizzen top was aiming at Commodore Hopkins, nearly six feet away from Fitz. But a slight vibration in the mast moved his muzzle about an eighth of an inch as the charge in the breech exploded, throwing off his aim.

The ball hit Fitz at the scalp line of his forehead, above his left eye, and depressed his cranium into his brain before ricocheting. Fitz's hands relaxed, dropping his rifle and ramrod. Then he collapsed to the deck.

His squad of Marines stopped firing and stared at their beloved lieutenant. The nearest gun crew also paused until their gun captain began clubbing and prodding them with his linstock.

"Evitt, McLocken—take the lieutenant into the cockpit. Handsomely now," ordered Corporal Marshall. "The rest o' you get back to your duties."

Fitz was dead before the men lifted him from the deck. They laid him across two chests which were tied together to make an operating table in the cockpit. A bright lantern swung wildly from the beam overhead, and it shook with each broadside fired or received.

Fitz was the first casualty taken below, so other than Dr. Harrison and his mates, the only occupants of the space were two prisoners—Governor Browne from New Providence and a British midshipman taken from an earlier prize. Dr. Harrison bent over the patient. He lifted an eyelid, then bent to listen for breathing and felt his pulse.

The doctor looked at the two Marines and said, "Best get back to your duties, men. He is gone."

The two frigates continued to sail on through the darkness, steering just a point east of north. Their only illumination was the almost continual muzzle flashes of over twenty cannons. *Alfred*, John Barry's former merchantman, *Black Prince*, was one of the newest and stoutest ships afloat. Her gun crews were well led by Lieutenant John Paul Jones, and her Marines were selected from skilled and determined marksmen.

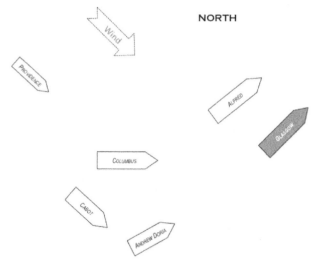

Glasgow was a fine frigate from the world's greatest navy. Her gun crews were buoyed by centuries of training and discipline. They maintained a devastating rate of fire—and accuracy was all but guaranteed as the two ships sailed on within a pistol shot of one another.

The cockpit on a warship—where the surgeon did his grizzly work—was located below the waterline to provide as much safety as possible from enemy shot. As luck would have it, however, *Alfred* rolled to larboard, exposing her starboard bilge, at the same time *Glasgow* rolled to larboard, depressing her guns.

One shot penetrated the frigate's oak hull planking and killed the British midshipman incarcerated therein. This was only one of many shot piercing each ship betwixt wind and water. Pumps ran continuously now on both contestants to keep ahead of the water flowing in. The two carpenters and their mates were continually harried to patch or plug the damage as best they could during the terrible din of the fight.

"Frigate approaching, sir. Two points on the larboard quarter," the master's mate reported to Howe.

The captain turned his attention to his wake and saw *Columbus* maneuvering to rake his stern. *What these rebels lack in gunnery and discipline, they seem to make up for in sheer numbers and audacity.*

"Where's my clerk?" Captain Howe demanded.

"Here, sir," the midshipman replied.

"I believe it would be prudent to jettison the dispatches and the signal book at this time."

"Jettison the dispatches and signal book, aye, Captain." The teen went below to gather the documents and put them in the weighted canvas bag.

Howe knew that secret documents would be sinking into the depths of Block Island Sound within moments. He also knew he could not maneuver to avoid the rake, nor was he concerned with it at such a long distance. The most prudent course open to him was to stand on toward Newport and continue pounding the rebel frigate.

He noticed that she seemed to ride lower in the water—a good sign. But then, *Glasgow* also was becoming sluggish as she began to settle again. *I shall have to send more men to the pumps.*

DONT TREAD ON ME

Captain Nicholas forced an impassive visage as he walked aft to Corporal Marshall. The corporal moved forward to occupy the space vacated when Lieutenant Fitzpatrick fell. He saw the private Marines, Owens, Evitt, Mickery, Dougherty, McLocken, and the rest who were still standing to their posts.

They continued to load and fire, but it was not easy to distinguish their faces in the dark because they wore masks of grime and powder soot. Several seeped blood from holes and scratches caused by tiny bits of splinter and metal shards. Corporal Marshall squeezed off another shot, grounded the butt of his musket on the deck, and reached for the ramrod. Nicholas laid a hand on his forearm, and he stopped his motion.

"Captain?" he said with a grin.

"What is your report, James?"

"Ain't the same without Lieutenant Fitz, sir."

"I feel the same. What else?"

"The boys is down to a handful of cartridges between 'em, Sir."

"Send a couple below to the magazine. Get some for the men in the barge, too."

"Aye, Cap. Owens. . ."

"What is it, Jim. . ." He looked up and saw Nicholas standing there. " . . . er, Corporal?"

"Take Dougherty and get down to the magazine. Tell Mr. Thomas that Captain Nicholas wants four hundred more cartridges. Take three hundred to Mr. Parke and bring the rest back here—on the double."

"Right. Let's go, John."

Both privates laid their muskets on the deck along the taffrail and trotted off toward the companionway. They got as far as the wheel. Two nine-pound balls arrived on *Alfred's* quarterdeck together. One came across the cap atop the bulwark, and the other came through the bulwark—crashing through and sending splinters and iron flying across the deck.

The same broadside that killed Privates Owens and Dougherty also instantly wounded others, severing the tiller ropes and smashing the wheel block. Farther forward, the main brace also parted. With no control of her rudder and very little of her sails, the wind forced the frigate's stern around to starboard as she went in irons, head to wind.

Alfred's stern, composed of glass and the thinnest planking on the ship, squarely faced *Glasgow's* entire larboard broadside. She went dead in the water.

Corporal Marshall watched, transfixed, over the taffrail as *Glasgow's* gun crews worked frantically to reload before she sailed on past the stricken rebel, and they lost their chance to deliver a punishing stern rake. He watched in horror as, one by one, the menacing black muzzles poked out through their ports.

"Down!" Marshall yelled.

The remaining Marines on the quarterdeck dropped flat on their bellies as the broadside fired from the British frigate. Balls came crashing through the stern, causing havoc on the gun deck and main deck.

Miraculously the balls flew under, over, and around the Marines, but none were wounded. Then, *Alfred* was left helpless in *Glasgow's* wake—the second Continental ship forced to break off the action.

"Back the foretopsail," shouted Captain Howe. *What remains of the foretopsail, at any rate*, he thought.

Arresting *Glasgow's* motion allowed his gunners to continue their raking fire. *Alfred* lay there under *Glasgow's* guns, pitching and rolling, which allowed several rounds to pierce her bilges below the waterline. Howe watched the devastation his frigate inflicted with satisfaction.

"Sir, there are a frigate and a brig coming up hand over fist."

Howe scowled at the interruption but turned his attention to the south. Sure enough, *Columbus* and *Andrew Doria* were approaching. Further, it looked as if they meant to board if they could. Crowds of men with weapons filled the fo'c'sle's. Howe couldn't allow that to happen. His exhausted crew would be swamped by waves of fresh rebels. He would have to abandon his current victim.

"Sheet home the foretopsail. Set the courses. Look lively there!"

Glasgow picked up way, sliding through the water to the north. She fired a couple of more shot from her quarterdeck guns, but then even they would bear no more.

"Twenty-eight inches o' water in the well, Captain," the carpenter made the report. "Just keeping up with it."

"More men to the pumps."

"That's no good, sir. We already got full crews and are relieving with fresh men each ten minutes."

Tyringham thought about the predicament. He knew that the press of full sail was causing the hull planking to work, possibly opening and closing the seams and allowing water to seep in. He also knew that there were two frigates and two brigs chasing him that he could not fight forever.

"Carry on, he said. See if you can get at any more shot holes. If you need more men to shift dunnage or ballast, inform the first lieutenant."

"Aye, aye, sir."

DONT TREAD ON ME

Marines were mixed with seamen on the tiller ropes in the steerage. Captain Saltonstall was beside himself to get *Alfred* back into the fight. Lieutenant Seabury shouted orders down the hatch, and Mr. Maltbie relayed them to the men hauling on the tiller ropes.

With the block shot away and ropes parted at the block, the wheel on the helm spun impotently. The only way to control the heavy rudder was using large groups of men to pull it one way or another. It would not allow very fine steering, but as men on deck worked feverishly to knot, splice and wrestle canvas back into place, it would allow the ship to at least move in the right direction while other repairs were conducted.

A single battle lantern swung in dizzying spirals from the overhead. The space was stuffy, moldy, and smelled of too many sweaty and grimy men cramped together and exerting themselves strongly.

The group on the starboard rope was holding the rudder hard over to starboard while men on the fo'c'sle backed what was left of the jib. The officers on the quarterdeck were praying that the sail would hold enough wind to push the bow back around to the north so *Alfred* could pick up way.

Midshipman House looked like a chimney sweep with the addition of large patches of dark blood splattered about his smoke-covered clothes. He approached Saltonstall who was harried on every quarter with reports and questions. George waited for the only pause that could be considered a break in the stream of petitioners and saluted the captain.

"Sir?"

"What is it, boy?"

"Captain, the men are encumbered by the bodies. Should we put them overside?"

"You will NOT," roared Saltonstall. "Take them to the orlop. We are here within biscuit-toss of New England. They shall go ashore and receive a hero's burial."

"Aye, sir." The midshipman scurried away to grab some hands to help carry their fallen shipmates below.

Lieutenant William Jones literally leaned against a tree asleep. He was on the bluff of Brenton's Point facing south over the water, which could not be seen for the fog. Dawn would break in a few hours.

Jones was exhausted after riding and working all the previous day, then installing the battery, then sighting the guns on the British squadron, giving orders for the bombardment, then riding to Brenton's Point battery. He fell asleep on his feet leaning against the huge fir tree. A militia private poked him.

"'Tenant. TENANT'."

Jones shook himself. "What is it?"

"Sounds like thunder over the water."

Jones cocked his ear and listened to the rumble. Occasionally the fog to the south would flash lighter for a moment.

"Not thunder, Private. That's gunfire. Is the battery ready?"

"A few more timbers on top o' the earthwork and we'll be ready to start loading the guns."

"Excellent. It appears we will be just in time. Soon—perhaps today—the Narragansett will be rid of the British Squadron."

Lieutenant Cummings stood on *Columbus'* larboard gangway. Nearly a dozen of his Marines crowded in the bows—perhaps a dozen more in the fore and maintop—competing for space to load and aim their muskets and rifles.

There was little for Cummings to do as the frigate sailed along about a hundred feet to leeward of *Glasgow's* wake on her starboard quarter. He knew that below him, on the gun deck, Lieutenant Arnold was frustrated that none of his nine-pounders would bear —but not nearly as frustrated as Whipple.

Cummings frequently stole glances at the captain. He was forcing himself to present a calm appearance, but the Marine officer was sure that the frigate's captain felt like jumping about and stamping his feet. He grudgingly admitted, silently, that there was no faulting Whipple's seamanship.

Every sail that could, in good conscience, be set was, and they were drawing perfectly. But there was no denying the fact that *Columbus's* bottom was foul, and she was very deeply laden with the booty captured from New Providence. All the ships in the squadron were in the same condition—a fact that primarily accounted for their inability to overtake the enemy.

Ding-ding, ding—five thirty in the morning. Whipple looked at the Marine who rang the bell and scowled. He looked at *Glasgow*. No nearer and no farther this last two glasses. Jets of water were spurting from every scupper, and she looked low in the water. Two nine-pounder muzzles were poking from her cabin where they had been dragged around to serve as stern chasers.

The captain's eyes continued to survey everything, and everything he saw annoyed him. He felt impotent. Yawing and firing a broadside occasionally yielded little more than a pock-marked sail here and there. Each time left him a half cable farther astern. His eyes met Cummings' briefly before the Marine averted them. This incurred Whipple's ire.

"It appears your officers have nothing better to do than skylark, Captain," Whipple said testily to Captain Shoemaker. "If you cannot keep them profitably employed, I will find some useful activity for them."

"I will attend to it, Captain," Shoemaker replied levelly and strolled forward along the larboard gangway, stopping next to Lieutenant Cummings.

"Don't look at the captain anymore, Robert. You are making him nervous."

"Puts me in mind of a cat picking his way through a pack o' wild dogs."

"Just don't make it any worse."

"Right."

Flame and smoke out of *Glasgow's* cabin. Half a second later a ball skipped through a wave alongside the main chains, showering the two Marine officers and the quarterdeck. Captain Shoemaker wiped his face on his sleeve and watched *Andrew Doria* luff until the seven six-pounders comprising her starboard battery bore on the English frigate's wide-open stern cabin.

"Fire!" Captain Biddle ordered.

A loud full-throated crack accompanied the fire and smoke and was followed immediately by rumble and twang and the guns fully recoiled. Immediately, the crews began swabbing and reloading.

"Put up your helm." The quartermaster deftly spun the wheel so that the brig's head would fall off the wind and follow the frigate again.

Before the bow began to swing, *Glasgow's* larboard chaser belched. A nine-pound ball crashed through the starboard bulwark and empty arms chest on the quarterdeck, smashing the box into kindling. Splinters and twisted chunks of iron hinges scythed through the air.

One of the pieces sliced into the soft thigh of young John Bromfield. It broke his femur and laid the muscle open to the bone. The ten-year-old drummer boy collapsed to the deck in his own blood. Lieutenant Craig was there in three steps. He scooped the boy into his arms and stared into his ashen face.

His chest was still moving ever so slightly. As he held him and watched through watery eyes, Sergeant Kearns grabbed a scarf from a sailor and bound the wound. He then used a stray bit of line to apply a tourniquet. Craig passed the unconscious boy to the sergeant.

"Take him below and tell the surgeon to do everything he can."

By the time the drama was finished *Andrew Doria* was back on course in Glasgow's wake. The next rounds delivered from *Glasgow's* stern chasers were for *Alfred*, chasing alongside *Andrew Doria* on her larboard bow. One ball pierced her fore topsail, and the other smashed squarely into her mainmast.

The upper rim of the new sun flashed with all the brilliance and promise of a new day, dazzling and bright with hopeful illumination. No sooner did it make its appearance than it was hidden by a bank of fog closing off the vista to the east.

Lieutenant Maltbie lowered the sextant from his eye and inspected the numbers on the drum next to the index line. He glanced over at *Andrew Doria* and *Columbus*, noting their relative positions was unchanged. Then he looked at Captain Saltonstall and shook his head. *Glasgow* was still about two and a half cables in the lead and had been there for three glasses past.

Maltbie used the sextant, normally a navigation instrument, to measure the angle from the enemy frigate's waterline to main topgallant masthead. If the angle remained the same, so did the distance to the ship.

"No change, sir," Maltbie said to Saltonstall with disappointment in his voice.

Captain Nicholas stood near and heard the report. He looked aloft at the tattered ribbons of sails, saw the water being pumped out through the scuppers by the hogshead, and looked around at the shattered spars, bulwarks, and other splintered deck fixtures. Irish pendants streamed out to the wind, remnants of the severed rigging from every mast and yard.

Several splashes of color were now evident around the decks where blood was showing in the morning light. Continental colors were clearly evident now at the masthead, as were the British colors on the chase. Samuel watched Dudley force his eyes to meet those of the Commodore. No words were exchanged.

It was quite some time since *Alfred* luffed up and released her broadside. The first lieutenant made his appearance on the quarterdeck.

"Captain," Jones said to Saltonstall, "the starboard battery is ready to fire. I request you come head to wind, sir. There is every likelihood that we can knock away a spar or perhaps even her steering."

Saltonstall listened to his request in silence, then turned and looked at the commodore. Hopkins was looking past *Glasgow* to the headlands on Rhode Island's coastline. They were opening Narragansett Bay and stretches of land were visible low on the brightening horizon as fog patches blew in and out. The shake of his head was barely perceptible, but Dudley read it.

"No, John. It's no use. There are bound to be others there, even now. The fleet is in no condition to deal with fresh British frigates that are probably standing out already."

Jones's frustration boiled to anger, but he managed to keep his tongue still as he stomped below to the gun deck.

Captain Nicholas looked at Lieutenant Parke in the barge. Their eyes met. Parke's face was dark from powder stains, and exhaustion was written in the lines on his face. Several Marines had sunk to the bottom boards of the barge, resting against the gunnels, and dozing. No one on the weather decks was speaking. Few even moved.

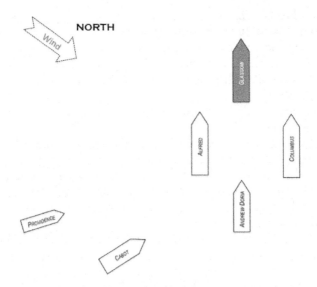

The commodore walked back to the taffrail and looked at the rest of the Continental Fleet trailing the flagship. *We tried. By thunder, we tried. Every last man gave his best last night. Our ships are too heavily laden with the stores captured in New Providence. I cannot risk the materiel so vitally needed by His Excellency, General Washington. We must see the rest of our prizes into port.*

He turned around and rested his back against the rail. He wanted the fresh sea breeze to clear his head, but the wind also carried the smell of burned powder with it. He would wait to be refreshed later.

Smoke puffed from *Glasgow*. A ball screamed over his head. Another smashed into the thick trunk of their main mast, shaking *Alfred's* timbers. Hopkins' bloodshot eyes sought and found his son.

"Midshipman Hopkins, would you and Mr. House be so good as to hoist the recall."

"Aye, sir," the boy replied after the briefest pause.

"Captain Saltonstall, you would oblige me if you would haul your wind and shape your course for New London."

"As you say, Commodore." The captain issued a string of orders to bring *Alfred's* head through the wind to begin the final leg of their voyage. He then ordered Lieutenant Jones to house his guns and the remainder of the crew and Marines to secure from quarters.

Looking around the horizon, he saw most of the other ships making motions to follow his example. Then, the morning fog of Block Island Sound closed in, blanketing him from the world not immediately visible on his own frigate.

Captain Nicholas caught himself starting to make a comment to Fitz. A pang of regret stabbed his heart for a moment. He went to the waist to talk with Lieutenant Parke while his Marines began to secure their arms. If the wind held and the fog cleared, they would be in Connecticut by evening.

The screaming shriek of the eighteen-pound iron ball streaked overhead. The sharp crack, like a pistol shot, heralded the parting of the mizzen topsail brace as the ball passed through it then splashed midway between *Rose* and *Nautilus*. Several of the men on *Rose's* quarterdeck flinched or ducked. Captain Wallace did not.

While he was clearly a brave officer, his unflappable air this morning was due more to his fury than his courage. His sortie on the previous day was prematurely curtailed by what he considered two bumbling buffoons.

Today he was awakened by bombardment of his squadron from an unseen shore battery that apparently materialized from nothing during the night. It was decidedly not composed of light field pieces. The iron raining down about his ears was clearly fired by heavy artillery. *Would there be no end to the foolishness of these rebels?*

"The cable has been buoyed, Captain. Shall we slip?"

"Slip? Slip the anchor cable! Have you lost the use of your faculties?" Wallace could not believe what his first lieutenant was saying. "We will not slip our anchor and run from these traitors like naughty schoolboys. You may heave around on the anchor and get the frigate underway immediately it is catted."

Wary of his captain's temper, *Rose's* first lieutenant chose to follow the order rather than question it. He had more respect for his captain than the battery on Coddington Point. He noticed a hole open in *Nautilus's* main topsail while he was giving the order to weigh the anchor. Newport had clearly ceased to be a viable port for the British squadron.

DON'T TREAD ON ME

The Rhode Island Militia private was true to his word. By the time the sun rose on Brenton's Point, the two eighteen-pounders were mounted on stable plank decking, a magazine was built twenty yards behind, stable earthworks were thrown up around the battery and the magazine, and the gun implements were arrayed and ready for use. Further, a target, *HMS Glasgow*, lay at anchor barely three cables distance.

Even the eighteen-pound shot was stacked neatly in racks in the magazine. One of the militia privates was a carpenter and brought his tools to the project, which he used to quickly fashion racks for the round shot. Lieutenant Jones lacked only one ingredient to complete his task—powder. For some reason he could not possibly fathom, the logistical men had not deemed it necessary to assign powder to the supplies delivered to Brenton's Point.

"Private," William Jones spoke, "Can you ride that horse?"

"Course I can, 'Tenant. She's my horse, ain't she?"

"Good. Return to Newport and find the quartermaster. Tell him we require the powder that should accompany these guns. Do you see the frigate down there?"

"Course I do, 'Tenant. Why, she's the ol' *Glasgow*, ain't she? 'Pears to be in pretty sorry shape, she does."

"Yes. I agree with your assessment. I desire to sink her with this battery before she sinks of her own accord. Now then, tell the quartermaster to send along powder for at least two hundred rounds, as fast as ever he can. If he has no powder or if he drags his feet, ride to the battery at Coddington and have them send along all the powder they can spare, up to half of their store."

"Yes, sir, 'Tenant. All the powder I kin gets."

He swung easily up into his saddle and trotted off toward Newport.

Well then, if I have no powder, the least I can do is resume my duties of observing and reporting. Jones retrieved a pencil stub, portfolio of papers, and his long glass from a saddlebag. Extending the glass, he took in the condition of the English frigate.

The first things he noticed were jets of water shooting from the pump scuppers. This prompted him to look at the waterline. Having observed *Glasgow* daily for several weeks, it was immediately apparent to Jones that she was considerably settled into the water.

She enjoyed at least two feet less freeboard than usual. He made a note, and before he continued to observe, he sat with his back against a huge old pine tree and propped his portfolio on his raised knees.

The frigate's topsails and courses hung loose and flapped lazily in the light morning breeze. There would be no point in clewing them up or attempting to furl them. Either activity would be an exercise in futility as they all hung in ribbons and small patches of scorched canvas.

Starting with the main course, William mentally sectioned it into four quadrants and began systematically counting the holes. Since much of the sail resembled a large rag, he had to extrapolate in many cases. His final assessment of the main was that it had been pierced no fewer than one hundred times.

He made a note and continued. He finished counting the holes in the fore course at eighty and estimated ninety holes. He wondered how she managed to come to anchor because there didn't appear to be enough running rigging left to control the sails and capture the wind.

He saw that the main mast was much damaged. So damaged, in fact, that carpenter's mates were preparing to fish it where it was obviously sprung so that it could stand the strain of a moderate blow.

Topmen were aloft now unbending the foretopsail and sending the scraps to the main deck, and with the yard bare of canvas he could see why. It was so shot-through and splintered that it would need to be replaced.

His assessment continued thus for the better part of an hour. It was clear the frigate would need to be docked before she could again be an effective combatant. Halifax for sure; Plymouth most likely. That was if she escaped his guns. Here was his chance to strike a major blow for freedom and he was hamstrung by a lack of powder.

April 8, 1776
New London, Connecticut
Inn of the Disavowed Crown

"Out o' the door, you lazy cur," Whipple said with very little emotion and stepped over the canine-shaped lump stretching across the open door. Snout, who was occupying his favorite warm-weather position, did not budge from the tavern's open doorway. When still a pup, Daniel Uncas named him.

Like many of his race—Mohegan Indian—Daniel sailed in the West Indian trade and frequented the Disavowed Crown when home. The Crown stood on the same patch of ground for decades. The appellation, Disavowed, was added to Crown several years ago, after the *Gaspee* incident. Standing foursquare on Water Street, the establishment faced the waterfront.

Captain Whipple's mood grew worse daily since the battle with *Glasgow*. For two days Arnold and Trevett suffered the brunt of his temper, struggling to serve as intermediaries with the Marine company. The fog that delayed their entry into the Thames River only served to magnify the foul mood.

Well, that was just too bad as far as Whipple cared. *Disloyal officers made for a disloyal crew.* He would deal with them after this meeting. Hopkins summoned all the captains to a gathering at the Crown.

"Captain Whipple?" the serving girl asked when he stepped over Snout and paused.

"Yes."

"The commodore is in the great room on the second floor, sir. Please follow me." Whipple made no eye contact with the other patrons while he walked behind the girl up the stairs. William Grinnell followed Captain Whipple with a sheaf of papers in his hand—the log of the battle as well as the condition and state of readiness of the frigate.

Several men were already gathered in the large room overlooking the wharves and anchorage. The room was the first at the top of the stairs and ran east and west from the rear to the front of the building, occupying roughly a third of the upper floor.

The rest of the top floor was divided into cramped, squalid bedrooms let to mariners without a current berth. Two windows allowed illumination along the wall to the south and another at the end opposite the entry door provided a sweeping view of the river.

A long table ran the length of the room and a sideboard loaded with food stood against the wall with the door. Whipple stepped in and stopped just inside the door. The food was to his left, and he faced down the length of the table and through the east window.

"Abe!" Commodore Hopkins came from the other end of the room and shook his hand firmly. "Thank you for coming. Come in and refresh yourself. Is that Mr. Grinnell with you?" Hopkins gently nudged Whipple aside and shook the clerk's hand. "Glad you could come, sir; glad you could come." Hopkins was smiling at both men.

Whipple took in the room with his eyes. Bottles were already open. Captain Saltonstall, Lieutenant Jones, and Captain Nicholas were already present. Lieutenant Rathbun of *Providence* sat across from Jones, but of his captain, John Hazard, there was no sign.

Two other men were also present. They wore militia officer uniforms.

"You haven't met our guests, Abe. This is Colonel Henry Babcock and his young associate, Lieutenant William Jones—both of the Rhode Island Militia. They bring news and intelligence they will report when the group is assembled."

Handshakes, bows, and pleasantries were exchanged.

Abe Whipple grinned when he shook hands with the young lieutenant and said, "Lieutenant Jones and I have met, although he wasn't a lieutenant at the time—merely an intrepid patriot with initiative and ambition for our cause."

Jones smiled and bowed his head, blushing under his wind-burned face.

Whipple took a seat beside Rathbun, and Grinnell took the next on that side.

"Coffee and a plate," Whipple said curtly to the girl.

She bobbed and replied, "Yes, sir." She filled a plate with fish, cheese, and bread.

More men walked in while the girl continued taking food and drink to the men in the room. The commodore embraced his son when he entered the room; then abruptly released him when he flinched from the pain. Captain Hopkins' left arm was in a sling, and his coat hung loosely over his shoulder.

"How are you, my boy?"

"It is healing nicely, Father--little more than a scratch, actually. I am much more fortunate than too many brave men."

Several of the other men rose and congratulated Captain Hopkins on his honorable wound. Eventually, the room filled. More chairs were brought in. A bench was set along one wall to accommodate some of the midshipmen and junior lieutenants who were towed along to serve as clerks and scribes.

Ships' captains, Marine officers, and senior lieutenants filled the chairs around the table. The general roar of conversation made it difficult to distinguish a single thread of discussion. Commodore Hopkins and Captain Nicholas watched and listened with satisfied countenances. They occasionally shared a thought, but mostly they merely observed and let the men in the room relax and warm to one another.

Eventually, the conversation subsided, and men looked to Commodore Hopkins. He smiled and stood. He was framed ideally with the view of his anchored fleet in the window behind him.

"Gentlemen," Ezek began, "I'd like to begin with a count of casualties from the battle and the material state of your ships. Mr. Rathbun, would you please begin the proceedings?

John stood. "Captain Hazard asked me to represent him, Commodore. He reports that he is indisposed today."

Ezek nodded. He was not surprised at the captain's absence. Many of his peers and not a few inferiors already commented on his noticeable absence during the battle with *Glasgow*.

"*Providence* suffered no casualties from the battle, sir. We are, as is the rest of the fleet, much ravaged by illness and weighed down with cargo from Nassau. *Providence* will be ready for sea when we have offloaded the cargo, watered, and made up our crew shortages."

After a moment he said one more thing. "Captain Hazard desired me to state that he remained close to the prizes during the engagement to ensure that no enemy could retake them while the fleet was distracted elsewhere." He sat down without making eye contact with any of the others.

"Thank you, John," Commodore Hopkins said after the officer sat down.

The group listened to several other reports from smaller vessels and prize commanders. No battle casualties were reported, but death and disability from fever had taken the lives of one in five of the men who set out from Philadelphia earlier in the year.

Captain Hopkins pushed himself up with his good arm and slid his chair back with his hams. "I am very sorry to report, sir, that my master, Seymour Sinclair, as well as two private Marines, George Kennedy and Patrick Kaine, were killed in action with the British frigate. We also had Lieutenant Wilson and six more hands wounded. The men are all expected to survive, sir."

Hopkins inhaled slowly to steady his voice, then continued. "But I am deeply bereaved to report that Lieutenant Wilson succumbed to his wound in the middle watch this morning. *Cabot* was much shattered by the battle, but she is sound below the waterline. I imagine the brig's company can put her to rights topside within a fortnight; but we will likely need to procure some spars, cordage, and canvas."

Lieutenant John Paul Jones stood as Captain Hopkins resumed his seat. "Captain," he said, "I had the pleasure to still be topside when you set about the enemy cruiser. To open the fray as you did, attacking a hardened enemy of twice your displacement and gunnery . . . why, sir, it was nothing short of intrepid. I am acutely distressed by the loss of Captain Wilson but will never forget having witnessed this heroic event. It will be a cherished hallmark in the historic annals of our young nation."

A general and enthusiastic approbation accompanied Jones' praise. Hopkins looked down at his empty plate, and his father beamed from the end of the table.

The commodore waited for the praise of his son to subside before calling on the next report. He waited until last for the big ships. "Commodore Whipple, may we have your report?" Whipple was slightly pleased that Hopkins has used a complimentary title, reminding the room of his days in charge of the Rhode Island Navy.

Whipple cleared his throat. "As you know, sir, *Columbus* was in the rear of the leeward column. I had sixteen men away in prizes and suffered from a similar proportion of fever to the remainder of the fleet. Despite my utmost endeavor, I was not able to bring the frigate alongside the enemy. I had one man wounded lightly and some incidental damage delivered by the enemy's stern chasers."

"Thank you, Commodore," Hopkins said. "I notice that you are not accompanied by any Marine officers today."

Whipple frowned and his ears reddened. He considered the three Marines in a state of mutiny but chose not to share this embarrassment with the other officers in the room. He instead inclined his head to Hopkins and said in a neutral tone, "That is so, sir."

"I trust they are well," Hopkins persisted.

"To the best of my knowledge, Commodore, they are all in a fit state of health." Whipple pressed his lips into a straight line.

Realizing that he would have to wait until a more opportune moment to discover the truth of the matter, Ezek Hopkins decided to probe no more and turned to Dudley for the flagship's report.

"I shall defer the Marine report to Captain Nicholas," Saltonstall began. "*Alfred* herself is severely knocked about in hull and rigging. We had seven wounded among the sailors. The main mast is much shot through and was fished by the carpenter and his mates the morning of the battle. Tiller blocks and ropes were shot away and are still knotted. Much rigging and canvas will need replacing, and she was pierced by seven nine-pound shot below the waterline. Even today the pumps are going every watch to keep ahead of the inflow. A prisoner from Bolton was killed in the cockpit by one of the balls. *Alfred* will need to be docked or careened at the least."

Captain Nicholas took up the report. "Marine casualties were few in number but overwhelming in character. Privates Owens and Dougherty were killed in action and will be missed by their shipmates. Tragically, Lieutenant John Fitzpatrick, Fitz, was killed during the battle. He was universally loved for his spirit and care of the men. I despair when I contemplate the task before me of corresponding with the new bride he left in Philadelphia fewer than three months past." The room fell silent for a moment. It seems there was not a man present who was not touched by Fitz during their short cruise. After a moment of reflection, the commodore nodded to Colonel Babcock.

Babcock said, "Gentlemen, I am most sorry for the losses you have sustained. I feel the poverty of not having known the gentlemen you lament. I have asked Lieutenant Jones to come along to your meeting this morning, therefore, to report that your loses were not in vain."

"Sirs," William Jones began as his stood. "You have my sincere condolences for the loss of the brave men in your company. It is in tribute to their sacrifice that I report to you this morning the tyrants have been driven from the Narragansett. While you were shattering *Glasgow*, my men and I were erecting batteries near Newport. It seems that the batteries, combined with the valiant actions of you gentlemen have convinced the scoundrel, Captain Howe, that Rhode Island is no longer conducive to his presence. *Rose* and *Glasgow* have taken their consorts and left the region. We are free of their marauding. Congratulations and thank you!"

Babcock stood and opened a newspaper that was lying on the table in front of him. "Your victory, gentlemen—and yes, I call it a victory—follows closely on the British departure from Boston. They fled last month, without the firing of a shot! His Excellency, General Washington, was invited to address the Massachusetts Legislature on the occasion of his great feat of dislodging the interlopers. I would like to read you the final portion of his address." He looked at Commodore Hopkins.

"Please proceed, Colonel."

Babcock held the paper up to benefit from the full light of the window at his back, found the place to begin, and read to the fleet's officers.

Boston has been relieved from the lawless domination, the cruel and oppressive rule of those sent by a tyrannical sovereign to trample upon the rights of humanity. This great metropolis is open again to its free and rightful possessor.

That this welcome transition has been accomplished without the blood of our fellow citizens and soldiers being shed can only be ascribed to the merciful and omnipotent hand of Almighty Providence. May that Being, who is powerful to save, and in whose hands is the fate of nations, look down with an eye of tender pity and compassion upon the whole of the United Colonies; may He continue to smile upon their counsels and arms, and crown them with success, whilst employed in the cause of virtue and mankind.

May this distressed colony and its capital, and every part of the wide extended continent, through His divine favor, be restored to more than their former luster and once happy state, and have peace, liberty, and safety secured upon a solid, permanent, and lasting foundation.

~~The End~~

. . . Just the Beginning

Observations and

Remarks

M arines that I know, of whom there are many, like to claim that the US Marine Corps was born in a bar. More specifically, The Corps was born in Tun Tavern in Philadelphia.

Several years ago, during a visit to the historic city of Philadelphia, I was disappointed to discover that this famous tavern no longer exists. It has essentially been reduced to a plaque under the Interstate 95 overpass near Penn's Landing.

The Second Continental Congress authorized the formation of the Marines. As we all know, it takes more than an act of Congress to make a reality. In this case, it took men—hundreds of them. Samuel Nicholas was the first Marine officer appointed. About six months later an innkeeper named Robert Mullan was appointed to be captain of marines on the new frigate *Delaware*.

After several months of detailed research, I have concluded that one or both of these men either owned or managed Tun Tavern and/or the Connestogoe Waggon. Further, one or both of these establishments were significant locations involved in the early recruiting of Marine enlisted men for the Continental Fleet and other Marine units during the Revolution.

The first cruise of the Continental Fleet established for all time the inseparable bond that is the United States Navy—Marine Corps Team, with combined amphibious operations at the heart of this partnership. Since the spring of 1776, US Marines have "fought in every clime and place they could take a gun."

The raid on New Providence is historically regarded as a success. Certainly, it achieved Commodore Hopkins' tactical objective; the colony was captured, and military stores were returned to America for the use of the Army and Navy. It could even be argued that the fleet action in the Block Island Sound was successful. Small war vessels were captured, and the new Navy did drive off the British post ship *Glasgow* without losing a ship. And, combined with land forces, they did evict the British Navy from Narragansett Bay, making it a safe refuge for commerce and naval operations.

These successes may seem even more admirable in the perspective of the time. Almost none of the naval or Marine officers in the tiny Continental fleet had any combat experience. When the battle with *HMS Glasgow* began, it is possible that many, perhaps most, of the Continental gun crews had never fired a cannon at an enemy ship. The most gun drill any of them had did not exceed two months and was probably a lot less.

All of the Continental warships were converted merchantmen. Contrast this with their British enemy that had centuries of discipline and training. English officers were bred to command for generations, and *Glasgow* was built, from the keel up, to serve exclusively as a warship.

Within a few days, the Continental fleet settled into port in Newport, Rhode Island. There they were beset by politics, recrimination, minimal funding, desertion, inadequate manning, and politically motivated courts martial. Regrettably, many of these characteristics have become a part of the American political subculture.

Thankfully, although undeniably present, they are vastly overshadowed by the more noble attributes of Courage, Honor, and Valor. Since that momentous day in November 1775, the United States Marine Corps can be proud of having continually demonstrated its motto: Semper Fidelis.

AFTER you finish reading the book, please go to the link on Amazon https://www.amazon.com/David-Perry/e/B00G04V4T6 and help other people enjoy the story by writing a short review. Even one sentence is extremely helpful in letting readers know about the story. Thank you.

Salty Talk

Athwart

Across or crosswise; also, from side to side or transverse. To lay athwart means to be across something.

Back Water

To row a boat backwards, either to stop its forward motion or move it backwards.

Backed

Of wind: a counterclockwise shift in the direction from which the wind is coming. Example, The wind backed from north to northwest.

Of sails: turn a sail so that the wind is blowing on the side of the sail that is facing the forward end of the ship or boat. Example, The captain backed the foretopsail.

Of water: to row a boat backwards. Example, The oarsmen backed water to stop the forward momentum of the boat.

Bells

Life at sea is divided into watches. Watches are regulated by bells. At four hours long each, there are six watches in a 24-hour day. Each watch is divided into eight bells, being struck every half hour. During the age of sail, the elapsed time of the watch was measured by sand running through the half-hour glass. Every half hour is struck with one more bell than the preceding half hour. At the end of the four hour watch, eight bells are struck. Then, the cycle is repeated for the next watch. Bells are struck in pairs, followed by the remaining single bell. For example: one o'clock sounds like "ding-ding"; and two thirty sounds like "ding-ding, pause, ding-ding, pause, ding."

Bosun (Boatswain)

On sailing ships, this is a warrant officer (below a commissioned officer such as Lieutenant). The bosun is responsible for the rigging and use of sails, anchor, and similar equipment. He is assisted by bosun's mates who are seamen that have specialized in the maintenance, use, and repair of this equipment. Modern navy ships may also have a bosun, but this person is generally a commissioned officer of junior rank. Bosun's Mate is an enlisted designation in the modern navy.

Bowhook

The Bowhook is not an item of gear aboard ship but rather a crewmember of a ship's boat. The bowhook handles lines forward when the boat is coming alongside a pier or ship. The bowhook also tends fenders and serves as a lookout.

Bow

The front or pointy end of the ship or boat. Sometimes called 'bows' referring to the starboard side of the bow and the port/larboard side of the bow.

Brace

A brace is a line (rope) on a square-rigged ship (ship with square sails). The brace is used to pull the yardarms (ends of the yard) forward or aft, allowing the sails to be trimmed so that the ship can sail at different angles to the wind.

Broadside

Refers to the guns (cannons) on the side of a sailing ship that point outward, at right angles to the longitudinal centerline of the ship. To fire a broadside means to discharge all the guns on one side of a ship simultaneously. A rolling broadside begins at the forward end of the ship, firing all the guns on one side, one after the other in quick succession ending at the rear of the ship.

By (sailing by the wind)

A vessel sailing *by the wind* is sailing with the wind forward of the beam. The beam is the direction on either side of the vessel that is straight out (perpendicular) from the centerline. Simply stated, the vessel is sailing at an angle into the wind. "Fore and aft" rigged vessels with triangular or trapezoidal sails along the centerline (like a modern sailboat) sail closer to the wind (point more directly into the wind) than square-rigged vessel with square sails on yards that are rigged perpendicular to the centerline.

Cable (Length)

This is a unit of measure, but it is based on the actual length of a cable, which was the very thick hemp line (See "Line") that ran between the sailing ship and the anchor. This line was 1/10th of a nautical mile (See "Mile (Nautical)"). Hence, the unit of length termed "cable" is 1/10th of a nautical mile, or 200 yards.

Clew

Noun - the lower corners of a square sail or the aft corner of a triangular sail. Verb - 'clew up' means to draw the clews up to the yardarm, making the sails ineffective for sailing but getting them out of the way quickly if the ship is going into action. When sails were made from canvas, and ships fired cannons with lots of sparks and fire, sails were clewed up out of the way to avoid catching fire.

Close

Sailing *close to the wind* means to sail into the wind at an angle. The more directly a ship sails into the wind, the closer it is sailing to the wind.

Ensign

The national flag of the country flown on a ship. Also, the lowest officer rank in the modern US Navy. In the eighteenth century, it was the lowest rank in the British Army.

Fake (or Flake)

Laying a line (rope) on the deck in a loose but organized manner, sometimes as a series of figure eights atop one another.

This allows the line to run freely when necessary without fouling or hockling in a block or other constriction.

Fathom

This is a unit of measure equal to two yards, or six feet. The word itself comes from an ancient English word that means (very roughly) "a hug or outstretched arms." This may seem a strange word to use unless you picture how it was used. It is traditionally used to describe the depth of water. If you measure the water using a small line with a lead weight attached to the end, when you retrieve the line, as you bring it up, you stretch your arms with a length of the line between your hands one "fathom" at a time. By counting the number of times that is done, the person making the measurements (the leadsman) can announce to the captain "four fathoms" or whatever the depth he counted.

Incidentally, the famous author and humorist, Mark Twain, was named for this term. On Mississippi riverboats, a leadsman was frequently used in this treacherous river. His lead line was marked with different materials to easily recognize the number of fathoms. If he called out to the captain "By the mark twain," he was saying the depth of the muddy river was exactly two fathoms—by the mark.

Flemish

When a line (rope) is laid down on the deck in a tight, flat coil. It is a decorative way to store a line, but not practical because if needed the line may not run freely, and the tight coil may not allow the line to dry well if it has been wet.

Gammoning

The thick, heavy lines (ropes) wrapped around the bowsprit that secure it to the cutwater of a sailing ship.

Glass

Glass is a very versatile word in the nautical language of past centuries. It generally means three different things that must be derived from the context. It can refer to the barometer in a phrase such as "the glass is falling." This would mean that barometric pressure is going down and this generally portends a storm. If there were a phrase such as "turn the glass" then the reader would know

the reference is to an hourglass and the sand has run out so it must
be restarted. The third meaning is that of a telescope.

Helm

The ship's steering wheel. May also refer to the area around the
wheel and the apparatus that holds the wheel.

Hockle

This is a twist or knob in the line that forms when the line is
twisted in the opposite direction from the natural lay of the fibers.

Knot

This is a measure of speed equal to one nautical mile (See "Mile
(Nautical)") per hour. The term derives from the method used to
measure speed on a sailing ship before electronics. A crewmember
stood near the stern (See "Stern") of the ship and threw a line (See
"Line") over the side that had a drag attached to the end. The
crewmember would then let the line run off a reel and count the
number of knots that ran off the reel in a preset time. These knots
were tied at calculated intervals to indicate the speed of the ship
during the given time period. The crewmember would then
announce to the captain the number of knots, indicating the speed
of the ship.

Large (sailing large or going large)

When a vessel is sailing large or going large, it is sailing with the
wind abaft the beam, or in very simple terms, the wind is pushing
the vessel.

Larboard

The left side of the ship when facing the bow (front). Sometime
during the nineteenth century larboard was replaced by port to
eliminate confusion with the similar sounding *starboard*.

League

This is a unit of measure that originally meant, "the distance a
person could walk in one hour." This was taken to be three miles.
The term was used at sea to mean three nautical miles (See "Mile
(Nautical)").

Line

This is the naval term for what most people call a rope.

Loom

The round shaft of an oar.

Mast

The vertical spar that supports the booms and yards which hang the sails. The arrangement that most people refer to as a mast on a ship is usually a collections of masts, more or less fastened together vertically. In order, from the deck skyward, these are the lower mast, the top mast, the topgallant mast, and the main mast.

The most common three masted ship has, from forward to aft, the foremast, main mast, and mizzen mast.

Mile (Nautical)

A nautical mile is exactly two thousand yards (a statutory, or land, mile is 5,280 feet, considerable less than the 6,000 feet in a nautical mile. You may be thinking that sailors coined this term just so their mile could be longer than the soldiers' mile. Not so.

If you dig deep enough, most nautical terms and traditions have very practical roots. There are ninety degrees of latitude from the equator to the north (or south) pole. Each degree is divided into sixty minutes. A nautical mile equals exactly one minute of latitude. Using this unit of measurement makes it very easy for navigators to measure distances on the most common type of nautical charts.

Port

The left side of the ship when facing the bow (front). Sometime during the nineteenth century, port replaced the term larboard.

Point

A direction of the compass. In modern times, the compass is divided into 360 degrees, with 000 or 360 being north, 090 being east, 180 being south, and 270 degrees being west.

In former times, the compass was divided into 32 points. So, one point was equal to 11.25 modern degrees. North, South, East, and West were the four cardinal points and each quadrant was further divided. All 32 points listed in clockwise order with corresponding degrees are:

North 0 deg 0'
North by East 11 deg 15'
North Northeast 22 deg 30'
Northeast by North 33 deg 45'
Northeast 45 deg 0'
Northeast by East 56 deg 15'
East Northeast 67 deg 30'
East by North 78 deg 45'
East 90 deg 0'
East by South 101 deg 15'
East Southeast 112 deg 30'
Southeast by East 123 deg 45'
Southeast 135 deg 0'
Southeast by South 146 deg 15'
South Southeast 157 deg 30'
South by East 168 deg 45'
South 180 deg 0'
South by West 191 deg 15'
South Southwest 202 deg 30'
Southwest by South 213 deg 45'
Southwest 225 deg 0'
Southwest by West 236 deg 15'
West Southwest 247 deg 30'
West by South 258 deg 45'
West 270 deg 0'
West by North 281 deg 15'
West Northwest 292 deg 30'
Northwest by West 303 deg 45'
Northwest 315 deg 0'
Northwest by North 326 deg 15'
North Northwest 337 deg 30'
North by West 348 deg 45'

Poop Deck

The poop deck is a raised, partial weather deck. It is usually aft of (farther back) the main deck. On larger sailing ships, it is the farthest aft deck, usually over the captain's cabins.

Quarter

Ships have two quarters: the starboard and port (larboard) quarters. The quarter is half of the rear part of the ship. Draw a line down the centerline of the ship from the stern and stop about a quarter of the way forward, the right of that line is the starboard quarter and the left is the port (larboard) quarter.

Sally Port

A protected point of entry into a secure location.

Scuttlebutt

This term represents the source of water for immediate consumption aboard a sailing ship. It was a cask or butt that had been "scuttled" by making a hole in it so that water could be withdrawn for drinking. Since the sailors tended to congregate around the scuttlebutt, the word took on a secondary meaning in the Navy for gossip.

Sheet

Contrary to the belief of many lubbers, the sheet is not a sail, but rather the line (rope) that controls the angle of the sail. On a square sail, it is attached to the clew (lower corner) and generally led aft to hold the corner of the sail against the wind. In some cases, it may be replaced by a tack, which generally holds the clew straight down to the deck or bulwark.

On a jib or staysail, the sheet also attaches to the clew (the aft lower corner of the triangular sail) and holds it against the wind so the wind can fill the sail. On a triangular mainsail, with its foot attached to a lower boom, the sheet attaches to the boom and controls how far the boom/sail can swing out toward the side of the ship or boat.

Spar

A mast. The arrangement that most people refer to as a mast on a ship is usually a collections of masts, more or less fastened together vertically. In order, from the deck skyward, these are the lower mast, the top mast, the topgallant mast, and the main mast.

Starboard

The right side of the ship when facing the bow (front).

Stern

The back or rear of the ship or boat.

Sternway

Moving the ship or boat backwards. In the days of sail and oar, it was accomplished by turning the ship into the wind so the wind would press on the front of the sail, moving the ship backwards. A boat without a sail could be rowed backwards, called backing water.

Tackle

An arrangement of lines (ropes) and blocks (pulleys), generally fasted between the sides of a gun (cannon) carriage and the side of the ship used for adjusting the train (side-to-side aim) of the gun or pulling it up tight to the bulwark or gun port.

Truck

A flat metal cap on the top of a mast or spar. Also, the wheel of a gun carriage.

Weather Deck

A weather deck is a deck that is exposed to the weather. It is not covered by an enclosed structure or higher deck.

Yard

This is the spar (long cylindrical beam) hanging perpendicular to a mast on which the sails hang or are furled.

Ship Nomenclature

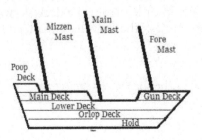

Sail Plan

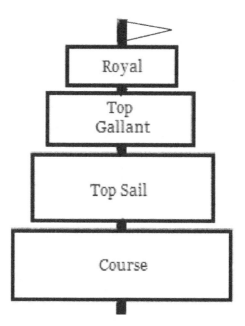

Principal Characters

This novel contains 144 characters, three of which are fictional and were created from the mind of the author. These purely fictional characters include Lawson Bellows of the Virginia Loyalist Navy, Finnestere, who is portrayed as Lord Dunmore's butler, and Betty Hugg who is the fictional daughter of the real historical figure, William Hugg.

Following is a partial list of the actual historical figures used in the story and a short profile of each. The information contained here was acquired from detailed historical research and was then used to name the characters, develop the timelines, and outline the events. While the names listed below are people from history, conversations and thoughts attributed to the names in this book are from the author's imagination (except in rare instances where an actual conversation was recorded for history).

If the reader would like a complete list, she or he can sign up for the author's newsletter and request the list via email at dave@daveperrybooks.com.

Anderson, Thomas

A corporal in the Continental Marines, Thomas Anderson went aboard *Columbus* on December 16, 1775. He was promoted to sergeant on August 16, 1776.

Ayscough, James

Lieutenant Ayscough, captain of the British Sloop *Swan* served on the American Station during the American Revolution. During the period of time involving the *Gaspee* Affair, Ayscough was known by the locals as a British naval officer who treated Rhode Islanders fairly. He died in 1798.

Babcock, Henry

Colonel Henry Babcock of the Rhode Island Militia served in both the French and Indian War and the American Revolution. He was an eyewitness of the battle for Ticonderoga in the latter war. A lawyer from Yale, he was born in 1736. In April 1776, the Rhode Island legislature removed him from command of his troops because it determined he was mentally unstable. He died in October 1800 in New London, Connecticut.

Biddle, Nicholas

Nicholas Biddle was born in Philadelphia on September 10, 1750. He was one of the first five captains that Congress appointed in the Continental Navy. His father was William Biddle and his mother, the former Mary Scull.

Nicholas went to sea in the merchant service when he was fourteen, joined the British Navy as a midshipman in 1770, and resigned three years later. In 1773 he sailed on an expedition to explore the Arctic with Captain Lord Constantine Phipps. It was on this expedition that he became acquainted with Horatio Nelson.

On March 7, 1778, his American Frigate, *Randolph,* engaged a British ship of the line twice her size. Biddle fought the battle bravely until, twenty minutes into the fight, he and 304 of his crew were killed when *Randolph* exploded.

Bromfield, John

John Bromfield was a Marine drummer assigned to the Continental Brig *Andrew Doria.*

Browne, Montfort

Browne was the governor of the Bahamas from 1774 to 1780. He was a British army officer and also served as lieutenant governor of West Florida.

Bulloch, Archibald

The great-great-grandfather of President Theodore Roosevelt, Archibald Bulloch was born January 1, 1730, and died on February 22, 1777. He served as a delegate from Georgia to the second

Continental Congress. He died in Savannah while preparing the defenses against British invasion.

Burke, Edward

Burke was a Marine sergeant on the continental frigate *Columbus*. He was promoted to lieutenant in New London after the Battle of Block Island Sound.

Chambers, William

William Chambers was captain of the *Mississippi Packet*, a vessel that was in New Providence Harbor when the Continental Marines made their first raid on the island.

Cogan, Issac

Cogan was a private in the Continental Marines. He entered the rolls on the frigate *Alfred* on December 15, 1775.

Coggins, John

A warrant officer in the Royal Navy, Coggins was Bosun on HMS *Bolton*. After the brig-sloop was captured, he was sent with his captain and two other shipmates to jail in Windham, Connecticut. They all escaped in a boat, but the other three drowned. Bosun Coggins was recaptured.

Craig, Isaac

Isaac Craig was born about August 1741 in Hillsborough or County Down, Ireland. After moving to Philadelphia, he became a master carpenter and cabinetmaker. One of the original Marine Corps first lieutenants, he was assigned to the brig *Andrew Doria* in November 1775. He was promoted to captain in October 1776 and became a captain in the Army in March 1777, even serving in the War of 1812. He died in Ohio at age 85 May 14, 1826.

Cummings, Robert

Robert Cummings, or Cumming, was a Marine Lieutenant on the Continental frigate *Columbus*. He was one of the three Marine officers who had some sort of falling out with Captain Whipple and were listed as deserters. However, all three were officially transferred or reassigned from *Columbus*.

Dayton, Henry

Lieutenant Henry Dayton was probably from Newport, Rhode Island and may have ridden with Whipple and Trevett on board *Katy* to Philadelphia when Congress formed the Navy and Marine Corps. He served as Lieutenant of Marines on the sloop *Providence*. He may have been commissioned a Captain in the Rhode Island Militia in 1799.

Dickenson, James

James Dickenson, lieutenant of Marines, was aboard the frigate *Columbus* on January 24, 1776, after collecting one month's advanced wages. There is no record that he was aboard when the fleet departed in February.

Dougherty, John

John Dougherty was a private in the Continental Marines. He entered the rolls on the frigate *Alfred* on December 16, 1775. He was killed in action in Block Island Sound on April 6, 1776.

Dunmore, Lord

John Murray was the Fourth Earl of Dunmore, a Scottish peer. He was named the governor of New York in 1770 and Virginia in 1771. After the American Revolution, he became governor of the Bahaman Islands for nine years.

Edgar, James

As just a boy, young James Edgar was the drummer in the Continental Marines. He enlisted on the Continental frigate *Alfred* on December 8, 1775.

Evitt, Richard

Richard Evitt was a Marine private assigned to the Continental frigate, *Alfred*. He enlisted on December 17, 1775. He deserted from the frigate on September 3, 1776.

Fitzpatrick, John

John Fitzpatrick was commissioned a second lieutenant in the Continental Marines. His commission from Congress was to the

Continental frigate *Alfred,* dated on November 28, 1775. While details beyond service on *Alfred* are not certain, it can be surmised with strong confidence that before the American Revolution, Fitzpatrick was a tanner in Philadelphia, and a widower with four very young children. He married Elizabeth Prior at Christ Church on February 8, 1776. In his report covering the Battle of the Block Island Sound, Marine Captain Nicholas wrote that Lieutenant Fitzpatrick died at his side from on *Alfred* during *Glasgow's* first broadside. He was "shot by a musket ball through the head." Deeply grieved by the tragedy, Nicholas wrote "I have lost a worthy officer, sincere friend, and companion, who was beloved by all the ship's company."

Hacker, Hoystead

Hoystead (Hoysteed, Hoysted, probably pronounced HIGH-sted) Hacker was commissioned a lieutenant in the Continental Navy on December 22, 1775, and he was promoted to captain on January 20, 1776. He was the first commander of the 8-gun schooner *Fly.*

Hallock, William

William Hallock was commissioned as the first captain of the Continental schooner *Wasp,* probably in December 1775 in Baltimore, Maryland. He later commanded the Continental sloop *Lexington.*

Hardy, Joseph

Joseph Hardy was a midshipman on the Continental sloop *Providence.* He served during the cruise to capture New Providence and Battle of Block Island Sound. Later, Hardy became a Continental Marine officer.

Harrison, Joseph

Joseph Harrison was the original surgeon on the Continental frigate, *Alfred.* As such, he became known as the first surgeon in the US Navy.

Hawkins, Mary

Owner of a tavern in Alexandria at the corner of Royal Street and Cameron Street in the 1770s. She owned five slaves who worked there.

Hazard, John

Little is known of the Pennsylvanian John Hazard, Captain of Continental sloop *Providence*. He was the first officer to hold that position. He was court-martialed in Providence, Rhode Island on May 8, 1776, due to his actions in the Battle of Block Island Sound. The author has not found the verdict and/or sentence but does note that command of the sloop was awarded to John Paul Jones immediately after the trial.

Hopkins, Esek

Esek Hopkins lived from April 26, 1718, to February 26, 1802. An accomplished merchant captain and privateer, he served as the only Commander in Chief of the Continental Navy during the American Revolutionary War. The raid on Nassau in New Providence, in which he led his fleet, proved nominally successful, but it set a precedent for Navy-Marine Corps combined amphibious operations for centuries to come as well as proving a very successful tactic for the tiny Continental Navy during the Revolution. Unfortunately, it caused no end of political problems for Hopkins, which ultimately resulted in his removal from command. He was the father of Midshipman Esek Hopkins, Junior and another revolutionary navy captain, John Burroughs Hopkins.

Hopkins, Stephen

A great patriot and brilliant man, Hopkins was born March 7, 1707, in Providence, Rhode Island. Cousin of Benedict Arnold and the elder brother of Esek Hopkins, he was a shipping merchant, delegate to Congress, fiery patriot, signer of the Declaration of Independence, and a drafter of the Articles of Confederation. In 1774, he freed his slaves and introduced a bill in the legislature to ban the importation of slaves to Rhode Island. He died in Providence on July 13, 1785.

Howe, Tyringham

Howe was posted captain of the *Glasgow* on January 11, 1775. He commanded *Glasgow* at Boston and at the Battle of Bunker Hill in June 1775. Shortly after that, he took his frigate to Rhode Island. Tyringham was first commissioned lieutenant on September 10, 1765, four years later being promoted to commander of the sloop *Vulture*-14 on 28 December 1770. In September 1772 he took his sloop, *Cruizer*-8, to the North American station. Captain Howe later saw significant service in North America commanding *Thames*-32 until she paid off in 1782. He died the following year in 1783.

Huddle, William

Very little is known of the biography of Marine Lieutenant William Huddle. He was in command of the detachment of five Marines on *Wasp* during the voyage to New Providence in 1775. There is no record of when he left the schooner.

Jones, William

Born October 8, 1753, in Newport, Rhode Island, Jones served in the Rhode Island Militia, the Continental Army, and as a Marine officer in the Continental Navy.

Kaine, Patrick

Patrick Kaine enlisted and served as a Marine private on the Continental brig, *Cabot*. He was killed in the Battle of Block Island Sound by a broadside from HMS *Glasgow*.

Kearns, Robert

Robert Kearns was a sergeant of Marines on the Continental brig *Andrew Doria* during the raid on New Providence and the Battle of the Block Island Sound.

Kennedy, George

George Kennedy enlisted and served as a Marine private on the Continental brig, *Cabot*. He was killed in the Battle of Block Island Sound by a broadside from HMS *Glasgow*.

Marshall, James

James Marshall was a Marine corporal assigned to the Continental frigate, *Alfred*. He enlisted on December 14, 1775.

Mason, Christopher

Lieutenant Christopher Mason was captain of *Nautilus* during the Battle of Block Island Sound.

McLocken, John

John McLocken served as a Marine private assigned to the Continental frigate, *Alfred*. Private McLocken enlisted on December 24, 1775.

Mickery, Samuel

Samuel Mickery was a Marine private assigned to the Continental frigate, *Alfred*. He enlisted on December 16, 1775. Shortly after the Battle of Block Island Sound, he deserted from the frigate on May 1, 1776.

Mullan, Peggy

In 1685, Samuel Carpenter built the first brew house in Philadelphia. Around 1740 the name was changed to Peggy Mullan's Red Hot Beef Steak Pub at Tun Tavern. Peggy Mullan was presumably the proprietress of the popular establishment at that time. By the 1770s, Peggy's son Robert was the proprietor of the eatery and public house.

Mullan, Robert

Living in Philadelphia during the American Revolution, Robert Mullan was the manager of the Tun Tavern. He is reputed to have been the "chief recruiter" for the new Continental Marines. He was commissioned a lieutenant of Marines on June 25, 1776. It is possible he died sometime before 1794.

Murray, John

Born in Tymouth, Scotland in 1730, he was also known as the 4th Earl of Dunmore. He became a notorious governor in the colonies of North America and died on February 25, 1809. See Lord Dunmore.

Natty, Ol'

A slave of Samuel Morris in 1769, Ol' Natty served the fox hunting club. Eventually, he purchased his own freedom and continued to serve as Knight of the Whip and became master and commander of all the hounds. He was paid £50 per year, a house, a horse, and an assistant.

Neilson, Alexander

Most likely from Philadelphia, Alexander Neilson may have been from Maryland. He served as Sergeant of Marines on the Continental frigate *Alfred* from December 8, 1775.

There is evidence that he may have wed Mary Clouser on January 12, 1776, in Philadelphia's Second Presbyterian Church. He was commissioned a lieutenant aboard *Alfred* by October 1776. In later life, Neilson may have served as an officer of artillery in the Continental Army.

Nicholas, Samuel

A Philadelphia socialite who became the first Commandant of the Marine Corps, Nicholas was born in Philadelphia in 1744 to Anthony and Mary Nicholas. Anthony was a blacksmith.

Samuel may have sailed on merchant ships for Robert Morris as a supercargo. On November 28, 1775, he became the first, and therefore senior, officer in the Marine Corps. Congress promoted him to major in June 1776.

In 1778 he married Mary Jenkins. Samuel Nicholas was a Marine, real estate speculator, innkeeper, Quaker, and Mason. Major Nicholas died on August 27, 1790.

Owens, Thomas

Thomas Owens was a Marine private assigned to the Continental frigate, *Alfred*. Private Owens enlisted on December 21, 1775. Sadly, he was killed in the Battle of Block Island Sound on April 6, 1776.

Parke, Matthew

Born in Ipswich, England in 1746, Matthew Parke moved to Virginia for a while after living with his grandfather who was the governor of the Windward Islands. Parke was commissioned as one of the first Marine officers in Philadelphia on November 28, 1775. After a very eventful career in the Marines, he died in Boston on December 28, 1813.

Pratt, John

A lieutenant of the New Providence Militia, he led a detachment of around thirty men from Fort Nassau to garrison Fort Montagu against the Continental Marines.

Prior, Eleanor

Eleanor was a resident of Philadelphia who married a John Fitzpatrick on February 8, 1776.

Richey, Robert

Robert Richey was a private Marine during the American Revolution. Private Richey enlisted and was assigned to the Continental frigate *Alfred* on December 8, 1775.

Saltonstall, Dudley

Captain Saltonstall was born in New London, Connecticut in 1738. He was a merchant captain and privateer captain during the French and Indian war. Saltonstall was the first captain of the Continental frigate *Alfred*.

It is reputed that he and his first lieutenant, John Paul Jones, did not get along. Despite other commands, he was dismissed from the Navy after the Penobscot failure. He met with some success as a privateer captain. Saltonstall died in 1796 in the West Indies.

Seymour, Sinclair

As a warrant officer, Sinclair Seymour served as the sailing master of the Continental brig *Cabot*. Master Seymour stood his post on the quarterdeck as he was killed in the first broadside from HMS *Glasgow* in the battle in Block Island Sound.

Shoemaker, Joseph

Little is know of Captain Joseph Shoemaker before he took command of the Continental Marines on the frigate *Columbus* under Abraham Whipple in December 1775 or January 1776.

Shoemaker is listed on the ship's muster as having deserted sometime before November 1776. In 1782 Major Nicholas swore an affidavit leading to the conclusion that Captain Shoemaker left *Columbus* May 2, 1776.

Sneyd, Edward

Although commissioned as a Royal Navy lieutenant, Edward Sneyd served as the captain of HMS Brig *Bolton* during the Battle of Block Island Sound.

Sterling, Robert

Robert Sterling was a major in the New Providence Militia during the time the Continental Marines invaded the first time (1776).

Strobagh, John

John Martin Strobagh, probably from Philadelphia, was a lieutenant of Marines on the Continental sloop *Hornet*. He probably suffered from seasickness and resigned his commission on May 14, 1776. He was commissioned in the Continental Army, rising to the rank of lieutenant colonel. He died on December 2, 1778.

Trevett, John

Born in Newport, Rhode Island in 1747, Trevett was a naval midshipman early in the revolution. He later became a Marine Corps officer who served in several major battles, including the Marines first amphibious assault. He died on January 22, 1823.

Turner, Thomas

Sergeant Thomas Vernon Turner of the Continental Marines died of fever on *Andrew Doria* on April 3, 1776.

Uncas, Daniel

Native American Mohegan mariner, Daniel Uncas, was from New London, Connecticut. He participated in the construction of the frigate USS *Confederacy* as a rigger and sailed in her crew as a Marine after completion.

Vanluden, Israel

Private Marine Israel VanLuden enlisted on the Continental frigate *Alfred* on December 19, 1775. He was discharged on November 7, 1776.

Wallace, James

Sir James Wallace was born in Norfolk, England in 1731. He was a distinguished British naval officer. He served as governor of

Newfoundland after the American Revolution. He died in London on March 6, 1803.

Welsh, John

John Welsh of Ireland is reputed to have come to Philadelphia specifically to fight in the American Revolution. He was commissioned Captain of Marines on the Continental brig, *Cabot*. He entered the brig with 40 Marines on January 4, 1776. Captain Welsh served honorably and successfully on several commissions during the war. He was killed in action on July 28, 1779, in the landing at Bagaduce.

Whipple, Abraham

Born in Providence, Rhode Island in 1733, Whipple was a seafaring man. He was a leader of the raiders in the *Gaspee* Affair and a successful naval officer. He was also the Commodore of the Rhode Island Navy and later Captain in the Continental Navy. After the war, he established Marietta, Ohio as a maritime trading center. He died in Ohio on May 19, 1819.

Wilson, John

Lieutenant John Hood Wilson (sometimes James Hood Wilson) was the First Lieutenant of Marines on the Continental brig, *Cabot*. Lieutenant Wilson was killed in action with HMS *Glasgow* on April 6, 1776.

Naval Service

Hymns

THE MARINE CORPS HYMN
Anonymous

From the Halls of Montezuma
To the shores of Tripoli;
We fight our country's battles
In the air, on land, and sea;
First to fight for right and freedom
And to keep our honor clean;
We are proud to claim the title
Of United States Marines.

Our flag's unfurled to every breeze
From dawn to setting sun;
We have fought in every clime and place
Where we could take a gun;
In the snow of far-off Northern lands
And in sunny tropic scenes,
You will find us always on the job
The United States Marines.

Here's health to you and to our Corps
Which we are proud to serve;
In many a strife we've fought for life
And never lost our nerve.
If the Army and the Navy
Ever look on Heaven's scenes,

They will find the streets are guarded
By United States Marines.

ANCHORS AWEIGH
George D. Lottman 1926

Stand Navy out to sea, Fight our Battle Cry;
We'll never change our course, So vicious foe steer shy.
Roll out the TNT, Anchors Aweigh. Sail on to Victory
And sink their bones to Davy Jones, Hooray!

Anchors Aweigh, my boys, Anchors Aweigh.
Farewell to foreign shores, We sail at break of day-ay-ay-ay.
Through our last night on shore, Drink to the foam,
Until we meet once more. Here's wishing you a happy voyage
home.

Blue of the Mighty Deep; Gold of God's Sun
Let these colors be till all of time be done, done, done,
On seven seas we learn Navy's stern call:
Faith, Courage, Service true, with Honor, Over Honor, Over All.

ETERNAL FATHER (WITH USMC VERSE)
William Whiting 1860

Eternal Father, strong to save,
Whose arm hath bound the restless wave,
Who biddest the mighty ocean deep
Its own appointed limits keep;
Oh, hear us when we cry to Thee,
For those in peril on the sea!

Eternal Father, grant , we pray,
To all Marines, both night and day,
The courage, honor, strength and skill
Their land to serve, Thy law fulfill;
Be Thou the Shield forevermore
From ev'ry peril to the Corps.

Navy Blue and Gold
Commander Roy de Saussure Horn, Class of 1915 1953

Now college men from sea to sea May sing of colors true,
But who has better right than we To hoist a symbol hue:
For sailor men in battle fair Since fighting days of old,
Have proved the sailor's right to wear The Navy Blue & Gold.

Final Information

For more detailed enjoyment and involvement check out these resource links:

www.daveperrybooks.com

https://www.amazon.com/David-Perry/e/B00G04V4T

I would love to hear from you. You can write to me at dave@daveperrybooks.com.

Made in United States
North Haven, CT
29 April 2022

18736453R00134